Sheila is a retired teacher of Modern Languages and English as a Foreign
Language (EFL)
Until Lockdown she had only written a few articles for magazines and some
Christian Poetry. Inspired by attempting a memoir of her spiritual journey, she
decided to use her experiences in Education, travels in Europe, Canada and
Australia to create family stories dealing with anthropology, racism, spirituality
and mental health, indigenous art and belief systems and relationships,
counselling and sexuality. In her retirement she studied Romanian, Creative
Writing, Indigenous Spirituality and Post-Colonial Theology. She also did
Prison work and teaching for the Probation Service.

My book is dedicated to my family and friends who encouraged me to get published and also to my dear friends in Aachen, my late husband's Scout Exchange partner and family from 1954.

Sheila Longman

THE DEVIL'S SANDBAGS

AUSTIN MACAULEY PUBLISHERS™

LONDON • CAMBRIDGE • NEW YORK • SHARJAH

A CIP catalogue record for this title is available from the British Library.

ISBN 9781398477858(Paperback)
ISBN 9781398477865 (ePub e-book)

www.austinmacauley.com

First Published 2022
Austin Macauley Publishers Ltd ®
1 Canada Square
Canary Wharf
London
E14 5AA

The title comes from a myth about Aachen Cathedral.

Aachen Cathedral has a large, decorative, metal door where the catch is carved, depicting the Devil's thumb. According to a much-repeated myth that Charlemagne could afford to build the cathedral by making a pact with the Devil, the townspeople fooled the Devil who slammed the doors in anger, trapping his thumb. He was so angry that he decided to destroy the cathedral and the town by burying them under sand from the sea, which he carried in large bags. He was fooled again by an elderly lady and gave up, thinking he had miles to travel. He emptied the sand forming two high hills to the north west of the city. Thus was Aachen saved from the Devil's Sandbags.

The myth became a symbol for the life and work of Dorothea Manning.

Dorothea Manning spent several weeks in Aachen every summer for over ten years.

In England she was a busy teacher in a London Comprehensive School teaching German to A level with some French. In Aachen she was a member of the RAF (Rote Armee Fraktion) with special duties to help the groups organise demonstrations, propaganda, posters and terrorist activities. She was known as Diane by her fellow revolutionaries. They knew it was her cover name and she never knew the real names of the others.

Dorothea experienced danger and trauma in her time as an undercover agent. Her controller helped her stop the work and return to a more normal life.

After nearly 30 years of marriage, motherhood and a successful teaching career as Head of Modern Languages, she heard once more from her controller. She was recovering from the grief and bereavement of losing both her husband and son a few years ago, when the unexpected call came. She had never told anyone about her ten years of secret work. She had been recruited while she was in her first year at Oxford. She hardened herself to act without emotion, to be a liar and to betray those who considered her as a friend and to have sexual relationships which were merely part of the deception.

The call from her controller, whose name she had never known, caused emotion which was foreign to her. Why did he invite her back to the Intelligence Service Office after three decades of no contact?

Why now, when she was just getting back on her feet and learning to live again after devastating loss? Dorothea has to juggle past and present, experience fear and danger and find love, while looking back on the years of terrorism in Germany and looking forward to a new life.

Chapter 1

The rosebay willow herb caught the golden light of the setting sun. It grows higher than the fence and waves in the breeze above the brambles by the railway side. The gold sunlight hits the fir trees on the hills behind. Small grey clouds move not too slowly across the last light of the grey sky. This view through the conservatory window always affords a sense of joy, as does the view from the lounge window: a large, full-leafed tree where sparkling, blinding sunlight flickers through as the sun sets. It has to bring a sense of joy, a sense of relief. There were still some good things in life. This is a lovely corner in which to feel sad. Geraniums bloom outside the kitchen door. All the doors are glass so light floods through all the rooms. All the guests love the light and comment on the views. When the weather allows, they can see more of the hills, the valley and the skies from the garden. Pots of fuchsias, banks of bright orange montbrecia, roses and shrubs, present a welcoming, simple open space with a bird table on the lawn.

Dorothea was making a good recovery three years after the deaths of her husband and son. She was experiencing enough renewed energy and inner drive to take up some activities, to travel again, to teach again. The voice on the phone was like a cruel joke. She was learning to live again when another past, never forgotten but pushed down, hidden, secret, broke into her calm and sunny corner. Dorothea had last heard that voice thirty years ago.

"I am so sorry to call you unexpectedly, Dorothea. You will receive a letter from the new young boss of our section. I decided to ring as well and make contact with you personally."

"Rainer, how did you know my phone number and address after all this time?" She grasped the phone to her ear. "Silly question. Forgive me!"

"I have retired officially but I have been called in to close some files. It is partly a question of identity. You may recall that one of the long-hunted women terrorists was released in the nineties when she was serving a life sentence in Lübeck. She was unrepentant and it caused a lot of controversy.

There is a fear that the RAF still exists, perhaps underground. The department want to have a good look at who belongs, who is in contact with them."

"Identity? So long ago. Not sure I can help."

"Lotte retired some years ago. She was so nearly blown, she just got out in time. She could be there when you come."

"Lotte! I'd see Lotte?"

"You will, but only in the formal interview. It is up to both of you if you want to keep in touch after that."

"Rainer, she saved me, got me through that terrible year of 77."

"Yes, I remember. Doro, after the formal part I would like to talk with you. Would you be willing to come to lunch with me and have a talk? I know you have had a few sad years."

"Of course, you do. Did you ever see Richard and Edward?"

"I'll explain when we meet." Dorothea was troubled, interested, fascinated. Did he know everything about her second life as a wife, mother and teacher?

"Yes, Rainer, I will have lunch with you."

"Thank you, Doro, I am looking forward to seeing you again soon. The details will be in the letter. It is neither an investigation nor an interrogation. I have been called in just like you. I think the new boss wants to tie up some loose ends and close some files and make sure about the present RAF situation."

She had a hundred questions in her head but was unable to ask any. She was still in shock but she really wanted to know how he was, what he was doing in life, whether he had a family.

Somehow, she could not imagine him as a father. She could understand why they had been called in but she could not imagine what he wanted to speak to her about.

She put down the phone and stood like a statue, paralysed, staring ahead. Her right hand went to her throat which felt sore and dry. Her eyes felt prickly but she shed no tears. Anger rose up inside her. She was able to get a glass of water and sit in the lounge. She had left that life she had lived for ten years in the formative years of her adulthood. She had put all her energy into playing the role demanded of her, making big sacrifices in every aspect of her life, her mental health, her psychological state. When she agreed to marry Richard, she made an equally gigantic effort to play her new role. She encouraged herself to feel, to have normal emotions, to enjoy her marriage relationship and her first son. As Diane, she had deadened all real emotion. She hardened herself to focus on her task in the RAF. Why was she being made to face it all again now?

Before the letter arrived, she spent time writing e-mails to her German friends. She was aiming at normal conversation, normal friendship linked with her long teaching career and nothing to do with her undercover work, her time in Aachen. She was looking forward to visiting friends in Dresden. After the reunification of Germany, she had opened communications with schools in the old East Germany and began exchanges between the classes in her English school.

The letter was on the mat one day, when she returned from grocery shopping. She abandoned the shopping and took the letter into the lounge.

"Smart, thick, headed note paper." She unfolded it.

"You are invited to attend…we would be very grateful if you would agree to attend…no actual compulsion. I could refuse. What could they do to me?"

Doro watched the swaying pink flowers and walked into the garden to look at healthy, life-giving blooms, the blue sky, and the passing, white, fluffy clouds. She had already agreed to go in her phone call with Rainer. Now she sat and wrote a formal acceptance. Her anger did not stop the force inside her, the drive to attend the meeting and to sit and talk with Rainer.

There were a few days before she had to make the journey to London. The address was an office block in a high-rise building in Tottenham Court Road, and not in the main Headquarters. It was quite near Russell Square where she had had many of her debrief meetings with Rainer in those ten years. They had never met at this address. It was probably a new block with some floors taken over by the Intelligence Services. If it had rained during the debrief, they went to a safe house in a side street near the British Museum. Some emotion was attached to Russell Square even though Doro had done her best to deaden her feelings.

One incident could account for the rise of strange emotions. The worst year in her RAF role was 1977. Events in Germany that autumn had been dramatic and tragic for many and had impacted England, Europe and many other parts of the world. In her personal experience she had suffered in a physical way which nearly broke her as she was preparing to leave for England and the new term at the end of the summer holidays.

She had met Rainer as usual in the Square and they sat on a bench near the water fountain. Rainer had held her in his arms as she told her discomforting story. He had never ever touched her. He understood that she was at breaking point. He calculated what she needed to begin a recovery and did what was necessary. Russell Square held a precious memory in all the pain.

In her two free days she allowed herself to recall how Rainer and Eliza had recruited her at Oxford and arranged for her to be trained for undercover work. She wondered how, at such a young age, she had agreed to tread such a path of deception.

"The RAF members were ready to die for their cause. I had no cause. They believed in what they were doing. They had an aim, a motivation. I had nothing except the awareness that my information could possibly prevent an act of terrorism. I did not act out of patriotism or even love for Germany. Why did I ever go along with it all?"

She could not sleep the night before she was due in London. She felt nervous but did not know why. The wording in the letter and Rainer's words on the phone had been reassuring. On the train to Waterloo, Doro remembered her teenage feelings. She had been overawed by Rainer and was clearly attracted to him. She felt she was falling in love with him. He never made any move on her over those early years so she learned to kill any feelings she had for him or for anyone else. She had nevertheless felt an inner compulsion to do whatever he asked of her when she was Diane with the German group.

She walked slowly across the Thames to Trafalgar Square, along Charing Cross Road to Tottenham Court Road. She was early so she had a coffee in a cafe and thought about how she had escaped from her RAF work. She left the secret world to marry Richard. He knew nothing of her secret life when he proposed to her. She had met him when he came to her London church to play the organ. He was a quiet loner who lived for music. He did not find it easy to chat and share himself but she felt relaxed with him. Spending time with him was such a relief after her weeks in Aachen. The events of 1977 broke something inside her and she began to withdraw her focus from the RAF group. She made less effort and longed to feel free. Rainer seemed to agree that it was time for her to withdraw and made it as easy a transition as possible.

Her anger at having to face those years again had not left her, but she pressed the button at the door, feeling grateful that Rainer had set her free when she needed to leave.

Chapter 2

The first few minutes were very awkward. Doro heard the buzz that opened the outer door for her. The office was on the fourth floor. She stepped out of the lift and saw a grey ponytail in front of her.

"Could it be?" She stepped to one side and saw that indeed it was Lotte. "Diane!" They hugged. "How are you?"

"Not pleased to be here, but pleased to see you again."

"Are you well?"

"Yes, thanks. I lost my husband and son a few years ago. I'm just learning to live again."

"I'm sorry. We must chat and share when this is over."

"Where do you live, Lotte?"

"In London. Here's my card. Where do you live? You contact me."

"A village outside Guildford in Surrey. I will! When did you leave Aachen?"

"In 1990 after the reunification. Everything changed. The RAF wound down. The groups causing trouble now are right-wing and anti-foreigners."

A door opened and a besuited young man with a mop of curls smiled at them and held out his hand.

"Ralph. Thank you for coming. Come in."

They walked over to a long table where another besuited young man with premature grey hair, sat behind a pile of files.

"You must be Lotte. This is Martin, my second in charge. You must be Diane."

Three chairs in a row faced Ralph and Martin. Lotte and Diane sat next to each other and left the third chair for Rainer. They heard the buzzer and the sound of the lift. Rainer soon walked through the door. His thick hair was smartly cut and totally silver, He wore a leather jacket and a jumper without shirt and tie. He smiled and put his hands on the shoulders of his two colleagues.

"Lovely to see you both again." They turned and looked up at him as he took his seat. Ralph talked them through the release of Irmgard Möller who had been serving a life sentence for her part in bombing a US base, killing several people. Although she refused to repent in any way, she was released in the late 1990s after being arrested in 1972, to be greeted by her supporters. The Press showed her smiling face as she came through the prison door.

"Were you aware of this?" There were three nods.

"As Irmgard came out, so Ingrid Jakobsmaier went in. She was arrested after escaping for 20 years."

"The RAF, what was left of them, declared an end to the guerrilla warfare but they did not totally disband."

"You probably know the books by the other RAF members, Bauman and Cohn-Bendit, virtually expressing a change of mind."

"Yes." They nodded again.

"We have some intelligence that some less well-known RAF members have been meeting up again. We will speak to you all individually but we are asking you to have a good think back to the '70s and '80s. Recall names, involvements with the Stammheim groups, plans of attack, chosen victims. First of all, Martin is going to show you some photographs. We have some of the group you were with as they were, and some of them as they are now and some others of present-day members who you may be able to recognise."

"Let's start with those." Martin spread out eight photographs of elderly people along the table. "Are they an Aachen group?" asked Diane.

"They meet in Cologne mostly but they come to Aachen to see some of the old members you will know. Names later."

Doro felt that she had been away from such people for so long that Lotte, who had seen them in the past 15 years, would have a better chance at recognition. Rainer would have seen all these in his files. He did not go to Aachen himself. He was not a field agent.

Doro looked with Diane's eyes at the grey-haired men and women. Lotte picked up the photo of a man and placed it next to a woman and stared down at them.

"Diane, the French couple that joined us in 1972 or 3. What do you think?"

"She was Felicity and he was Raoul. They came from Alsace and in 77 they were linked to the kidnapping and even murder of Schleyer."

Doro pulled her arms across herself and held herself tight without folding her arms. Her worst year had been mentioned in the first 15 minutes.

Rainer pulled the photos to himself.

"We might have some of them younger. Keep them to one side."

They considered the other photos but there was little reaction. Diane picked up a woman with very short grey hair.

"Could that be Ilse?"

"Ilse, who slept with all the men?" Doro shuddered a little as she remembered her own sexual encounter with the leader. In her naivety, she thought she was having an affair with him and was shocked to return to the commune one day and find him in bed with Ilse, having sex while others were going about their tasks in the same room. It was part of their anti-bourgeois doctrine. That was about her first lesson in killing emotion and becoming like an automaton.

"Okay. Let's see the historic photos." Martin put the three recognised photos in a blue folder and opened an old grey one and spread-out pictures of inferior quality. There was young Lotte and young Diane and four men and two girls. Lotte ran easily over all the names. She picked up Ilse with her pixie hair style and cheeky smile.

"Ilse." Diane sat in silence. She was overcome with the power of her memories. There was the leader, Manfred and his aides, Volker, Jürgen and Ulrich who joined with Angelika who glowered in the final photo. She tried to say the names but could only whisper. Rainer looked at her and saw she was trembling and had closed her eyes. He knew she was not expressing a broken heart but was having a reaction to the cruel way Manfred had treated her in a time of need. It had nearly broken her.

"Let's have a break." Rainer said and stood up and offered her his hand. She took his hand and walked towards the door. Manfred's photo was in front of her so she pushed it away as she left the room. Ralph called for some coffee and Rainer walked with Doro to the end of the corridor and put his arms around her. She unlocked her own arms and held them at her side as she leant against him. She could not prevent the pain of the past swamping her and bringing her to tears, not just tears but sobs as she relived the events, she had suppressed inside her for many years.

Chapter 3

Dorothea had first met Rainer in a room in her Oxford College. Rainer and Eliza had sat at the table discussing their notes together.

"We are looking for a girl who has a good level of German. She needs minimal family attachments in England. She needs to be adventurous enough to break rules, go against traditions. She needs to be cool headed, calm and not hold strong religious convictions. She must be emotionally self-contained, even hardened," Eliza read out her notes.

"Here's the file on Dorothea Manning. She is in her first year. She gained As in German, French and English literature. She is doing BA German with subsidiary French. She's nearly 19 and look at her, passable, slim, pretty but not sexy."

"Trouble is brewing in many left-wing groups in both France and Germany. The activists are recruiting groups of radicals and have strong leaders in both countries. They are fanatics and consider Zionism and imperialism as the enemy," Rainer reminded Eliza.

The Bundes Republik Deutschland (BRD) was rebuilding their state after the war, regretting the division in 1961 into two German states. The Wall was built not just across Berlin but across the whole of Germany, breaking the Deutsche Demokratik Republik (DDR) away into the Iron Curtain under the control of Russia. The left-wing groups of the West maintained contact with similar groups in the East. The Intelligence Services discovered a growing link with Palestine through the PLO. There was a growing paranoia in the West of these groups who accused the state of repression, hypocrisy and fascism.

"Can we stop this turning into a real threat, a revolution? If it happens in Germany, it will spread to France, Italy and even England."

"That's why we need to infiltrate the groups and learn what they are planning."

"Let's talk to this girl and then we can decide who controls her if she accepts. It is asking a lot of a teenager."

Dorothea had signed up for some extra language conferences to be held in one of the modern Oxford Colleges. She knew she would be interviewed and was not surprised to see a man and a woman sitting behind a table. They greeted each other as she sat down on the single chair holding a folder.

"Have you brought your work with you?"

"Only my last long dissertation."

"Please tell us the title and why you chose this subject."

"It's called *Karl Marx and the Acts of the Apostles*. I decided to read *Das Kapital* and as I read, it struck me that many of his ideas, not revolution or overturning the state, but the ideas of having things in common and sharing and caring for each other, were very similar to the teaching of the Apostles in the early church."

"Are you a church goer?"

"Not regularly. I appreciate the liturgy and the music; so peaceful, but I don't go along with the strict rules."

"Such as?"

"Women's roles, keeping quiet, covering their heads. No sex outside marriage, the threat of hellfire."

"Could you read us some of your dissertation? The beginning, a central argument and your conclusion."

Doro was rather surprised but she opened the folder and began reading. Rainer and Eliza paid intense attention.

"So, you agree that communal sharing is important for society?"

"Yes, it's a worthy aim."

"Would you agree with demonstrations, revolution, violence as an expression of this aim?"

"Politics. I would accept demonstrations, peaceful demonstrations. I would not accept violence."

Rainer stood up and offered his hand to her. "I'm Rainer. We have asked you here for this interview as we have a different motivation, an ulterior motive."

Dorothea looked at him then at Eliza but said nothing.

"We want to recruit some young German speakers for a special job, a very special job. We are going to explain the situation among Marxists in Germany and then explain what we need." Eliza took over.

"If you decide it's not for you, we will send you to the course you applied for and we will ask you to sign some papers, the Official Secrets Act. If you agree to have a go, we'll send you for special training, meet with you regularly and then send you on your first assignment in Germany.

Dorothea was stunned. "If I refuse, do I go on the course about the language of Marx and Hitler?"

"Yes, you do."

"How did you choose me?"

Eliza opened a file and read her notes.

"Dorothea is a loner and very self-confident. Her parents died in a road accident three years ago so she moved in with a grandmother. In spite of her grief, she worked hard at her studies. She went on exchange visits to Cologne, Berlin and Stuttgart. Her German is of a high standard and she could pass for a native most of the time. Her grandmother was her last living relative except for her aunt who lives in Scotland. She has virtually no contact with her mother's sister as they had fallen out many years earlier. She has a few close friends but does not easily mix socially. She seems very self-contained. She reads and listens to music and enjoys concerts."

"You think I could do the job you want?"

"We do."

"Can you tell me more? Are you MI6? Can I do both my studies and this work? I want to become a teacher."

Rainer outlined the groups which were growing in Germany.

"They live in communes and eschew the mores of traditional society. They are becoming revolutionaries and want to overturn the state which they consider as fascist. They have troubling international links in the Middle East. They are anti-Zionist and anti-imperialist. They feel that justifies attacking properties and people."

Then he described what they needed. They already had some full-time undercover agents in all the countries who spoke all the languages.

"We need young people like you to infiltrate the groups as students, on a part-time basis. They have several German students joining communes in this way. You would need a cover name and a cover story. You would tell them you are a student or a teacher of German in an English school as a suitable background, but that your sympathies lie with the Marxist groups. You explain that your dissertation caused you problems with the college authorities.

You were interrogated as a possible left-wing activist. Before you go, you would link up with such a group in Oxford and in whichever town you end up teaching in. We have an undercover, lady agent in a group in Aachen and we are thinking of sending you there. She would recruit you and 'sell you' to the others. You would regularly spend time with them in the academic holidays and would be one of half a dozen student agents in Cologne, Aachen or Düsseldorf."

"Take half an hour and have a drink or snack, the come back and tell us your thoughts," Eliza finished up.

"Can I leave the building?"

"No, there's a bar one floor up." Dorothea had imagined she could go out and not come back but she realised they had controlled everything.

She left the room, took the stairs and went into the pleasant bar. It was bright, light with soft armchairs. As she sat, she immediately realised the implications of taking on such a task. She would be two people leading two lives. She would have to keep at a distance from close friends. How would she explain her regular trips to Aachen? She would have to lie. What would she have to do? She would have to give secret information. She could not imagine what the training would entail. She did not want to back out. She was fascinated and attracted but she wanted to ask more questions for clarification. She felt she could live a secret life and become another character that was a Marxist working to effect change in society. She had a sandwich and a glass of wine and knocked on the door when the 30 minutes were up.

Rainer and Eliza had discussed her and felt quite optimistic that she could handle the job. They needed to discuss her thoughts on boyfriends, sex and marriage.

"She may have to have sex in the commune. She probably will. We'll have to sound her out." Eliza agreed to tackle that.

Dorothy sat down and waited for their comments. "Do you want to know more?" asked Rainer.

"I do. What is the task exactly? How would I be trained? How would I get and give information?"

"Good questions. A delicate area first." Eliza began, "You would live in the same commune and build relationships with the boys and girls. You may need to have sex with the men. It's how they behave."

"I'm a virgin."

"That could be an advantage. When the invitation comes, you could explain that you are a virgin but you are so convinced of the cause that you are willing to let the man take your virginity."

Rainer said that it sounded hard but free love was part of their belief system. He asked if she had a boyfriend, she could have sex with first if she preferred to feel prepared.

She sat up straight and stared at him. "I would be expected to have sex?"

"Think about it and decide on a plan."

"I do not have a boyfriend I want to have sex with. I'd rather wait and see what happens in the commune and see if one of them wants to take me on."

Eliza looked at Rainer and smiled.

"I will tell you what you can do for us and then I will meet with you again soon and begin the training and introduce you to our agent.

"You will help with the literature, posters, leaflets and folders. You need to get as many names as possible, even though we know they all have cover names. When they trust you, they will take you to demonstrations and to meetings and you can encourage other young people to join. With the short stays, we think you would not be used for anything violent or to work with explosives."

"Can I really avoid violence?"

"We do hope so. While you are at Oxford, you must not jeopardise your studies. I will meet you in a safe place in Oxford. Please leave us now and we will ring you to tell you when and where to meet."

Dorothea left the room after signing the secret papers and walked back to her room. She preferred to live in student rooms although her grandmother had died. She did not want to live in that house, so she arranged for the house to be let. She sat rather stunned when she returned.

"So, you want to be her controller?" Eliza asked Rainer. "Will you seduce her before she goes?"

"Only if it is necessary. I think she will take her own action and will be ready once she is accepted in the commune. I will see her in the safe house until she finishes her degrees and then meet her wherever she gets a job. I shall encourage her to choose London."

Instead of going on the course, she was given the address of the safe house. It was a flat in a small, modern block built by the footpath along the river. It was a pretty, idyllic corner.

Rainer opened the door and let her into the lounge.

"Sometimes I will have to stay here. No one in your college must know you spend time with me here. I will never meet you in college. Once you are in Aachen we will meet here or in the London office according to the situation with the groups."

Rainer described her cover story for the time she was in Aachen. She would be known as living her cover in England. She would be a church goer, a girl with Christian beliefs who loved liturgy and music but she would really belong to the Marxist group.

He told her about Lotte, an English woman who was known as a left-wing activist, a supporter of demonstrations and revolution and of urban guerrilla warfare. Lotte would come to England to meet her, give her any information she needed then take her to Aachen to meet Manfred, the leader.

Rainer talked her through commune life and gave her some vocabulary including 'anti-fascist activities'. The members were clever, dedicated, bold and brave, anxious to fight for their cause and to find targets to hit at imperialism, such as department stores and US air bases.

He checked out again that she would be ready to live like a revolutionary without keeping to Christian morals about lies and sex.

He sat with her in the lounge and talked about his department in the Intelligence Services trying to find ways to infiltrate Marxist groups.

"Lotte helped set up the commune in Aachen. It is not an obvious place for a Marxist group. They usually choose big, industrial towns. It's a popular tourist town with a border with Belgium and Holland. It has an attractive, historical cathedral with masses, organ concerts and the tomb of Charlemagne. There is an amazing legend that Charlemagne made a deal with the Devil to build the cathedral but then the Devil tried to destroy both cathedral and city when the townspeople fooled him."

He said it was a beautiful town which had been badly bombed in the war. The cathedral was not destroyed. The Town Hall had been damaged but had been fully restored. There were Roman remains, good museums, a healing spa and lots of restaurants, special local food and many metal statues around the city centre.

She did not stop him to say that she had been there once. She decided to tell him later rather than stop him in his flow.

The more she met and spoke with Rainer, the more she felt attracted to him. She felt she was falling in love with him. She was overawed by him, admired his thick, dark hair and his smart suits. She hoped he might show an interest in her but wondered if he would lose his credibility if he were known to sleep with new recruits.

On her next visit to the riverside flat, she greeted him with the continental kiss on both cheeks but he drew away from her and did not respond. He sat away from her and she thought he was making it clear he was not intending to have a romantic liaison with her. The training moved to more common sense and technical matters; secret letter boxes, cameras, phone numbers, playing her cover role in both England and Germany.

She decided on attending Christ Church chapel for services and Marsden chapel for evensong.

She felt joy and excitement when she was next due to meet Rainer.

She saw that any effort to flirt with him was useless. She knew he would have understood her efforts but she backed right off and instead told him that she was willing to do anything at all that he needed her to do, anything to serve him and to please him. She knew that she was not going to succeed with him and wondered if he had a partner already.

Lotte came to the flat with Rainer and she and Dorothea hit it off immediately. Lotte checked her cover story, tested her and questioned her. They both went to meet the Marxist group in London. Dorothea became Diane.

Lotte told her about the leader, Manfred. "He will question you, interrogate you. Have your story straight."

She had to have her cover straight for the Aachen group. She had to be an inspiration to the young revolutionaries. She had to think like a left-wing activist and talk and act as if she thought that killing enemies was acceptable.

She told Rainer that she had once visited Aachen when her exchange family in Cologne took her there on a day trip. "What a beautiful city! What history, what charm!"

The weeks of training by a whole team were very intense. Doro learned not only to stand up to people and fool them but how to use the tiny technology she was given. She had a lot of reading material; news bulletins about revolutionary activity in Europe and Intelligence Service reports on the worrying increase of student unrest.

She was completing her BA and preparing her MA when Paris erupted. The force took everyone by surprise. Hundreds of students sprayed graffiti on the Sorbonne and smashed the lecture theatres in the new university buildings at Nanterre.

Doro felt hesitant to travel to Europe and spend the summer among the unrest. While students demonstrated, Baader and Meinhof set fire to department stores and robbed banks. There were arrests, some settings free and escapes. Baader and Meinhof had their names forever joined by her audacious, armed attack which got Baader free from prison. The groups were often called the Baader Meinhof Gang for years to come.

Chapter 4

Diane was introduced by Lotte to the Aachen commune. She claimed to have met her in a London Marxist group. Dorothea learned as Diane, to look confident, bolshy and cocky and hide all sign of nerves. Manfred and Jürgen interrogated her. They had learned how to question and intimidate a person with harshness. She managed to impress them and they offered her a beer. With Lotte, she had entered an elegant looking building in the town centre and was led up the stairs and ushered into a small room with a single bed in the middle.

Shelves of documents were all around the walls with three hard, upright chairs squeezed in by the side of the bed. Diane sat with her back to the door and argued about the arguments in *Das Kapital* and she realised that she knew it better than them.

"Welcome to the guerrilla warfare!" said Jürgen.

"I'll do whatever you want but actual shooting and bomb making is reserved for the full timers, I gather."

"Just so. It takes a long time to plan an attack and you are only here for four weeks at the most."

"How are you finding your cover as a student at Oxford?"

"There are a lot of left-wingers. We manage to get together. I enjoy my studies and I hope to teach eventually, but then I will have preparation to do." Manfred stood up and stepped forward to be right in front of her. He cupped her head in his hands and kissed her passionately, thrusting his tongue into her mouth. She remained cool and unsmiling.

"You are good to have around. You know so much and feel so strongly."

"I feel strongly too, that women are equal and have choices. Women's liberation is important to me." She grabbed his arms and thrust them down.

"Well done!" said Jürgen and he came and kissed her on the cheeks.

She tried to prepare herself for what was to come. She tried talking to Jürgen, to understand how he had become involved with the group. He told her that his father had been a Nazi and had been executed for war crimes. He hated him and all that he represented so he looked out for revolutionaries.

They opened the door and showed her the large central room. There were several low beds, a central table and chairs, and an old aluminium bath tub. There were cupboards and files around the wall.

A small kitchen, standing room only, was at one end with showers and toilets at the far end. There were three other smaller rooms, each with a bed and shelves of literature. One room was like a study with a large desk and piles of box files. Papers were piled high on the desk.

"Your first job, get this lot out into the market place and at the university, just outside the entrance. Don't go in, you will get arrested." Manfred grabbed piles of leaflets and thrust them towards her. She smiled at him.

"Have we got a printing press?"

"A floor down, there's an office we can use."

Ilse came in and laughed as she saw Diane standing next to the bath tub.

"Don't worry, there are showers but some of us like to bathe naked and break the middle-class standards."

Diane did arrive back one day to find Ilse in the tub with Ulrich washing her with soap suds and kissing her.

On that first night she slept on one of the low beds in the common room and was grateful that she was left alone.

The German police were on edge. There were demonstrations against the Vietnam War and against the visit of the Shah of Persia, the students were loud and angry. Diane joined in all of the demos and saw on television news that in Berlin and other big towns, the police were shooting real bullets at the crowds. One student was killed so more demos followed. Manfred came back with her when they ran from the police lines. He took her hand and led her to a small bedroom.

"Madam, Diane, will you let me make love to you?"

"I'm a virgin," she told him.

"So? I'll be gentle." She sat on the bed and let him undress her. *No nerves. Hard as nails*, she told herself. It was not as bad as she expected. He wore a condom and treated her gently with caresses and kisses. There were even aspects she could enjoy but inside she had deep regret that her first sexual encounter was not with someone she loved. She smiled at him and kissed him. "Thank you." She put on a good act and put her arms around him.

25

Lotte went to the market with her before she caught her train back to England and checked out that she was coping, could put up with the sex and could stand being in such violent demos.

"Who do you have sex with?" asked Diane.

"Volker."

They said their goodbyes and she got on her train with a strong sense of relief and achievement. Rainer had arranged to meet her in the safe flat. She rang the bell and saw him come down the stairs. She longed to leap up and hug him but he stood straight and stood back to let her in. She held back and made no effort to greet him.

"How are you?" he asked showing her to an armchair. "Glad to be back. I don't like all of those in the commune."

"How do they treat you?"

"I fight my corner. The leader took me so I let him deflower me." She looked down. "They swop around a lot." She took in a breath and pulled out her camera and notes.

"They are in touch with Andreas Baader and know his plans for fire bombs, banks and US bases. Here are the names they mentioned in a meeting. He looked at the list; Holger Meins, Ulrike Meinhof, Rudi Dutschke, Carlos Ramirez, Daniel Cohn-Bendit and Horst Mahler, a lawyer.

"They spoke of attacking the Springer Press and of killing ex-Nazis who are in important positions today."

"Well done! They mentioned all those things in the commune?"

"Yes. Manfred calls a meeting and sometimes he rants in anger. He believes we need to be more radical to shake up the fascist state."

"He sounds dangerous."

"I think he has that potential. They have the use of a printing press in an office in the same block. I don't know who it belongs to. They collate literature but there is no evidence of actual explosives in the flat."

"Any photos?"

She passed him the camera. "Photos of the members and of the posters and leaflets they asked me to distribute."

"They must have access to explosives. See if you can find out where without causing suspicion."

"Sixty-eight was a big year for them because of the student demonstration in Paris and Germany. I'll try to sound out Ilse who sleeps with all the boys. Angelika came with Ulrich but shares him with her."

"Do you have to steal?"

"Not yet. Manfred said we could easily be caught stealing in a shop. We have enough money from the last bank raid."

"You have done so well, Diane! Your first report. Very impressive. Nearly all the well-known names."

Rainer checked her examination dates and the week she could return before spending the summer of 1970 with the group. By then the RAF 'Rote Armee Fraktion' became the official name but they were also called the Baader Meinhof Gang because of Ulrike's successful attempt to free Andreas Baader from prison. He fled abroad and several of them spent time in Jordan for training in arms, weapons, explosives.

Diane gained some interesting information during her next week with them. They had made contact with the PLO and Manfred was very angry about the arguments and splits in the Palestinian Liberation Groups. All they had in common was their hatred of Israel.

Manfred spoke several times about Carlos, known as the Jackal. As violence escalated in the next few years, he had shot three policemen in Paris and had escaped. This fired up the Germans to attack police stations.

Manfred asked Diane for sex. He did not demand it. She always complied and asked him for more responsibility. She offered to help pack explosives and work the printing press. He agreed to discuss it with Jürgen.

In those early 1970s, Manfred seemed increasingly angry. The death of Ohnesorge, the student shot dead at the demo against the Shah of Iran, sent him into an angry outburst. Angelika, Ulrich and Volker left to join the Cologne group. New people joined; a French couple from Alsace, Kurt, Hans and Anne. Lotte welcomed them in and helped them settle. However, in 1974 a prisoner on hunger strike died. Holger Meins was a hero and had a huge funeral and demo on his behalf. Manfred was furious.

"No one should take the coward's way out. They should fight. We need them!" Aachen did not see the violence of the big urban cities.

This was also the year when Doro left Oxford with her first-class German degree and Master's Degree and applied for a teaching post in a school in South London. She had advice from Rainer, Eliza and Lotte.

"With such a degree, you would normally get a post in a grammar or private school. Go for a new Comprehensive and meet up with left-wingers. Make this your sacrifice for the Marxist cause!"

She took a post in one of the large, new modern, mainly glass buildings in South London. She rented a flat within walking distance and found one overlooking a park for her sanity.

The headmaster interviewed her with his deputy and the Head of Modern Languages. They asked why such an Oxford graduate would want to be in a Comprehensive school. She convincingly lied about her views of social justice and a fair education policy. She was able to act her role.

She kept to herself as much as possible in London. She explained that she would still like to attend some of the Oxford language conferences. This meant she could easily meet her controller and continue some training as Manfred allowed her to handle explosives in the commune and in another centre with Ilse and Lotte.

In her last report, sitting on a bench in Russell Square, she was able to tell Rainer of the plans to target ex-Nazis. They planned to kill some and kidnap others. The RAF had a list of names of men who had been important Nazis but had escaped justice by offering much needed business acumen to help rebuild the economy. She had no access to that list. It was well hidden from all except Manfred.

In 1976 Diane noticed a change of atmosphere when she went for her week before Christmas. The new members had blended in quite well but they were aware of Manfred's angry outbursts. Not long after Easter Ulrike Meinhof had been found dead in her cell. In those early summer days, he had sat at the table, banging it with his fists.

"No way did she kill herself. She was murdered. She was a brilliant writer, a staunch revolutionary. They killed her because she succeeded so many times in attacks." Diane sat opposite him, saw him put his thumb on a crane fly and systematically pull off its legs then brush it to the floor. Diane looked at him with distaste. Ilse came and sat on his lap, cuddled and kissed him and then they went to bed.

None of the groups believed that Meinhof had killed herself. Demos and further attacks took place as the year progressed. Diane managed to turn her two lives on and off. She was able to handle explosives in the commune, sending the possible targets to Rainer. By the time her week before Christmas came, Manfred had reached explosion point.

He rejected Ilse, stormed around the flat and then shouted at Diane for living with one foot in the corrupt, bourgeois, fascist society. He yelled that she was keeping to the false morals of a dying society.

"They will all die out. Marx will win!"

Diane tried her peacemaker act but he grabbed her hand and dragged her into the bedroom. He pulled off her lower clothing, held her arm and pulled off his own clothes, and then he violently spun her over, pinning her arms underneath her and raped her from behind. She could not move but she could yell. She was helpless as he raped her for a prolonged time. No one came when she yelled. As he slid off her, she shouted,

"Why rape me? I do not refuse you! What's the matter with you?"

He left naked and went to the shower. She hardened herself to endure what he had done and did not weep. She played the role of a commune member she thought was being demanded of her.

As she returned for Christmas, she feared for Manfred's mental state. She also recalled that he had not worn a condom.

It was a relief to start the New Year with her classes and she did her utmost to put what had happened out of her mind. She did not even report the rape to Rainer. She just could not face talking to him about it. She did not weep but she let her anger rise. By the time she was ready to travel to Aachen to pack explosives with Kurt and Raoul, she realised she was pregnant.

She was sickened to think that Manfred's rape had given her a baby. She planned to book an abortion on her return to London.

Diane asked Lotte to walk into town with her and they walked through the beautiful square behind the Spa. She told Lotte what had happened.

"We are all aware of his dark moods. I think the others may see the Cologne leaders and ask for him to be removed."

In the flat she refused to make eye contact with Manfred.

"I suppose an apology is beyond you!" she said angrily. He did not reply. She continued her packing.

"I suppose you think that your first-class studies and your fist class job and your English life are exonerated by your handling of explosives!" She did not answer.

"Ulrika gave her all!"

"Baader and Ensslin have children. Don't they matter?"

"Children? No, they don't!"

He stood up and made her stand. He touched her abdomen.

"Don't tell me you have a baby in there!" He pressed her and she began to feel fear.

"Your baby. I am having an abortion in London."

He slapped her face hard and knocked her to the ground.

"I'll save you the bother." He pulled her up and punched her hard several times until she was doubled over in pain. He slapped her face, punched her stomach over and over again. He was out of control, yelling and was about to kick her when Lotte came in. She bent over Diane, stood up, pushed him away hard and pulled out her pistol.

"Go!" she yelled. "Leave the flat!"

"No hospital. We cannot risk that. No doctor!"

Diane was bleeding heavily and in a lot of pain. Lotte fetched water and towels and mopped up as best she could. She left the blood on the floor and concentrated on Diane's condition. She could hardly breathe.

Manfred would not leave until Lotte promised not to call an ambulance. "It will be the end of us all."

"You upper class bitch. You expect the best of everything." He grabbed the bowl of red water, swiped the floor with the towel, gathered up some pieces and poured it all down the toilet.

Lotte put a cushion under Diane's head. She had fainted. Lotte sponged her head and her bruised and battered body. She sat her up and gave her some pain killers. She slept on the stained floor for at least an hour.

Lotte comforted her and said she would return to England with her and get her to a hospital. She contacted the other RAF leaders and told them that Manfred had committed a criminal act and that he could have killed Diane. Three leaders came and took him away with them, taking a suitcase.

"Manfred, you should be arrested," said Lotte.

The rest of the group returned soon afterwards and were horrified. Ilse and Felicity helped her dress and sat with her through the night.

Lotte warned Rainer and he arranged for her to be met by an agent who would take her to a private clinic. The clinic personnel had an understanding and knew they should not ask Diane any questions.

Diane said she had been beaten up by a mentally ill man and had a miscarriage. She was given the good treatment she needed and spent two days in bed.

"I am very sorry for your loss," said the doctor. "We have cleaned you up and made sure that the entire embryo has come away. We'll check on you again in a few weeks. I am very hopeful that you will be able to conceive a child in the future. You have bad bruising and you have lost a lot of blood. I hope you can rest for a few days."

Diane hoped she could recover enough to return to school for the start of the summer term. She got Lotte to check her facial bruises and that she could walk normally. She wanted to return to Aachen in summer but she stipulated that Manfred should be nowhere near her.

Aachen had a new leader, Bruno, who had heard what had happened to her. He treated her very well. She learned that the Palestinians were planning to hijack a plane and demand the release of the Stammheim prisoners. The fact that Diane had returned after such an attack on her, helped convince the group of her trustworthiness and dedication. All through those summer weeks, she was aware of tension, a greater degree of paranoia in the country. The group often discussed kidnapping and hijacking and explosions. She was glad to leave all that behind and start the new school year. She could never have guessed what would happen in Germany that autumn.

At half term she went to meet Rainer for the first time since she had been in the clinic. It was a beautiful autumn day, golden sunlight on golden leaves. She sat on the bench watching the children and the dogs playing. Rainer came and sat next to her and immediately held her in his arms. She leaned on him, did not touch him and did not cry.

"I am so sorry," said Rainer several times. He continued to hold her. "Are you up to date?" he asked.

She pulled away and looked at him.

"I wonder what I have achieved," she said. She had already given all the vague warnings. Hanns Martin Schleyer had been kidnapped, the PLO had hijacked a plane which was stormed by German forces in Mogadishu. The Palestinians had been demanding the release of all the Stammheim prisoners. The hijackers had all been shot dead. Shortly afterwards, the remaining prisoners, including Baader, had been found dead in their cells, some shot, some were hanged, another was stabbed. It was called a group suicide pact. The body of the ex-Nazi, Schleyer, was then found in a car boot near the Alsatian border.

Shocking events, one after the other entered Doro's head and joined with the horror of the attack by Manfred. She felt the vertigo as she thought about the swirling, black cloud filling her mind.

"Such a lovely day," she said as she turned her head around and looked at normal people, normal children and normal activities.

"How is your school work going?"

"Quite well. I'm okay at school. No one gives me a hard time except some of the teenagers. It is a relief to be there after what happened."

"We'd understand if you did not want to go back to Aachen. If you are prepared to return, we are close to finding out about the Palestinian links. The new leader is very involved with them. In Germany, they are looking for new targets since the funerals."

"Schleyer was a dreadful man. The RAF people have children of their own. It is all so upside down."

"Diane, you will recover slowly. You need to take care of yourself in England. Go to concerts, plays, whatever. You should have a holiday soon."

"You know, Aachen is such a lovely town. The Devil didn't destroy it. His sand is on the hill outside. I've been up the hill to the restaurant on the top. I've seen the lovely view all around. His sand made it even more beautiful. It's a pity I can never have a holiday there." Rainer was not quite sure what she was talking about.

"I'd like you to see our psychologist before you go back to Aachen."

"Am I achieving anything?"

"More than you can understand. It is a very delicate situation now after all the dramatic events this autumn. Violence could escalate. One of the terrorists did not die. She survived her stab wounds. But I do not want you in the hands of a psychopath. Get some support, please."

"It can't make it any worse."

Sad, subdued, she left him on the bench and walked across the square watching the playing families.

Chapter 5

For the past six years, Doro had worked at the Dale School, her first teaching job in a large Comprehensive School. This was her second life. She spent more of her waking hours at the school but the heavy overshadowing of her special job never left her. It dominated all her decisions. She could not take on too much extra work nor accept a promotion which would mean she needed to be in school during her Aachen weeks.

She could not spend much leisure time with colleagues. After the rarefied atmosphere of Oxford, she found it difficult to adjust to a Comprehensive School. Poor white children from poor family backgrounds and a large proportion of Afro-Caribbean children took some getting used to. Pupils thought of her as strict, cool, hard but fair. Fellow teachers admired her self-contained character, no parties, no getting drunk. Most of them preferred the tipsy, light-hearted company of the non-Oxbridge staff. She wasn't the only one, but she was asked why she did not take a first job in a grammar or private school.

"I am privileged. I have sympathies with the left-wingers who fought to get Comprehensives accepted and to give a higher standard of education to all children, no matter what their backgrounds."

"And you think that is what this school is doing?" She smiled without answering. "Go and help the bright ones who would have been in a grammar school and find themselves teased and mocked here, brought down by the masses."

She did in fact do that. Identifying the high flyers was not difficult but persuading them that trying hard, learning and achieving could be cool was a different story.

All teachers soon learn that there is more to teaching than standing in a classroom. Life comes in and unsettles the routine. Students have disagreements and fights; they fall in love, have sex and try drugs and drink.

There is truancy, damage to property, theft of property and nearly 2000 pupils to keep safe. Life within the tall glass windows was often more difficult than life in the commune.

Miss Manning did very well. She took over the responsibility of all the German. There was less German than French, so she helped with two French classes each year, but took German up to O level and A level. Spanish was considered easier for the less bright pupils, so in year 9 the majority chose Spanish. Her workload was achievable.

As a form mistress, she had a tutor group across the age groups. From year 7 to year 13. There were four to five of each year represented in her registration group. They were part of a house system. Each pupil was put in a house named after a famous person for the duration of their time in the school. It was one way of dividing up the huge school and getting the age groups to mix; the older ones were expected to help and encourage the younger. There was good as well as bad influences within the groups.

She had to deal with issues which were huge in teenage lives.

One of her groups from year 8, came after school to tell her that her best friend was pregnant. "Our neighbour has boys and Judy came around to play in my house. The boys next door came and joined us and that's how Judy got pregnant. She won't tell her mum," explained Sue.

Miss Manning asked Judy to see her and discussed what Sue had told her.

"She's joking. I'm not pregnant. It's not true!" Judy laughed.

Sue and Judy stood together. Sue insisted that Judy was just scared and swore that she was pregnant.

"We'll have to call in your parents whether it is true or not," Miss Manning insisted. Following that there were a few quiet days.

"Miss, Judy really is pregnant. She is really scared." Judy was called in.

"This cannot go on. I shall ask your Housemistress to invite your parents in and talk with the Head Master." She dismissed them once more.

School was closing up, cleaners were coming in, sports teams were changing, and the choir was meeting for practice. The Head suddenly appeared at her classroom as she was closing drawers and cupboards.

"Miss Manning, please come now to my study."

She followed him.

"I have some parents here to speak to you."

Judy and her parents stood just behind the door. Her father looked very angry. "How can you listen to such lies?"

"I told Judy and Sue that I was about to ask the Head of Year to invite you in. Sue insisted, even in front of Judy, that Judy had said she was frightened and was really pregnant," Miss Manning tried to explain.

They calmed down and the Head asked for the foundation of the story.

The poor teacher told them Sue's story about the boys from next door who came to play when Judy was visiting. They agreed to call in Sue with her parents the next day. There was no pregnancy. Sue was attention seeking in the most disturbing way.

Carol, however, was pregnant. Doro found her crying in the cloakroom one Friday evening and sat with her to ask what the problem was, if she could help her at all. Carol said she had rowed with her parents about her boyfriend and they had forbidden her to see him. The teacher said what she thought might help and was about to leave her when she helped her take her coat down. She looked very pregnant. Miss Manning challenged her.

"Everyone knows I have put on weight!" She smiled and set off home. Doro was convinced the girl was pregnant but it was Friday evening and there was no one left in school to tell.

On Monday morning the Head called Miss Manning in again.

"Your tutor group is having a time of it!" he said. "Carol's parents rang early this morning to say that she had run away to Cornwall with her boyfriend who had bought camping gear."

They had asked the police to help and the couple were found in the hills and were brought home. Carol was three months pregnant. The boy was a black lad from Brixton from another class in her year. They were both 15. He was expelled but Carol was allowed to stay for another three months. She gave birth to a boy who was put up for adoption. Carol sat and wept with Miss Manning when she returned to school. Carol said she cried for her baby every night and prayed for him every day. Doro felt for them all. A mixed-race, illegitimate baby at 15 was not acceptable in 1969.

The person of Diane had only just begun to exist. It was summer 1970 before she felt she had become an accepted member of the Aachen group. In England she shut down her emotions as she did not want to become promiscuous and have sex in Aachen and then with another man in England. She worked at remaining withdrawn from that side of normal life.

She thought life at the Dale School was very fulfilling. She found herself wanting to tell Rainer about school life as well as giving reports on Aachen. He did not want to sit and chat. He did not want to hear of her school life. Which life was real? She was not at all sure as she succeeded in cutting herself in two.

The student rebellion reached the Dale School on the ether. Years 11 and 12 staged a school strike. A politically minded parent contacted the Guardian who sent a photographer. There was a photo of one boy and a few girls holding placards. On most of them were the words: 'We want coloured tights!' Not quite anti-imperialistic slogans.

'Freedom to wear our own clothes' was written on the boy's placard.

They objected to wearing black tights with their uniform when coloured tights, yellow, blue, red and green filled the shelves of the local shops. This was the current fashion. Even the teachers wore them.

Doro liked to tell the story in later years. Compared to France and Germany, it was a joke. All the students were expelled and they were accepted at a more radical school the other side of London. Two of the girls were in Miss Manning's tutor group. Life returned to normal.

In 1966 Guinness had published some huge posters to commemorate the anniversary of the Battle of Hastings. It depicted the Bayeux tapestry with soldiers holding glasses of Guinness. The previous teacher had stuck one right across the wall on top of the notice board. Doro considered that it should go as it was out of date, dog-eared and irrelevant four years after the event. She asked two tall boys to help her. She put a chair on a desk and stood as high as she could as they pulled on the corners.

"The corridor's on fire!" yelled a boy.

"Oh, yes! What a thing to try." She carried on until the poster was peeled down.

"Miss, really! It is on fire!" The teacher balanced on the chair and turned around as far as she could. The corridor at right angles to her room was a wall of fire. In the next minute the alarm was sounded and the school was evacuated. Miss Manning and the boys jumped down and filed out in the opposite direction. The glass walls overlooking the court yard began to turn black. Opposite the windows there was a wall of wooden lockers. Some vandalising pupils had filled the lower lockers with paper and set light to it.

"We had arson this week," she told Rainer in Russell Square. "It's worse than the terror in Germany." She laughed.

36

"You are doing a wonderful job, Diane, coping with school adventures as well as the Marxists."

At Easter she heard of some of their plans to contact Baader and Meinhof and possibly take a car bomb to Stammheim, the prison in Stuttgart. He was pleased to hear that because he had received other intelligence about the same event, so this was a confirmation. In those early years of the '70s, Baader and Meinhof were more in prison than out. Rainer encouraged her to keep going after so many years. Doro wondered what he did with his time. He was always very up to date on the news of any bombs or kidnapping but he seemed to fade away as she put down one life and took up the other. Her only real relaxation was attending concerts. She had joined a local Anglican church which often gave public concerts.

After the death in prison of the hunger striker, Holger Meins, one of the RAF terrorists, there were renewed demonstrations, totally expected, but Lotte became more and more concerned about Manfred. She reported to Rainer and to the Cologne group leaders. Manfred had been broken by the death of Ulrike Meinhof but did not direct his anger towards the bourgeois system which he considered responsible for her murder. As the dreaded year of 77 approached, Doro put more and more effort into her school work.

She started a German club and tried to get some of the black students to join. She arranged to call at the home of one of the girls she had invited.

"You have a lovely singing voice, Melda. Could you come and sing with us on the Carol Concert? We are going to sing three or four in German."

Melda asked her parents who were happy to see Miss Manning at their door. Melda had quite a big, loving and caring family. Doro looked around. On nearly every flat surface was a coloured netting ruffle, mainly pink and green, sewn to fan out as a decoration. Family photos in flowery frames stood behind them. Melda's parents agreed that she could sing in the Carol Concert. On the day, Melda arrived wearing high heeled shoes and carrying a suitcase. Her parents had imagined that as it was a public concert, she had to wear evening dress. Miss Manning had some tactful explaining to do. She stood in her uniform with borrowed shoes and sang beautifully.

This was the Christmas week in Aachen when Manfred had violated her. The following Easter was when he attacked her and killed their baby. Lotte had rescued her, accompanied her to the clinic in England and amazingly, she recovered enough to go into the summer term. She also attended meetings with the psychologist recommended by Rainer.

Her sessions were on Friday night in north London so no one knew about her travels every two weeks. Doro fought the kind and understanding psychologist as she fought herself to maintain both outward and inward control. She worked hard at hardening her emotions and shutting down her pain instead of letting it out.

"Let it out. Let go. It will come back later in life if you suppress it."

She took no notice but concentrated on dealing with the present and her ability to cope. She made less effort to get information. What she gleaned she gave to Rainer but she spent most of her time with him talking about how she could get out without causing suspicion.

In 1978 she was relieved to see that Manfred had gone and was never referred to. Inside, something had changed and she felt she should stop.

A school friend invited her to an organ concert to be given by her personal friend. Doro went along to a central London venue with Monica and thoroughly enjoyed the traditional, well-known music of Bach, Buxtehude, Beethoven and Mozart. She was introduced to Richard Harlow; the performer and they all went for a drink together.

Richard was slim, well groomed, quiet and rather withdrawn.

Chapter 6

Quiet I can handle Doro thought as they sat in a pub.

"I so appreciated your concert," she said to him. "You have no idea what good it did me." He handed them a leaflet of his next concerts.

"I am doing Messiaen next. Not to everyone's taste." He smiled at her. "Combat de la mort et de la vie. That's amazing. I have heard that."

He smiled again. "Do feel free to come to any of them."

Doro felt a warmth come into her heart. She felt unthreatened by this organist. His conversation was undemanding. He did not ask many questions about her life. For just over a year, they met at concerts and went for drinks which progressed to meals. He shared a little about his family. He had remained single, had a London flat but was applying for a post in Surrey. His father was in a Care Home with Alzheimer's and he was planning to find a new home for him in Surrey if his application was successful.

Several events coincided. Rainer agreed to work on an exit strategy for Diane. She was told that once she had left, she should make no contact with any of the members including Lotte. After her final debriefing at the London Office, she would never see Rainer again.

Richard was accepted by Guildford where he would be organist in a historic church but also in charge of organising and playing at concerts in other churches including the cathedral.

Here was a full-time organist and choirmaster with whom he would liaise. Just at the right time he started taking Doro's hand, kissing her and putting his arms around her.

"Richard has asked me to marry him," she told Rainer. "And I want to say yes. He is a lovely, gentle and considerate man."

"You'll move to Surrey. That's a good reason to give for leaving!" He smiled at her. "The group will understand that you are changing schools, changing towns and getting married. They will understand. Most of them know what you went through." She stared into his eyes.

"Thank you, Rainer."

"You will have a pension for your services when you leave."

"Pension? I was not paid a real salary."

"That's how it had to be for your special job. You are owed a huge debt of gratitude and you will be given a large sum of money. It will help with your move."

"I'm grateful, Rainer. Thank you so much. Goodbye, Rainer."

The words echoed in her head. He stood up and opened his arms and she let him hug her. "I wish you all the best, a really happy life with Richard."

He kissed her on her forehead. "Goodbye, Dorothea." She gave him a hug, turned and walked out of the office without looking back. She could weep. She did not let herself. She walked to Russell Square via the back of the British Museum. She sat on a bench in silence and stillness. Her tactics had worked and she did not cry. She phoned Richard.

"Richard, I would love to marry you. I love you very much."

She was walking out to Trafalgar Square where she was about to meet Richard and suddenly noticed Rainer walking in and sitting on a bench. She was out of his line of vision so she watched him for a few minutes. He was just sitting like she had done, still and staring ahead and then he put his head in his hands.

"Twelve years. He's dominated my whole life for 12 years. It's over. I'm free." She did not know why she felt a deep sadness inside but she strode to Trafalgar Square to go into her new life.

She and Richard went to a concert at St Martin's in the Fields, then had a celebratory meal in a French restaurant a few yards away.

As 1979 ended, Richard took her to a jeweller to choose an engagement ring. She chose a diamond and then invited him to her flat. He gently suggested they got married in a London church where he had often played. She was happy with that. He was planning to go to Guildford to look at houses as he wanted a house in the country.

"What do you think?" She sat next to him and held his face in her hands and kissed him. "You have made me very happy, Richard." He kissed her back.

"Have you had boyfriends?" The question she dreaded.

"Just one, a few years ago. And you?"

"Also a few years ago, another organist."

"Richard, it is a privilege to be with you."

"Do you want children?" Another question she dreaded.

"If they came, I would be happy. If they don't, we'll find other ways to be happy."

"I'd love children," he said. She felt the pressure. She hoped she could give him children but the deep fear of damage was still with her.

They made love in her bed. The first time since the attack and she not only managed but gave all she could to make Richard feel loved and wanted.

"That was wonderful," she said.

"For me too." He kissed and caressed her.

"I love you, Doro, I love you." She responded with a passion which surprised her. Dorothea realised that her double life was over. She could be Richard's wife, perhaps a mother and a teacher in a different school.

She realised her isolation when it came to choosing a wedding dress. His friend, Monica who had introduced them was in the Music Department at school. She asked her if she would like to help her choose a dress.

"Doro, I'd love to. You two were made for each other. You have no relatives?"

"None. All alone in the world."

They went to Oxford Street and chose the dress. Monica persuaded her to have an off the shoulder dress, even strapless in silk and lace.

It was a magnificent dress and she looked like a princess. She really enjoyed seeing herself in the mirror. This is my life, one whole life, one whole person.

She went with Richard to see his church in Guildford and to visit estate agents. "When I sell my flat in London, I will have a large sum to contribute to the house."

"Let's see what the prices are like. We could hold back your money for decoration and holidays." He kissed her.

They were encouraged to look in a village in the Surrey Hills rather than Guildford itself. They both thought that being in the country would be wonderful. They were shown around a three- to four-bedroomed house in a quiet corner with a view of the hills. They both agreed to put in an offer. When back in town, she called in at the Education Office and gave them her details,

41

saying that in the new academic year she would be looking for a post teaching German. She also scanned the Times Educational Supplement.

Within weeks, her qualifications meant that she had schools competing for her. She talked it over with Richard and he encouraged her to have a change. She had worked in a huge London Comprehensive for years.

"Dear Doro, have a rest. Go for a grammar or a private school and use your language skills instead of battling with difficult pupils."

"Have you taught?"

"Yes, one to one, organ, piano and composition. In schools and in private homes. I love it."

"Your name is so lovely, Dorothea. It suits you."

"I am usually Doro, never just Thea."

"Why not? It suits you." They returned to his flat in London and made love on his bed. He stroked her, whispering, "Thea, my own Thea." She was filled with love for him and felt warm, healing power flow through her.

The farewell party at the Dale was an emotional affair. Doro was liked, respected and appreciated. The party was extra fun as the upper sixth linguists joined in. She was given lovely gifts suitable for a new home. She cherished the large vase for her hallway, bright, sophisticated and modern. Thea was so grateful that she had managed to get through all those years of teaching without anyone guessing her secret life. She had survived so much but she always doubted that she really achieved much for the Secret Services.

Monica and some other staff came to their wedding with the sixth form linguists. Dorothea looked stunning to them all as she became Dorothea Harlow. She felt waves of joy as she left more and more of her double life behind her.

They chose the south of France for their honeymoon. The perfume of Grasse lavender, the bright blue of the Mediterranean, the sun-kissed olive groves brought joy to them both.

Loving Richard was a cure for the abuse of Manfred. Richard loved her passionately but never did anything to frighten or disturb her.

She could let herself go and be quite innovative and adventurous with him. He nicknamed her 'Thea the temptress' but appreciated her efforts to give him pleasure.

Richard was a fairly withdrawn personality, even when he asked her about her parents and her past life, it felt very non-threatening. She managed to find satisfactory answers. He wanted to know about the accident that killed her parents and about her grandmother. She explained what she knew. She could have been killed with them on the motorway but she had an extra German class instead. She decided not to travel with them. They had crashed into the back of a juggernaut and were hit from behind by another lorry. The juggernaut had slammed on brakes to avoid a car pulling onto the hard shoulder. It did not make it in time. Doro had been close to her parents and was in grief for a long time. She loved her granny, her father's mother and was well cared for until the elderly lady became ill and died. She took her O levels and began her A levels still suffering the loss. Once she went up to Oxford, she let the house and took a room in the college.

Later she sold the house to buy a flat. Now she was about to sell that flat and add the money to the pension account so Richard would never know where it all came from.

Mrs Harlow took up a Head of German post in a private school just outside the town. The students were pushed to aim for Oxbridge or for Science and Technology in other prestigious Universities. Dorothea now had a different challenge, privilege instead of Marx, and well-to-do, middle-class families instead of the deprivation of her first school.

After two years of happy married life, Doro became pregnant, much to their delight. She still maintained anxiety about the condition of her body right up to the last moment when Edward was born. She was overwhelmed with love for him. Richard was thrilled and ever ceased to say so. He took his turn feeding and changing and hired a professional photographer.

It gradually dawned on Dorothea that she could make and keep friends and share her life. She had planned to return to teaching after maternity leave, but she could not bear to leave her son. She decided she could not do it so she resigned. The school did not want to lose her. She agreed to offer occasional cover and take some private tuition from time to time. Her greatest delight was to spend time with Edward. She sang, spoke only English with him. Richard was a little anxious that his salary alone would not cover all their needs. He took on some extra hours of private tuition between his church duties and his organising of organ concerts very regularly. Doro was thinking of restarting teaching when Edward went to nursery or play school. She then realised that she was pregnant again. They were really pleased and had fun choosing names. They learned that she was expecting a girl.

"Edward and WHO? Harlow?" he asked.

"Perhaps it will come to us when we meet her," said Doro.

She had visited Richard's father with the baby. He had settled in his new home but was not very aware of people around him. He recognised Richard, but that was all.

"What was your mother's name?" she asked.

"Evelyne Marianna Harlow."

"I like Marianna Harlow!" She smiled and kissed Richard.

They tried to prepare Edward for the arrival of his sister and more and more often, he sat on Richard's knee at the keyboard and played the notes. He greatly enjoyed this, banging sometimes, laughing and then tinkling a few notes gently and laughing with delight at the sound.

A scan revealed that the baby had an irregular heartbeat, so Doro was told to have bed-rest. Richard took Edward to play on the swings, to swim in the pool and run in the park while she obeyed.

Marianna was born and was immediately put onto a machine. They wept as they looked on sadly. They could not cuddle their little girl. Edward was allowed to touch her little hands. They sat stunned as the doctor told them that she was not likely to live. Her condition was inoperable. Richard stayed at home with Edward while Doro sat through the nights with her daughter.

She was dozing over the plastic box covering the tubes when the nurse came in to check the monitors.

"I am so sorry. She has gone." The nurse put her arm around Doro. They called Richard who brought Edward to say a final goodbye.

The loss of Marianne was a long-lasting blow for them. Edward was two and could remember touching his sister and knew that she was no longer with them. They gave her a beautiful funeral. They took Edward to Disneyland for a holiday that summer and Doro decided she should return to teaching part time now that Edward had a permanent nursery place.

Doro did not become pregnant ever again. She was grateful for her son but wondered if she had any internal damage which could have caused the heart defect which killed her daughter. She never asked. She and Richard both adored their son and resigned themselves to having just one son. They returned to their loving intimacy after some months. Doro felt that Richard was longing for another baby and kept an eye on dates, but after the next few years, he did seem resigned. She always did her best to make him feel loved and to show her enjoyment of his lovemaking.

Doro progressed from part-time to full-time and eventually became Head of Modern Languages in her original school. She enjoyed teaching German language and literature and only on a few occasions did a reference to recent German history come into her conscious thinking. She looked at the news and read about current events but was able to disassociate herself from it. These were the quiet years when she could totally forget. She was pleased that Edward favoured music above languages. He became more and more interested in science and felt he should pursue O and A levels in these subjects while keeping up music on the side. He was already a proficient pianist and could transpose music and compose for himself. At eleven he got a place in his mother's school. The next years passed without further dramatic incidents or tragedy.

Doro arranged day trips to France and exchange trips to both countries. There were mini dramas like there always are with teenagers and some memorable incidents. One of the return Channel crossings was hit by a storm. After a lovely day in Boulogne, the storm had hit mid Channel. Several of the staff as well as the children were taken ill. Doro and one male teacher were able to cope. All the others were being sick. Most people were being sick on the decks and in the corridors. Writhing bodies were on the stairs, the decks, and the benches.

A wave buffeted the ferry, causing a bang like an explosion. A woman lost control and screamed over and over. A man slapped her face.

The ship limped into dock and it was a terrible job to locate staff and children. Some had run to the toilet and not found their way back. They had been forbidden to open the doors and go on deck which had at least four inches of water swilling over the rocking deck. Doro counted the children onto the coach. One was missing. She asked about him and some said he was on the bench with them. They did not see where he went when they walked down to the coaches.

Olly was the sort of boy who would have disobeyed and gone on deck. The coach had to drive off and parked on the quay. Doro was not allowed back on the filthy boat. She called for someone in authority. They described where he had been on the boat and one sailor agreed to go and look for him. What anxious moments they had as the time went on. At last, the sailor appeared, carrying an unconscious boy over his arms.

"He had fainted and rolled under the bench. He's small so he was right at the back." With great relief, her colleague picked him up and held him upright.

"Olly! Olly! Come on, Olly!" An eye opened. The teacher patted his face both sides and asked for some water. Olly gradually recovered and asked what the fuss was all about.

It was 2.00 am when the coach arrived outside the school where a crowd of parents and the Deputy Head were waiting. Parents thanked the staff for coping so well and left quickly. They were told to take the next morning off school. Olly was still in the coach.

"Can we ring your parents?"

"Don't know where they are. I can walk from here, it's not far. I can get a key."

"I am coming with you." Doro put on her mac and walked with Olly who seemed bright and not at all bothered. The house was in darkness. Olly went to a flower pot and lifted it to get a key. He opened the door and put on the lights. The house was empty.

"They are still out. I'm OK. I am often on my own. I'll go to bed."
"I will ring in the morning. I hate to leave you after you were so ill."

Doro saw him in and saw him shut the door. After an almost sleepless night she rang his mother's number at about 8.00. Doro asked after Olly.

"He's still asleep. He's OK, why?"

Doro explained what had happened and that at two in the morning no one was at home. Olly had said nothing to her about being sick and fainting.

"Didn't you see my note with the number of where we were? It was under a heavy stone." This was one of the amusing stories that she could tell at dinner parties.

Richard and Doro had celebrated their tenth wedding anniversary in Canada. He had thought she might like to go to a favourite place in Germany but she could not make herself go there with her family for leisure. She bluffed her way through and said she would love to see the Niagara Falls and the prairies and big lakes. She had returned to Freiburg for the exchange visits but would not go again if she did not have to. They took Edward with them and he too loved Canada. They enjoyed the prairies, Toronto and Winnipeg and the vast lakes. Edward thought he might go and live there when he grew up.

Richard, Doro and Edward enjoyed many similar holidays over the years.

Edward applied for a Science and Technology course at Bristol and kept music as an important hobby. He brought a few girlfriends home but was more interested in getting into scientific research than settling down with a girl.

In his early sixties, Richard was diagnosed with prostate cancer. He made a good recovery after radiotherapy but the remission did not last very long. Within a year he was on chemotherapy. Over two years his wife and son saw him decline. He was put on a palliative care program. Doro welcomed care workers and nurses to her home.

Edward came home often to spend time with his father as the new tablets took their toll on his energy, his mind and his mobility. His cancer spread to his spine so he also lost mobility.

Edward was very upset to see this suffering. He loved and admired his father and found the pain hard to bear. He wanted to support his mum but he was aware of a profound inner strength within her. Richard died peacefully in a hospital bed. Vulnerable to infections he had been taken in for intense antibiotic treatment. Dorothea arrived in the ward to find Edward slumped over his father's chest as he tried to accept that he had gone. Dorothea sat and held her son.

They planned his funeral in the church where he had been organist and consulted his friends on hymns and pieces of music. Edward took a break from his research as he struggled to cope with the loss of his father.

"Your research might one day lead to a cure for cancer." Doro tried to encourage him and motivate him to continue with research. She feared he was too often alone as he spent hours in the laboratory. She felt he needed to spend more time in conferences and discussions with fellow scientists as a balance to his isolation. He went back to Bristol and left Doro alone for the first time since Richard's death.

She sat gazing out of the conservatory windows at the dramatic sunsets, the swaying trees, the buzzards gliding over the hills. She was surprised to admit that she had never told her husband about her secret work. Their loving relationship was part of another world and she no longer wanted to think about any part of her time in Aachen. When she let her mind recall Aachen, she had a sense of sadness that working with the RAF groups had prevented her enjoying the beauties of that part of Germany. She felt grateful that she had been able to escape the terrorist circle and enjoy nearly 30 years of happy marriage, happy motherhood and a happy life in all respects; teaching and leisure.

Less than a year after Richard's death, Edward's colleagues had noticed that he had a growing mole on his upper back and advised him to get it checked.

"Mum, I have a melanoma on my back. The doctor tells me they can operate and treat the area. It's a cancerous growth and could spread if I don't get it treated now."

"Ed, dearest, I am so sorry. Skin cancer is usually successfully treated. Can you have the operation in Guildford?"

"I'll ask."

Doro felt angry that he had to endure this just after the loss of his father. She read up notes online and spoke to her GP. He was confident that it could be treated and would never return and that he could lead a normal life.

She was waiting to hear where the operation would take place and planned to book into a Bristol Hotel if it had to be there. The phone rang and she guessed it would be Ed to tell her of the decision. It was the police from Bristol. Edward had been found dead in his room.

Shock and pain filled her as she tried to believe it. She asked a friend to go with her to Bristol to identify the body and find out how he had died. Renate, who was also a widow, had kept in touch with Doro after they had both retired from years of teaching. Renate offered to drive her to Bristol. She was glad of her company and support as she was handed a suicide note by her beloved boy.

He had planned his death with the awareness that he was abandoning his mother but he felt that he could not endure cancer treatment after witnessing the prolonged suffering and death of his father. He was unable and unwilling to go through something similar. He knew he had a strong mother who would be able to cope with the loss of both husband and son.

Edward had bought packets of Paracetamol from chemists in both Guildford and Bristol over several days. He had bought three bottles of vodka and poured it into six glasses. He had emptied the tablets into a large bowl. In his study bedroom he had threaded strong, white washing line over a hook which he had drilled into the ceiling. He had put on an organ CD and drunk two glasses of vodka, swallowing small handfuls of tablets. When he felt drunk, he stood on a chair and put his head in the noose he had made. Before he jumped off the chair, he had swallowed another glass of vodka. After he jumped, his death followed quickly.

He was lying in the mortuary looking peaceful and cleaned up, white and cold. Doro stood by him with her tears flowing.

"What a waste. He had so much to offer. He was afraid he would suffer like his father had suffered. My poor, dear son!" Doro said aloud.

She was treated with care and kindness as she dealt with all the aspects of his death; paper work, collecting his property, answering questions. The university said they would be holding a memorial service for him. On her last visit to the department office, a young lady was ushered in.

"Mrs Harlow, this young lady was a special, close friend of your son and wanted to meet you." An Asian girl, tall, slim and beautiful, presented herself.

"I'm Rabia, Mrs Harlow. I was Edward's girlfriend for the past six months." Her eyes were red and her cheeks tearstained. "He told me all about his father's death. I have known him three years but we have only been together for the past few months. I asked if I could meet you."

"I am so pleased to meet you, Rabia. Let me give you my details and take your e-mail. You would be very welcome at his funeral."

"Thank you. I am so sorry I was not able to stop him. I had no idea he was so depressed and in despair. I know he was afraid of cancer treatment." Doro and Rabia hugged each other.

It took Doro at least two years before she felt anything like normal. She remembered the psychologist she had seen in the 1970s and asked about bereavement counselling. After the memorial service in Bristol, she began some counselling but her divided life remains divided. She only shared about her sad and tragic loss and did not mention her secret past. Speaking out about her loss and grief enabled her to regain some inner strength. She was able to face the guilt that all relatives of suicides go through. As the third year approached, she started to realise she was more at peace, had some hope for the future and began slowly to make plans to travel and take up a new project.

It was at this stage that her old controller from the Intelligence Services contacted her.

The first interview had left her in a broken state, weeping and sobbing, totally overwhelmed and unable to cope.

Chapter 7

Rainer, her old controller, had seen her distress and taken her out of the room for a break. As he stood holding this shattered woman at the end of the corridor, he realised that she could not continue with the questioning. She needed serious help. She could hardly stand and began to sink to the floor. He was not sure what to do. If he let her go, she would collapse. He was rescued by Lotte. His precious undercover agent had realised there was a problem and had come out of the office. She came and hugged Diane with Rainer and spoke softly to each other.

"We must get her into the clinic. She is having the nervous breakdown she has put off all her life," Rainer said.

"I'll get a blanket and sit with her while you make the phone calls," Lotte replied. She told the new boss what was needed. They found some blankets and wrapped her up in the corridor. Doro was still sobbing deeply, trembling and beginning to groan. Rainer phoned for an ambulance and Lotte said she would go with her to the clinic.

"I am coming too. I can't leave her. I caused all this." Lotte went to see Ralph.

"We'll have to pause here. Our agent is having a breakdown. I hope you know what she suffered in her work for us. Rainer and I will go with her and I'm sure that we will be able to return to speak with you at a later date. We need to look after this precious, long-suffering woman."

Ralph said he would greatly appreciate reconvening in a week.

"No one realises the true cost, do they? So many agents turn to drink and drugs," Ralph commented.

The ambulance took Rainer, Lotte and Doro to the clinic.

"Lotte, thank you so much for coming and for caring. When you speak to her, when she comes out of this, please be careful what you tell her. I had arranged to speak to her after this session. She had agreed, probably reluctantly. She has no idea what happened. She's had a happy marriage but sadly her son killed himself after her husband died. She's been broken so many times."

Doro was sedated and put on some drugs to allow her to sleep for a couple of days. Rainer and Lotte took it in turns to spend several hours a day with her. Rainer took charge of the practical things. He found Renate in Guildford and introduced himself as an old friend.

He explained that she had been taken ill in London and was spending some days in hospital. Renate agreed to take her key and clear her fridge and check on her house. She wondered why she had never heard of Rainer and how Doro had been taken ill in London.

It was two weeks before Doro could leave the clinic. Rainer and Lotte saw her every day. They wanted to make a plan of action to get her home, to talk to her about Renate and decide on a cover story so the whole truth would not have to come out. Rainer agreed that Lotte was the best person to handle that. The day before her release, Lotte arrived in her room and found Rainer sitting by the bedside, stroking her hair and trying to calm her down.

"Shall we take her home together?" Lotte said.

"Good idea. We must meet Renate and find a counsellor based in Surrey."

Renate was phoned by Rainer and was sitting in Doro's house awaiting their arrival. Rainer had of course done the necessary research. Renate was from the Black Forest and had lived with her parents near Stuttgart during the war. Her village had not seen much action and they had all survived. Her father had been a regular soldier but he had died shortly after the war because there were no available medicines; he was not treated for appendicitis. She met and married an English man and moved to England. She trained to teach German, had no political leanings but carried the guilt of Nazism in her heart. Her children had married and lived nearby. They took care of her in her widowhood. She had retired just before Doro and they had kept in touch and she had proved to be a good friend to Doro when Edward died. Lotte and Rainer planned to tell her some of the secrets.

They all had tea in the lounge as Doro, still under the influence of medication, tried to understand exactly what was happening. Rainer talked her through what had happened to her and what their plan was for her immediate care.

She sat, sipping her tea.

"Thank you all so much for your help. I'll soon be better at home. There are some lovely walks near here. I have good neighbours who will do some shopping for me."

"Doro, take time. I'm coming to stay for a few days and Rainer will call very often."

"You can't do that, Rainer. It's too far."

"I have a surprise for you. I live about ten minutes from here."

"Since when?"

"Since I retired."

"I can't take it in."

"Don't worry, I will explain it all in little bits as you get better."

Rainer addressed Renate, "Thank you so much for your help. Doro needs a lot of support right now; she is having a nervous breakdown after a terrible ordeal she went through some years ago."

"You are both German, where are you from?"

"Renate, we are going to tell you some secret information. Do you think you can keep it secret from your children and your friends?"

"I am beginning to realise that I have not grasped the situation. It makes no sense. I have worked with Dorothea since 1985 and I have never heard her mention either of you."

"I believe we can trust you, Renate, it's a delicate matter." Lotte butted in. "We have German names, we speak German but we are English. They are our cover names. No point changing them now, we have known each other by those names for over 40 years."

"You were in the secret service?"

"We were. We have all retired now. We worked together on a specific project to help Germany deal with the post-war terrorism. It was dangerous work and Doro had some terrible experiences and now that she has lost her husband and son, the horror of them is catching up with her."

Doro was wiping her eyes and weeping.

"She needs to weep. She has held in her tears for 30 years, now they are falling and she will receive healing by letting them out." Lotte knelt by Doro's chair and hugged her as she sobbed. Renate looked on trying to get her head around it all.

"Renate, if she wants to talk about parts of her project, that's fine, but please do not ask her a lot of questions. Ask me or Lotte if you are frustrated trying to understand. Here's my card with email."

"You are such a gentleman and so kind to me. I am glad to help Doro get through this. I'm willing to stay some nights if it helps."

"Doro," said Rainer, "why don't you get some sleep. Renate has got food in for all of us. We'll wait for you."

"Of course, she has. One day you'll tell me how you found her."

"One day I will. Are you going to rest now? Would you like some of Richard's music?"

"Oh, Rainer, I would love that!"

Lotte administered medication and Dora slept.

"Renate, she was a very brave young woman. She suffered terribly but went on with the project for several more years before she was released to live a normal life. She met Richard, a lovely man and had a very happy marriage. Tragedy has followed her. She lost her parents at 17 in a car accident and her second baby, a little girl, died soon after the birth. As you know, she also lost her son to suicide because of his fear of the cancer which had killed his father."

Lotte stared at him. "How do you know all that?"

He smiled. "I think you know," he said softly.

"Where do you live?"

"There's a town called Godalming to the south of here. I live in a house in a side road, near the river Wey, just before you reach the town."

"Doro will be amazed."

"She will. Lotte, tell me how you are since you returned to England."

"I have a lovely flat near Regent's Park. I do some art work, I belong to the Goethe Institute, my second home, I cook and I relax."

"Well done, Lotte. I am pleased to hear that." Rainer smiled and looked like a different person. He even sat in a more relaxed way. She understood a lot more than she ever said and wondered how long he would keep it all inside him.

"Renate, tell us about your family." he asked.

She showed photos of her children, their wives and husbands and her grandchildren. Her son worked in an IT company, one daughter was a primary school teacher and the other was in social work.

Two hours passed before Doro came down stairs.

"Come and have some fresh air." Rainer took her arm and they went into the garden.

"You have a lovely view." She held his arm and they stood looking at the rosebay willow herb.

Lotte and Renate exchanged glances and went into the kitchen to prepare a meal.

Chapter 8

Lotte was pleased to see Doro wash and dress herself each day. She made coffee and planned lunch with her.

"What a lovely friend. You are lucky to have Renate."

"I am indeed. She came and identified Edward's body with me; she drove me to Bristol and back and she has a large family of her own."

"And now you have Rainer as a neighbour."

"What?"

"He's moved to Godalming."

"What?"

"I have only just found out. I have not seen him since I retired."

"I'm so confused. How? Why? What is he doing?"

"He will not want to be a nuisance to you but he will care for you while you need care. He will leave you alone when you don't want him around."

"I cannot get my head around how he found me and called me to the office after 30 years of silence."

"When you are stronger, I have a lot to tell you. You'll understand more then. It's too much for now."

"It was Manfred's photo. Seeing it filled me with horror and fear. I won't have to see him as he is now, will I?"

"No, you won't. It's too early to talk about it all."

"How did you get out? How were you nearly blown?"

"By Manfred. I was lucky to escape, but, Doro, learn it bit by bit. Be patient. Rainer wants to tell you, but he knows you are too fragile."

"When is he coming?"

"After lunch. He wants to take you out."

"When I am better, I want to know your names, your real names. I hate Diane."

"Of course, you would. You were only 19, so young and inexperienced. I wasn't happy with the decision but your information was like gold dust."

Doro was subdued by tablets but she felt her heart race at the thought of going out with Rainer. She found her 19-year-old self-longing to see him. He was less overwhelming now, more gentle, more human.

After lunch Lotte said she was staying at home. Doro felt so strange getting into his car, sitting next to him and being alone with him. She remembered the safe houses and Russell Square and her longing that he would show some sign that he liked her.

"I must pull myself together. I'm no longer 19, I am a few years off 60 and he must be over 60 now."

"Where are we going?"

"A walk by a lake, not far away, it's called Winkworth Arboretum."

"Oh, it's lovely. We went often and I have a Membership card."

"You agreed to have a meal with me in London. We'll have it one day in Godalming in the French Restaurant."

"I know that too. We had an anniversary meal there one year."

"Would you rather go somewhere different? I'm just getting to know the area and its delights."

"When did you move here?"

"Nearly a year ago."

Doro let it sink it. Why did he do that? What if they had met in Godalming? They walked down the steps in Winkworth and enjoyed the last blooms of the azaleas and the rhododendrons. At the bottom, the lake, reflecting the sky, stretched ahead of them with its wildfowl.

They found a bench.

"Just like the old days." She smiled. "You look so different; not just the silver hair but you are wearing very different clothes."

"I have to learn to put the past behind me. I love the casual clothes."

"You're looking good," she said.

"And so are you, Doro, in spite of all this."

"You hugged me once in Russell Square. I was falling apart and that hug meant so much."

"I'll never forget. I felt so wretched." He put an arm around her shoulders and they sat like that a few moments. She then turned to him and put her arms around his chest and he held her to him.

"Dorothea, I am so very sorry. I still feel wretched. Can you forgive me? It was my fault; I should not have recruited you and put you in such danger. More than that, I encouraged you to act out of character. I only saw the end results of the information on the RAF. I did not let myself think of what you would have to do. I am so, so sorry. I have never forgiven myself." Doro was trembling and weeping in his arms. She fumbled for a tissue and noticed he was weeping too. She fumbled for a second one and wiped his tears. He put his head in his hands and let go of her. They wept together; glad they had the place to themselves.

"Rainer, I would have done anything for you. I was obsessed by you until I learned to deal with my emotions."

"You were 19, not fully an adult, all alone in life. I took advantage; you were the perfect undercover agent. I am so sorry."

"We need to build on our past relationship but make it new, make it true, based on reality and truth."

"You are willing to do that?"

"I think I am. Start with your name. You dominated my life, all aspects of my life for 12 years. Something good must come out of it."

"I was never out of your life, Doro. I never stopped following your life."

"I can't take this in. Let's leave it there. My head is never clear. I live in a fog."

"I, as Rainer, nearly ruined your life. My name is Adam Chamberlain and I hope I can be a part of the rest of your life if you give me a chance. When you have had enough of me, tell me to go."

Doro stared at him. "You are Adam. You live near me. You have followed my life. My head is tired."

"I'll take you back now. You know this area much better than me. You choose a place for our next walk and talk."

"I need to think, Rainer…I mean Adam."

"Lotte doesn't know my name." He drove back, dropped her and drove off.

Doro needed to sleep again. She put on some music and lay on the bed. Lotte checked on her after a couple of hours. Doro sat up. "Lotte, I need to talk, to hear what you have to say, to understand what's really happening, but my head is not clear, I can't think clearly."

"You can ask to decrease the pills but it is a bit soon. What's on the top of your mind?"

"How you got out. What caused you to be almost blown? Why is Rainer living near me?"

"It's a long story. You have no idea what Rainer did for you but he took risks and put himself in danger. He doesn't want me to tell you but I think you need to know and it will help you get over the breakdown."

Those little dead-end chats helped Doro. She felt some hope that she would get stronger, that she would understand what Rainer or Adam was attempting to do, what he meant by some of his phrases, 'followed all your life'. Lotte was planning when to leave and to return to London.

"I'll always come if you feel you need me. I'm only a train ride away. I'll stay a few more days and I'll tell you what I think you should know. It will help you get things in perspective and help you make decisions. Renate isn't coming today so why don't we sit in your lovely conservatory. I'll have a glass of wine, you cannot yet."

Lotte asked Doro to recall the late '70s in the commune, the atmosphere, the tension, the plans for more bombs and the unreliable behaviour of Manfred. Just as an attack was being planned, to drive car bombs into a US airbase, when they least needed police attention, Manfred attacked her, could have killed her. He was taken away and replaced. Doro never asked, nor was she told what happened to him. Rainer was not a field man but he risked a journey to Düsseldorf to meet Gerd, his full-time undercover agent. He and Lotte met him in a safe house in a flat overlooking the river near the commercial centre.

Gerd was about to expose his group to the police, just before the bombing. The three of them discussed how to handle Manfred. The Cologne leaders were aware that he had a wide knowledge of networks, plans and contacts with the RAF leaders. He knew too much to be let loose but he was too unstable to trust with major operations. Normally they would want him brought to justice but that would be impossible without revealing Lotte and Diane. He needed to be out of the picture. He needed to be killed.

Rainer, Lotte and Gerd could not themselves make decisions. They would have to persuade Bruno and the other group leaders to put him in the firing line, or execute him. They did manage to get Bruno and the leaders of Cologne to meet to discuss Manfred. Rainer had no undercover agent in Cologne, so he risked going himself along with Lotte who was known and trusted. She introduced him as a sleeper agent from London who was concerned for the safety of his Marxist member from London. So far, so good.

Manfred exhibited psychotic behaviour when he met Rainer, shouting, banging the table, smashing cups and dishes. He caused a disturbance in the block of flats and had neighbours knocking on the door. They decided to move Manfred quickly. Bruno, Gerd and two other men including Jürgen, his right-hand man, took him to a van, gagged him and drove away, minutes before the police cars arrived with sirens sounding. The police officers came up the stairs, guns in hand. Manfred's ranting had used phrases such as 'radical action' and 'revolutionary zeal'.

Rainer, Lotte and other group members were still inside. They were asked for their ID when the officers noted the piles of boxes in the lounge. One had a closer look and yelled, "Explosives! A terrorist cell."

They radioed for more help and one of the members came through a door firing at the police. They fired back and injured the man and Rainer's arm was hit in the cross-fire.

Lotte grabbed a tea towel and tied it around his arm. They were all arrested and taken to a police station. Rainer was bleeding heavily and fearful that his arm was badly damaged, he asked for medical help. He and Lotte had a procedure for if they were arrested by the German police but he was unofficially there, in agony and hardly able to speak. Lotte was in a separate cell. They knew the specialist anti-terrorist police would soon arrive. Lotte asked to speak to the most senior police officer in the station. When he finally agreed to see her, she told him he should contact the British Embassy and use the code she gave him. Rainer was not an identifiable field man so it took longer for him to be seen. When Lotte spoke to the MI6 agent at the Embassy, she explained that Rainer needed urgent medical treatment. He was able to arrange for them both to be evacuated. Lotte was able to return to London with him and ask for the bullet to be removed.

Gerd let Rainer know that they had shot Manfred and disposed of his body. He was very relieved as he spent a few days in hospital. He had a shattered bone repaired below the elbow and was given physiotherapy to restore most of the movement in his left arm. He was able to move without problems by the time he next met Diane who had just been under medical care herself. Lotte had only just returned from her London trip with Doro when she had to go back with Rainer.

The Cologne group was blown. All the members were imprisoned. Bruno managed to build another group in a different flat. When Lotte returned to Aachen, she was under suspicion.

Why had she been allowed to go back to London and why had she been released? She explained that the 'sleeper' agent had been shot so she had to make sure he was treated in London or they would have been suspicious. No one knew he was a double agent. He was an undercover Marxist.

Diane was due to return to Aachen after her treatment for her attack and was willing to continue with her work as long as Manfred was not there. They were impressed. Lotte reported back to her wounded controller that she had been believed, mainly because Diane was willing to return.

"When Rainer held me in his arms to comfort me, he did so with an injured arm."

"He did not want you to know."

"Why ever did he do that? I'm sure the RAF would have killed Manfred."

"Stop and consider, Doro. Why would he take that risk to ensure your attacker was dealt with? He's always cared for you and watched over you all your life."

"Thank you, Lotte, you called me Doro now, it's hard to change the habit of a lifetime. Rainer told me his name. Not sure I will use it. What's yours?"

"Christina. I'll tell you my story another time."

Chapter 9

Doro was able to manage alone after two weeks. She was living in a dream state. The medication caused confusion in her mind. She had heard Lotte's account of Rainer's trip to Düsseldorf and Cologne to ensure that Manfred was dealt with. Her 1977 nightmare had become Rainer's nightmare. She and Rainer had talked of building a relationship, building on their past. It was still beyond her comprehension. Was he acting out of the guilt he so obviously felt?

She had trained herself to deaden her emotions until she married Richard. Now, alone, she was not sure about letting Rainer back into her life. What had he meant by 'sending him away'?

Renate looked in on her, ate with her and took her on trips to the countryside. She was very grateful.

Rainer's next visit would be difficult. She wanted to let him know that Lotte had told her about his trip and his injury and she knew Lotte would agree. He had checked on the clinic and found a psychiatrist willing to take on Doro's case in the Godalming Clinic. He recalled that she had used the word 'dominated' about his influence over her life, so he wanted to give her choices.

"Will you come and see my home and talk with me there?"

"Yes, I will, thank you." He arrived to pick her up. At the door he stood on the step and looked at her pull her coat around her shoulders. He took a step forward and greeted her with a kiss on the forehead.

She sat in his car feeling nervous and tired. He drove off the main road, down a stony drive. There were three houses at the bottom and he parked outside one.

"Welcome to Adam's home," he said. He showed her into his lounge which was the full length of the house, with glass doors which opened on to the garden and the river. His furniture looked new, two matching settees and a recliner armchair, coffee tables, bookcases and vases of flowers.

"Here's the kitchen." He walked out into a little corridor. The kitchen was large with a centre block with high stools. Through another door was the dining room which also had glass doors to the garden and river. It doubled as his study with a desk at the far end. The table had a glass top and six chairs.

"There's a toilet and wash basin near the front door, next to the stairs." He invited her to go up.

"There's my en suite bedroom and a smaller one opposite, not en suite."

Doro felt so strange seeing this home, talking with this man who in a way seemed like a stranger. She was longing to tell him what she knew, but nerves and confusion held her back.

"I'm so glad that you came, Doro, and that you are willing to talk with me." She put her hands on his elbows and stood in front of him.

"Which arm?" He looked down, avoided her eyes and remained silent for a while.

"Left," he almost whispered.

"Show me." He slowly removed his jacket and pulled his jumper over his head and dropped them onto a bed. She took his left arm and held it gently in two hands and looked at the deep, red scars just below the elbow. She moved forward and put both arms around his neck and he held her lightly. They stood still for a few minutes. He leant to her ear and spoke gently.

"Doro, everything in me wants to kiss and caress you. Don't feel rejected by me. If I did that now I would be taking advantage of you. I'm never going to do that again. When you have made a recovery and are off your meds and able to think straight, then and only with your assent would I do that."

"We are both damaged, Adam. That's wonderful of you." She wept in his arms and leant against his bare chest.

"Better get dressed." She wept, let him go and went downstairs.

She stood at the glass doors and watched the river. He came up behind her and opened the doors and took her to a little white bench.

"It's so lovely. You have made yourself a lovely home and decorated it so well. A place for healing."

"Coffee?"

"Please." They sat in the lounge on two separate settees.

"So, you risked being in Germany and you had Manfred killed?"

"In a way. I wanted to be sure you would be safe from him. The groups discipline their own. They would have killed Gerd, Lotte and you if they had ever discovered you worked for us. They probably shot him. Usually, they put a rogue agent on a dangerous assignment and make sure he got shot, but Manfred was too unstable. They could not trust him. Gerd and Bruno took assassins with them and took him into woodland. They probably buried the body or put it in the river." He sounded so matter of fact as he spoke from his other world.

"Lotte was saved by you going back to Aachen after the attack. No one could doubt your ardent Marxism after that. They believed her story of the 'sleeper' agent and she had only just got back from seeing you to the clinic. It was amazing."

"So Cologne was raided but not Aachen?"

"That is the most unlikely place to have a terrorist cell. Düsseldorf was raided. The police put a watch on it and followed the people who distributed the leaflets. Mainly they were blown because they were seen carrying the boxes with the explosives. Gerd tried to tell them they needed another centre for that work but they were fanatic about getting to a US airbase. Other groups in big cities were raided thanks to Gerd."

"Adam, you are Adam Chamberlain and you live in Godalming."

"I am. Try to change to Adam."

"Have you a family? Any lovers?"

"I have brothers and sisters, nieces and nephews. Our parents have died. Lovers? I've had a few over thirty years. Some out of duty, a seduction to gain an agent. Others were very short term."

"Do you know why?"

"I do. I'll tell you later on."

"How did you join the Intelligence Services?"

"I was recruited at Oxford. I had studied psychology and gone into research for my MA. The department wanted a 'people reader' to recruit agents and run them in the field, to be a solid base in London."

"How do you speak German?"

"My mother was a German Jew. She taught me and took me there. She took us to the concentration camp where many of her family were killed. They had put her onto the Kindertransport Refugee organisation.

"So sad. How did she cope?"

63

"She grew up with a Jewish family who were Reformed Jews. It made me hate Nazism and then the terrorism which presented itself as anti-fascist. They were just as ruthless, as you will recall."

"Are you Jewish?"

"No, my father was a Methodist but not very practicing."

"Adam, I am so pleased to meet you." she smiled at him.

"Dorothea, if you wish, you can see a psychiatrist in Godalming. One from the London clinic comes here regularly and is willing to take you on. See what you think."

"I don't have to go?"

"Of course not. You are suffering post-traumatic stress and you have so much to offer. You have a new life ahead of you and she is a specialist."

"Thank you, Adam. Can I go home now? I need to sleep."

Before she got out of the car, he took her hands in his and held them. "Doro, take care, get better. A walk tomorrow?"

"When I've made an appointment at the clinic. I'll show you a walk."

"Aufwiedersehen. Bis Morgen." He smiled and let her get out.

She turned before she shut the door and saw that he was crying.

"Adam, Adam, relax, please don't cry." She stretched her hand to his face.

Messiaen was playing when she sat in the lounge and allowed the powerful, dissonant, discordant, disturbing music wash over her and through her. She thought of Lotte Christina and wanted to do something special for her. She had been a totally unselfish undercover agent taking huge risks to save her and Rainer. She sat waiting for Adam to arrive and thought of some of his words which she had not taken in.

"Everything in me wants to kiss you."

"He's acting as if he loves me. He always totally rejected me. I wish I understood." The knock came and she went straight out to him.

"Straight along the main road to the A25." He obeyed. He drove up the hill and turned into the car park.

"What a splendid view!" he said.

"I live just down there." She pointed to a cluster of houses nestling on the far right below the hills. Motor cyclists were in the car park, revving noisily.

"Down and along." She pointed as they climbed down the grassy slope. The view of the distant hills and woods and the nearby farms below them gave them a sense of real pleasure.

"Look up at St Martha's Church and the cloud formations."

"Did you come with Richard and Edward?"

"Yes, often, picnics and rambles. You can walk for miles. It takes about three hours to reach my house."

"He was good for you, just the man you needed."

"You checked him out?"

"And Renate and Monica and your schools."

"Like a stalker. Like an agent."

"In a way. It's too soon to explain, but I will."

"When I'm off Meds and am level headed." He smiled and put an arm around her.

"That's right. I'm good at dominating. I am learning not to dominate, to accept, to let life flow." Doro took the hand on her shoulder and walked along with him hand in hand to the far end.

They saw an old wooden bench so they sat watching the dog walkers. Normal life was unfolding in front of them. She found herself trembling and had tears running down her cheeks.

"Adam, Adam," she said softly. "I have booked to see Dr Ford Lloyd next week."

"Well done, Dorothea, I think you need a few days away from me. I'll come if you need me or need anything, but take some time to yourself."

"I do need to think. I feel so confused. I'm so longing to understand."

"Dorothea, you did such harm to yourself for my sake. You killed all your natural emotions and put up with abuse. It harmed you. Your marriage did you a lot of good. Richard was such a kind gentleman. Now you have gone back into those terrible years and you need to be healed, to recover from all that harm, my harm."

They still held hands. "Why didn't you tell me about the rape? I knew nothing of it until the attack."

"Didn't Lotte tell you? I just could not bear to tell you. I need to think it through."

"Have you been to the villages down below?"

"No, not yet."

"Next walk." She smiled through her tears.

They walked slowly back to his car, loving the families, the children and the dogs. Her head was spinning as she sat in his car.

"Do you like art?" she managed to ask.

"Some." She remembered seeing an abstract painting in his lounge and a more traditional landscape in the dining room.

"We'll go to an exhibition in a few days. It's in a gorgeous Victorian house in the Surrey Hills, not a gallery."

"I'll look forward to it."

Doro was pleased to have a few days alone but as soon as she sat in silence, the fog returned. She was tearful but she wanted to think and find answers. Could she do that alone?

"Lies and betrayal, but it was to catch terrorists who killed innocent people and frightened the whole population," she said aloud.

"Manfred. There was nothing I liked about him. In the end he hated me, hated my privileged background and my general attitude. Did he really think that bombs would change the inequalities in society? The call to the London office was that genuine or was it a trick to break me?"

Rainer had totally rejected her and kept her at a distance for 12 years.

What was his motivation in following her whole life? Was he telling her he loved her? He was broken too. Why? She knew she had to be patient because he was holding back for her own good. How did he know how to judge all that? She Googled his name and found he was a retired specialist in German affairs in the Foreign Office.

"Oh, yes! In MI6!" she edited it aloud.

A German Jewish mother taught him the language. He had brothers and sisters who did not know what he did. It was all too unbelievable. She decided to write a list of what to ask him next:

1. A thank you celebration for Lotte
2. Eliza
3. Brothers and sisters

The visit to the art exhibition came before her first appointment.

She guided him along a winding, country lane. He had to turn off onto a bumpy, unmade path through the woods. The Victorian house was splendid, three floors with a conservatory at the back. Ivy and vines grew up the walls and wound around the drainpipes and nestled under the eaves. It was a romantic, attractive and inviting building called Fircroft.

Visitors were welcomed in a very friendly way. Adam decided to start in the garden so they walked through the trees, over soft, bumpy grass, along a woodland path and down uneven tiers to the lowest level. They admired the African black spring stone carvings, the metal work formed into kestrels, owls, fungi and little trees with leaves and fruit. Adam looked closely at one of the trees and walked around it.

"That would look good next to my bench by the river."

At £375 it was one of the cheaper art works. "How do you buy things?"

"They take your money inside and put a sold label on it. You have to come back for it at the end of the exhibition."

"Really? You can't take it now?" She smiled at him.

"It'll still be here in two weeks with the sold sign. See inside first, you might prefer a painting. Inside there were paintings on the walls, ceramics and glass on the tables and sideboards and two rooms with locked glass cabinets with Moorcroft ceramics and jewellery. Some of the artists and creators were in the rooms. Doro had a close look at the jewellery and liked a lot of it but felt it was too expensive for her. Adam really loved the abstract art and discussed it with the artist.

"I particularly like the colour combinations and the juxtapositions of the shapes. They had mood and power, atmosphere and challenge."

"Some were inspired by Bauhaus because of the recent centenary."

"How fascinating. I note the triangles. You like triangles. Your work is so varied. I am going to choose one for my new house." Doro was so surprised; this stranger who liked art and could discuss it was buying a painting.

"What do you think?" he asked her.

"Which one for the lounge wall?"

"That middle one has lots of subdued greys and blues and then a burst of yellow, orange and red. It's like hope, hope overcoming the darkness."

"You are right. Can I buy that one?"

"Yes, sir, pay my wife over there and I'll put a sold sticker on it.

Adam took Doro's arm. "Hope, just what we need. I shall think of you and all you have been through when it's in my room." She smiled, looking into his eyes. This was the uptight Rainer who had controlled her life.

He spoke softly to her, "I would like to buy you a present, please choose something you like. I would have no idea what to choose for you."

"Something you don't know about me? I am relieved!"

"I'm sorry. Give me more time to talk, not so long now. Come on, look at the lovely jewellery. I'm sure you like some of it."

He stood near the glass cabinets with her. "Where are your favourites?"

"I like all the enamel pendants and earrings." He stood back and looked at what she was wearing.

"A gift from my son."

"He had good taste. Do you like chokers?"

"With the right dress." He pointed to a silver choker with a small drop of fresh water pears, delicate and expensive.

"It's far too dear, Adam."

"My first gift to you ever. No. It's not."

"It's lovely. I'll have to get an invitation to somewhere smart to wear it." She smiled. Adam asked the artist's wife about the choker.

"You can take that today. The jewellery makers leave us a good supply." He saw it taken out of the cabinet and placed in a neat, shiny pouch. It cost over £100. Doro felt embarrassed but also delighted with his choice. She was uneasy that he was spending such money on her.

In the car, before they drove back down the bumpy track, he took her hands. "Dorothea, I had to buy today or I would lose the items. I had to take the opportunity. Please don't feel uneasy or suspicious. It is not a bribe or a pressure on you. In fact, I could keep it with me and give it to you on a future date. Good idea?" She gripped his hands and nodded.

"Tea?"

"Down the hill to Shere. There's a lovely cafe."

He was impressed by Shere, the ancient buildings, church and pub with stocks outside and a stream with ducks.

"I have things to ask. Let's sit outside." They took their places in the central square. "Lotte was wonderful. I would like to find a way to thank her, to celebrate our friendship. I would not have survived without her. She seems to be alone in life. Any ideas?"

"I owe her a lot too. She's not quite alone. She has a partner, a woman but they have kept their own flats. They are a couple. They go on holiday but they both wanted to keep their independence."

"She's gay? She told me she slept with one of the RAF boys in the commune."

"That was her sacrifice too. She never went after the girls. She could have done, it was tolerated, even encouraged but she was playing a role. She was marvellous. There were many arrests because of Lotte and you and many attacks were prevented."

Doro looked down and felt tears welling up.

"I'll have a think. I think they like shows and concerts and films. We could book them tickets and then take them out for a meal."

"Do you know her partner?"

"Yes, she's German."

"She said she would tell me her story one day. Can you tell me about Eliza?"

"Eliza worked with me from 1965 to 1971. She was trained like me in psychology and she took the terrorism very seriously. She found it hard to live with the bombs we didn't detect and she hated hearing of innocent people being killed. She turned to drink. She went to rehab and she struggled on in the department but she did become an alcoholic. She had to retire early and I'm afraid she died early."

"I'm sorry. Does the work break all the agents?"

"Many. I had some help before I left."

"Change the subject. Tell me about your siblings. Are you in touch with them? Where are they?"

"I'm the youngest. My oldest brother, Russell and his wife, children and grandchildren live in Greece. I go there for holidays. Steven and his wife live in Brighton. They have granddaughters, son and two daughters live not far away. My sister, Rosamund, and her husband live nearest to me, in Surrey, a town called Woking. Their daughter is divorced and lives with them. I am the black sheep, no wife no children. I share theirs, children that is!"

"I expect that's your sacrifice."

"When is Lotte coming to you?"

"Next week. We'll sound her out about shows and restaurants. And Adam, thank you so much for your lovely gift and for your support."

Chapter 10

Dr Ford Lloyd had a big file on the desk.

"Dorothea Harlow, nee Manning," she read. "Ten years an undercover agent in Germany. Orphaned at 17, widowed at 54, son committed suicide nearly two years later. Abused and beaten to cause a miscarriage. It is no surprise you have had a nervous breakdown. You have been very strong to withstand such traumas. Reports praise your secret life very highly. I am so sorry for your recent losses.

Dr Ford Lloyd had a lilting Welsh speaking voice and Doro took to her immediately. She gave Doro a specially written questionnaire to identify what caused her emotional pain. She was asked about sleeping, nightmares, eating and weeping. She moved on to her supportive friends. She was given some tasks to do before the next session.

"I want you to have a really good think about your feelings at the time you lost your parents and grandmother and then jump to the recent events which caused your breakdown."

She was pleased to have a systematic task to work on.

"I'm really keen to get off the medication or at least lessen it."

"Next time, depending on how you have coped, we can reduce it."

Doro thanked her and went to meet Lotte who had arrived with Adam. He drove them home. "I'll leave you two together to talk. See you tomorrow, supper at my house?"

Lotte was told of her progress and of the amazing transformation in Rainer, now Adam "He knows now that you know?"

"Yes, He's trying hard to stop dominating, as he said, and to apologies for recruiting me and asking me to do such ghastly things when I was only 19. He fears he has ruined my life and has caused my breakdown. He cries sometimes."

"That's good, he needs to. He has been involved in some terrible situations, deaths, betrayals, blown agents he lost. He acted like you; suppressed it all and got on with the job. He's supporting you now but he needs care and support too."

"He's being so sensitive and thoughtful. He says I must tell him to go away if I don't want him around. He fears taking advantage of me in my vulnerable state."

"That's so good."

"I feel as if he is treating me as if he loves me but he so rejected me for 12 years. It is so strange."

"What did you do when he rejected you?"

"I shut down. I killed tender feelings. I hardened myself."

"Perhaps I should not say this because he has never spoken to me about it, but I feel that he did the same. He was attracted to you from the start but killed his feelings for the work. I think that in spite of himself, he loved you in a devoted way. I know he followed your life. He could not love you so he was very pleased when you met Richard."

"Oh, Lotte, can that be true? I was overwhelmed by him, loved him and was ready to do anything at all for him, even sleep with a man I disliked. I find it hard to believe that we can rebuild trust and love after all that." Lotte sat next to her and hugged her.

"You've got to get better first. So has he. You both know it will be difficult."

"Let's eat, then Lotte, tell me your story."

Christina, now Lotte, had studied German in Berlin and worked for a firm of translators. She hated the divided country and what it meant for the citizens of a divided capital. She witnessed the building of the Wall in 1961, barbed wire and breeze blocks. She wept with her friends. She returned to England to complete her Masters in London. Marxist groups began to rise in the '60s. She had a similar recruitment; she applied for a course and was interviewed. She was persuaded to join the German Department of the Intelligence Services with the cover of working for the Foreign Office. After much question and answer, Christine was convinced she could do the job. Her point of decision was when she heard that the Marxist groups in the West were in communication with the Russians and the Stasi in its embryo form.

She finished her Masters and trained in an old army camp in Norfolk. She did weapons and explosives training. She produced pro-Marxist pamphlets, joined the London Marxists and built up a cover story. She met Rainer in 1963 when he became the controller of the German undercover agents. She respected, admired and liked him. By then she had realised she was more attracted to women rather than men. She had had some sexual relationships with boys at college but when she became an agent, she made the decision not to seek girls. She preferred to do her lying and betraying without sharing her life with a partner to whom she would have to lie. She sometimes went to lesbian clubs and had one-night stands as the years went by.

From 1963 to 1980 she was a Marxist terrorist. She had to plant explosives in cars and carry a weapon. She tried so hard to get the venues to Rainer or the West German anti-terror Police before the bombs went off. Some were stopped but not all. She had to face that innocent people would be killed by bombs she planted. She did not turn to drink or drugs but accepted that realistically she would lose sometimes. The leaders were very cautious about giving out a venue in advance.

When Doro came as Diane, she was concerned about this pretty girl being expected to have sex with the boys in the commune. She noted the inner strength of Diane and admired how she coped.

Christine had chosen Lotte as her cover name to remind her of her dear friend at university. When the Wall went up and was built more solidly, her friend Lotte joined the groups who tried to help East Germans escape. She helped meet people coming through the tunnels under the Wall. Sometimes she went in to help if there were a fall of earth. Lotte was 20 when she was shot by an East German border guard. The helpers were often betrayed by spies.

Christine was devastated. When she was recruited by MI6, she had the drive and motivation to become an agent, to give up her life and career prospects. She adopted the name of Lotte.

In 1977 when she had to make two trips to London to help Rainer and Diane with their injuries, she went to a lesbian bar and was surprised to meet a woman who recognised her. In Berlin University she had been close to both Lotte and Helga.

After Lotte was shot, they grew apart and lost contact when Christine/Lotte became a translator. Once she had been recruited, she kept away from old friends. She had had no contact with Helga for nearly two decades and yet in the London pub, Helga had noted the older woman with the ponytail. Full of the horror of what had happened in the commune; Christine/Lotte was open to receive the warmth of human friendship. Helga called her name and they both recognised a fellow student from Berlin. They passed a pleasant evening sharing their lives, for Lotte the cover story of her life. They made no plans to meet again but to her great surprise, she found herself back in London with Rainer, visited the same pub and met Helga again. She was invited to Helga's flat. This was not going to be a one-night stand but she would have to work out a strategy with Rainer. He did not want to lose her nor did he want to deprive her of a relationship. She was not always free to leave her Marxist group whenever she wanted, or to have visits from UK unless there was an emergency. She needed a story for the Aachen group, a story for Helga and permission from MI6.

The Aachen group was shaken by Manfred and by the violent events of that autumn in Germany, so they were ready to accept that Lotte had family commitments in England. If she did not keep them, it could cause suspicion. Helga was told of a special project, similar to the story Rainer told Renate. He had checked her out. She was a straightforward woman working for a marketing firm in London, using her German. She had not found acceptance of her lesbianism among her family and friends so she tried living in London. Rainer judged her to have integrity and discretion. After his arm had recovered, he met Helga in London and explained the importance of the work Lotte was doing for the Foreign Office. Helga could only relate to her on certain conditions. They could only meet in England, not Germany.

Helga had time to decide if she would enter the partly covert world. After re-unification, Lotte was able to retire and return to London. After being apart for so many years they decided to live independently while still being a couple. It had been a successful plan. Now, Lotte could go to Germany with Helga but never to Aachen, Cologne or Düsseldorf. They went to Berlin, Munich and the Black Forest area.

"Lotte, what a story! Thank you so much for sharing it. Do invite Helga here one day. I need to know what you enjoy doing; theatre, films, concerts. Rainer will explain more when we go for supper with him tomorrow."

"We both love film, but a West End show would be a real treat."

"Give us a shortlist."

"I want to talk to you about some films. We have them on DVD between us. I think they could be of real help to you."

"Sounds interesting. Tell me before you leave after our meal."

She phoned him. "Adam, I think I could drive Lotte to you, save you a trip."

"Have a try. Your medication warned about operating machinery but it did not forbid driving if you are feeling well."

Doro felt excited about driving again. She was nervous but soon relaxed on the familiar roads. Adam hugged Lotte and Doro and then they had drinks on the bench.

"I'll put the tree here," he said.

"You've bought a tree?" asked Lotte.

"A metal one, an artistic tree."

"You went back to Fircroft?"

"I did." Doro told Lotte about the exhibition. Adam had prepared a salad niçoise for them with ice-creams to follow.

"You have chosen a lovely place to live, Rainer. Will I ever call you Adam? You need to enjoy nature and let it heal you."

"And Lotte, I hope you will allow Dorothea and me to take you and Helga out for a treat, a show of your choice and a meal. We are so grateful to you for all you did for us. When Doro is stronger, we'll come to London and take you both out."

"That's so kind of you. If I had not accompanied you both to London, I would not have met Helga. Good came out of bad."

Chapter 11

Lotte arrived with some German cakes that Helga had made and a bag of DVDs. "How are you? How's it going with Adam?"

"Well, thanks. The doctor is very good and wise. I feel it's helping."

"Anyone who can untangle your past needs to be gifted and clever, patient, even brilliant." Lotte laughed.

"Adam's being very sweet and thoughtful. I still see him weep. He showed me his scars. He knows he needs to heal too."

"Pleased to hear it. You could do what Helga and I have done, be a couple but live in our own homes."

"I can't think that far ahead, too much I don't understand yet. I am suspicious about how we were called into the Department Office."

"Don't be, Doro. There is real concern when old RAF members meet up. They're being watched."

"Thank God we are out of it. Tell me about the films."

"I hope I have the right idea. Tell me first what general idea you have of the Marxist Groups, the RAF and the Baader Meinhof Gang."

"When I was training in the late '60s, I did read something by German psychologists about the post-war generation who had to face that their beloved parents and grandparents had been Nazis and even war criminals. I read about Vergangenheitsbewältigung and the Vaterlose Gesellschaft."

"Good. You can see how the young people gained the sympathy of several in the community as everyone struggled to survive and overcome the past. It was the Zeitgeist of 1960–80 Germany. The division into the DDR and BRD was mostly hated and resented; so many heartbreaking stories of families being split apart."

Lotte talked of the rise of left-wing groups who so hated what their country had done and wanted a new society to build justice.

Some feared that ex-Nazis would remain in positions of influence and accused the state of being fascist. There were a great many writers and film makers with left-wing sympathies and a group of New German Cinema directors got together to make challenging statements about fascism, ex-Nazis and the state's fears about radical Marxism. Böll, the writer had his offices raided in that atmosphere of fear. After the autumn events in 1977, seven film directors quickly made a powerful and challenging semi-documentary called 'Germany in Autumn'. It shows a variety of rather disconnected scenes but the whole is based on the two funerals, that of Schleyer and those of the Baader Meinhof Group in Stammheim Prison, who, it was said had made a joint suicide pact. There are some odd scenes. Each director made his or her statement in their own way.

"I did hear of it but I didn't see it. You have it here?"

"Yes."

"I did see a film a few years later when I was at the London school. It was called *Die Bleierne Zeit*, by a lady director, Margarethe von Trotte."

"Good, it's worth you seeing it again. With all your experiences you will understand more. Von Trotta really understood the conflict between the two sisters, based on the Ensslins. She also deals with the doubts that the families had about the suicides in prison."

"I remember so many dark scenes in prison and the unsmiling faces of the women guards."

"The third film is called *Stammheim*, the name of the purpose-built prison in Stuttgart. It deals with the trial of Baader, Meinhof and the last members of the group. You can feel some sympathy with them when you listen to their arguments. They knew how to make a case. It ends with their deaths. Do you think you would cope with that after your son's death?"

"I'm not sure. I've made myself watch documentaries on TV about suicide. Edward's was because of personal fear of cancer treatment after seeing his father suffer so much. If they weren't murdered, it must have been despair."

"I could see that despair in our group at times when they had succeeded in firebombing a store and car bombing a US air base, it seemed to be forgotten in the Press within a few days and there was not a single sign of any change in society. Over the last few years, the atmosphere changed; not so much 'terror is fashionable', like Robin Hood or Che Guevara, the romantic heroes, but more a lack of belief in fires and bombs. Ordinary citizens grew very tired of it all."

"Why do you think these films would be good for me?"

"You will see the group from another perspective and in another context. Most of your suffering was due to one man's character. Not all the leaders claimed the right to have sex with pretty, young recruits. The 'free love' in communes was by consent. It often went too far and was exaggerated but you were dealing with a sick, unbalanced, mentally ill man."

"That does sound helpful. Thank you, Lotte."

The DVDs were on the bookshelf for several days before Doro had the courage to see them. She decided to start with the one she had seen once before. She sat with a notebook and pen to jot down her thoughts and impressions as she watched.

With Dr Ford Lloyd, Doro had to look first at her teenage years when she lost her parents and then look at the recent events which caused her to break down. Facing her feelings, admitting them, talking through the ways she helped herself through was revealing. The deadening of her emotions had begun at 17 and not when she had arrived in the commune. Seeing the photo of Manfred had triggered the sense of horror, fear and dread which she had denied to herself. Her desire to be seen as strong, to cope, not to admit defeat had been her early strategy as she faced A levels, university applications all on her own.

The doctor enabled her to reduce her medication and planned to look next at her motivation for becoming an agent and her relationship with her controller. Doro both longed for and dreaded going over this ground.

The cormorants stretched their wings high in the trees on the island in Broadwater Lake. Swans glided around beneath the shore and varieties of ducks and geese rapidly moved to the banks in the hope of food if anyone stood next to the water.

Adam and Doro wanted to walk around the whole lake. Every few yards, was a fisherman in dark clothing, with rods and shelters, seats and boxes of writhing worms. Fishing was private and taken very seriously. At the far side of the lake stood some rough woodland and some open playing fields for football and cricket and a playground for children. Several people had long ball-throwers and let their dogs have long runs. Not all the dogs brought the balls back so the owners were having extra exercise too.

"Perhaps I'll get a dog," said Adam.

"Would he leap into your river, I wonder?" She smiled at the thought of a wet dog leaping into his beautiful lounge or kitchen.

"That's a thought!" He smiled. A spaniel stopped at his feet with a ball in his mouth. Adam bent down and stroked him.

"Let's have the ball then." The dog obeyed and dropped it. Adam picked it up and looked around for the owner. He saw a man in the distance calling him. He threw the ball in that direction and the dog sped off.

"You are a natural." She took his arm. "Does it still hurt?"

"Sometimes, like arthritis pain."

"Sorry, so, so sorry. I'm talking about you in my next session."

"I'm sure you need to."

"Will you watch one of Lotte's films with me?" She explained how Lotte had lent her some films and repeated the points she had made about seeing the groups in a different context.

"Of course, I will, which one?"

"Probably Stammheim, first for you."

"This is a lovely park so near to me. Thanks for bringing me."

"I love the lake, the birds, but rather too many fishermen. Edward played football here and there's a leisure centre over there with a pool." He smiled at her as they walked arm in arm back to his home.

"I've got the DVDs in the car. Watch one now?"

"Don't you need a sleep?"

"I don't think so. Let me know if I fall asleep in the trial."

"Such a sympathetic view of the attractive, intelligent young people who killed innocent people," Adam said.

"I cannot believe that such articulate, belligerent young people could kill themselves. Baader wasn't really intellectual. He was good-looking, charming, radical. Most of the others had a traditional middle-class upbringing, daughter of a pastor, journalist, lawyer, yet radical, certain, determined."

"Unfortunate collateral damage, all those innocent people killed or wounded."

Adam had provided a jacket potato with tuna and sweet corn filling. They ate with trays on their knees and saw a few scenes over again. Some of the most poignant arguments came in the dialogues between the team of judges and the individual terrorists. Even the well-educated girls called the judge names, showed no respect, shouted, left the court, stamped around.

Two of the terrorists died during the trial. Ulrike Meinhof hanged herself and Holger Meins died on hunger strike.

It was a sad depiction of the trial using the transcripts in the real court reports.

As Doro went to her car to drive home, she wanted to hug Adam but she held back and let him give her a peck on the cheeks.

In the doctor's office, sitting on a comfortable couch, Doro told her about seeing the films on the various aspects of the Baader Meinhof history. Dr Ford wrote notes and asked questions about her feelings as she watched.

"I'd like to come back to the films in the next session because I want to focus on your controller today. I think the films could be very important for you."

"I think so too. I watched one with my old controller and it helped both of us."

"You see him now?"

"Yes. I'll explain later. Can I begin at the beginning?"

"You can, Dorothea. I know him a little as he often used our clinic for his agents. I think he is a man of integrity who has regrets for his role in MI6."

"I think I am his greatest regret." Dorothea talked through how she was recruited at 18, trained at 19. She had thought about her motivation and spoke about her attraction to Rainer but also to the adventure of leading a secret life. She acknowledged that she had been immature and romantic. She admitted that she had fallen in love with him but had deadened her feelings when she saw how consistently he rejected her.

"I would have done anything he asked of me and I did!"

"Such as?"

"Having sex as a virgin with the group leader." Her voice broke and she began to cry.

"Were you ashamed? Were you hurt?"

Doro could not speak. Dr Ford gave her a glass of water and some tissues and sat holding her hand.

"It's OK; you need to cry because you have denied your real feelings and reactions. You have not allowed yourself to identify with what you felt and now it is all rushing in on you at once. You are facing abuse, self-disgust and dread of loveless sex."

Eventually she could catch her breath and speak.

"I loved him so totally. I was dedicated to him. I thought of him all the time. I was overwhelmed by him. I longed for the de-brief session just to look at him, hear his voice. I longed for him. Then I saw he rejected me, he kept his distance and never touched me and so I worked on myself. He's sorry now he took advantage of me."

"Dorothea, 'he took advantage' is a gloss over phrase. He abused you, he used you, and he disregarded your needs, your sensibilities, your lifestyle, and your standards. Abuse, that's what he did."

White-faced, she sat stunned and could not speak.

"What about anger?"

"I have been angry. After 30 years of no contact with him, he rang me. I'd been healed a lot by my happy marriage so I was angry to find myself back in contact with those years. Going there broke me."

"Angry with Rainer?"

"Not in my awareness. I lost my husband and son. I felt I had recovered and suddenly I faced my worst nightmare. I was angry with life, with MI6 but I suppose I was angry with him. You said he was a man of integrity with regrets. He has faced what he did to me and has said 'sorry' and he has wept with me and for me."

"Look at your anger with him. Acknowledge it. You cannot forgive unless you do."

"He is saying sorry to me. He is holding back from me because he says he does not want to take advantage of my brokenness. I'm so confused. He's said other things I don't understand. He says he's followed my life, all aspects as if he were following an agent. He knows so much about me. It's unbelievable and uncomfortable. He is acting as if he loves me."

"I've often seen broken and damaged agents. Some are so hidden from themselves that they can be ruthless. Do you know why he's followed you?"

"Why? No, not really. How? He knew about my husband and checked on him, my schools, the posts I held and my closest friends. When I broke down, he got my friend to look after my house and help me when I came home. We agreed on a cover story, not lies but not all the truth."

"What is your understanding of all this?"

"After his rejection, I could not believe he loved me, that he was in my life out of love. Now he is careful not to abuse me, declare love, hardly touches me, but he says he'll explain when I am better, stronger, or else he would be taking advantage of me."

"How would you feel if he said he loved you?"

"I think all the love I felt would come back but deep down I would doubt that we could mend our past."

"What did you feel about him when you married?"

"I thought I would never see him again. I did think of him but Richard was wonderful. We had a good marriage, good sex, amiable companionship, peaceful co-existence." Doro found herself crying again.

"He has cried too. He's really hurting and he's really sorry. He talks of the harm he did me."

"Good, that's honest."

"He needs to talk to you too, I think." They both smiled.

"The path to healing includes you both being honest. He needs to hear from you how you felt, what it did to you. You need to hear from him that he fully understands the way he abused you. You have both repressed your own feelings because of the work you did. I'm here to deal with you, not him; I want to see what you repressed in yourself."

Doro was exhausted and Dr Ford suggested she stopped for the day, but that for the next session she should jot down the emotions she had tried to destroy and that she should talk about what she had experienced watching the films.

After the session, Doro walked along the river, through the riverside park along the Wey. She had avoided the Broadwater Lake in the slight fear that Adam could be walking there. That thought reminded her of the last time she had seen him in 1980 when she had left the office for the last time and gone to sit on a bench in Russell Square. When she left the bench and walked to an entrance, she had seen Rainer go and sit on a bench with his head in his hands.

Chapter 12

Dorothea watched the film *Germany in Autumn*. She kept all her notes to talk to Lotte and Dr Ford Lloyd. This film she found was much more disturbing but she was not sure why. She asked Adam to watch it and give her his thoughts. After her last talk with the doctor, she felt so uncomfortable in his company; she was quiet and less able to share with him.

The Fircroft art show closed and he had gone to pick up his painting and his metal tree. He put in the tree but saved the painting until Doro could share the hanging. He called in on her.

"Would you come and help me decide where to hang 'Hope'."

"I need to be alone a while, Adam. I have reached a difficult stage with Dr Ford and I need to do some thinking."

"I did tell you to tell me to go away."

"Thanks. I'd love to see the painting hung but not yet. Sorry." He took her shoulders.

"Don't apologise to me! I am amazed that you talk to me even. I have caused you such harm, such pain. I hate myself for it. If you can forgive me, I may begin to forgive myself." Tears filled his eyes and Doro broke down sobbing. He embraced her and held her, leaning his weeping head next to hers. They held each other, clinging to each other.

"Doro, what's happening for you?"

"I'm not sure. I'm frightened and confused. I need to analyse exactly what you did to me. There is so much I don't understand."

"Analyse. Tell me. I'll explain soon. I cannot bear to see you in this state." He sobbed again; "It's all my doing, all my fault." She hugged him still, trembling and shaking, but his words gave her hope.

"Ring me when you are ready or just turn up at mine." He was wiping his eyes.

"We are two broken people. We'll work at mending each other." She held his hand then let him go and drive away.

Indoors, she let herself weep copiously. She was overwhelmed and longed to be alone. She put on a CD of Richard's organ concert and listened again to *Messiaen's Combat*.

I'm in a 'combat', she thought. *Can I forgive him?*

For three days she remained at home, alone. She wrote down her analysis and her notes on the film. She listed her emotions then and now.

She took deep breaths, did some exercises, walked in her garden, meditating as she looked at the hills. She then invited Renate to a pub lunch.

"You do look tired," Renate said. "Are you doing OK?"

"I'm working through a lot of things and why I had a breakdown. It's exhausting!"

"I'm going to have another grandchild."

"Oh, how lovely, Renate. When?"

"In about six months, my daughter is expecting a third baby."

"You'll be busy!"

"But, please tell me if you need anything, Doro."

"I will. I am so pleased to have you as a friend." She began to feel more normal after that but still hesitated to phone Adam.

One afternoon she drove to his home. He was digging in the garden. He dug in the spade as her car pulled up. He stood back as she got out and then hugged her. They stood hugging in teary silence.

"Can we ever mend?" she asked.

"I don't know."

"Let's put up 'Hope' and make it a symbol." She stood looking at the abstract shapes and loved it all over again.

They stared at the lounge walls imagining where it would look best.

"I could move the bookcase over to liberate more space on this wall." He got out a tape measure. "This could move more towards the kitchen door." He stretched it across the space.

"Yes, wide enough. My next project. What do you think?"

"I think your other abstract should go in this space and that 'Hope' should hang alone on that wall."

"Could work. Coffee? I like that idea."

"Just water please." They sat on the bench by the metal tree. She pulled out her notes. "Analysed?"

"You, you knew, knew that I loved you?"

"Teenage infatuation, I told myself."

"You asked me to have sex with a man I didn't love or even like?" He nodded.

"You, you abused my trust, you used me." He nodded again.

"You broke my heart but I only wanted to please you, to serve you. I loved you all those years. I killed my love. I killed all my feelings. I let a ghastly man use me for sex while seeing him have sex with other girls." Adam held his head in his hands like he had in Russell Square.

"I saw you in Russell Square," she said, "on that day I left for the last time. I sat a while thinking of you, remembering how I used to feel. You did not see me. I was leaving when I saw you arrive through another entrance and I saw you sit like this with your head in your hands."

"I sat there thinking of you. I knew I had lost you forever."

"Did you organise that call into the office?"

"Absolutely not. Ralph called us in. It was a wonderful chance for me to see you again, to tell you the truth, to tell you what happened thirty years before."

"Nothing to do with you?"

"No, nothing. Fate, destiny, karma?"

"I'm so relieved. I've been so frightened. I have not known what to think, what to feel, what to believe, how to understand your behaviour."

"Of course, you were suspicious. I hope I am not blowing it now but I cannot be silent any longer. Do what you will with this information."

He pulled up his head, rested his hands on the bench and sat straight and upright. He did not look at her.

"Dorothea Harlow, Manning as was, I fell in love with you in that first interview. Love at first sight. The more you coped in the commune, the more I loved you. I've never loved any woman the way I loved you. I longed for you, I was obsessed by you and I longed to tell you. I had to work at never showing you or anyone else, my feelings for you. I killed all my feelings and became disassociated from my real love. I suffered much inner pain and I was angry with Fate for bringing you into my life when I could do nothing about it. When you were so injured, I could willingly have shot Manfred myself. I made you

84

my secret agent for thirty years and I was really pleased you had such a wonderful husband. When you tragically lost him and Edward, I decided after a while to move house to be nearer to you. I would never have approached you, believe me, I would have been your guardian. The call into the office was like a miracle. Now I've said it. I loved you then and I love you now."

Dorothea looked at a broken Adam. Her heart was pounding as she had heard the words, she had longed for over so many years.

"Adam, I loved you then and I love you now."

"I treated you badly. I nearly destroyed the one woman I have ever loved. I need to learn to love."

"Adam, we are old enough to use our wisdom. We are so damaged. I'm not sure it can work."

"IT can work? What can work? We have to work at our love, not see if IT works. If we love each other, we can learn together, heal together. I need forgiveness, we both need healing.

"Have I blown it?"

"No, but we still need to hold back."

"With sex?"

"With lovemaking. We both long to make love, don't we? Let's wait until we can stop crying, I can stop my medication, we can have a stable relationship and make love from a stable, healthy position."

"You are quite right, my very dearest Dorothea."

"Could we watch *Germany in Autumn* together? I think it is relevant to us in some way."

"Of course, we could. I saw it a few days ago. It is very disturbing, isn't it? It's like a sob of mourning for Germany."

"We are too emotional right now, too upset and weepy." They were both trembling.

"I'll go now. Let's phone Lotte and ask her and Helga down for a meal so we can make a date to take them out."

"OK, my most beloved Thea."

"Richard called me Thea privately. But you can too. It was his name of love for me. It can be yours too."

"Sure? You have a lovely name. You can turn it around to Theodora."

"That's sweet. Goodbye for now, dearest Adam."

She drove home as if in a dream. She sat in the conservatory almost traumatised.

"He loved me. He abused me. I loved him. I forgive him. I love him. That's a good start. I must consider my anger, my pain, my self-hatred and see how to overcome them."

Lotte and Helga were waiting at the station for Adam to pick them up. "We are eating at Doro's," he announced.

She cooked salmon and pesto with salad and fried potatoes. Adam brought a fruit flan, much to her surprise.

"I cheated on the case and got one in the farm shop at Milford. Lovely place."

It was delightful to chat together. Helga and Lotte made a happy, relaxed couple who showed their affection for each other. For Adam and Doro, it was a relief from the tension of their deep, emotional sharing. Helga said they wondered about the show *The Book of Mormon*. They chose a date and Adam said he would order the tickets. He jotted down their favourite restaurants. Thai and Japanese were at the top of the list.

"There's a fantastic Thai restaurant in Guildford. It's on a roof high above town. It has great views as well as great food."

"We could get the tickets sent to you and the next day you could come down here again. We can put you up so you won't have to travel back late at night."

As they chatted, Doro looked at Adam and observed his face. Now and then he did the same and a few times they looked and smiled with the unavoidable look of love.

"That sounds lovely. Thank you for inviting me. I know you owe Lotte a great deal."

"We would not be here without her," Adam said. "Lotte understands a lot more than we have said." Doro smiled at Lotte and knew she understood that he had declared his love for her. Their pleasant evening came to an end.

Adam arranged the tickets and booked the Thai Terrace. As they relaxed in her conservatory, he took out the choker he had bought her.

"Will you wear it when we go to the restaurant?" She smiled and he took it out of the pouch. She tried it on with her tee-shirt. It was beautiful.

"I expect you have a blouse or dress to go with it."

"If not, I will invite Renate to come and help me choose one."

"It does look good."

Before this visit they planned to watch the film *Germany in Autumn* together. For some reason she wanted this to take place in Adam's house. Neither of them had watched many German films over the years. Doro's studies had included modern literature, dramas and poetry. She had read some philosophy and biography which touched on urban terrorism. She had read a biography of Böll who had collaborated on at least one scene in this film and written a novel about the exaggerated response of the state, the police and the politicians and most of all the Press, to the threat of left-wing terrorism. Böll had his offices raided and was harassed and criticised over his views which were seen as sympathetic to the terrorists. She had read his novel, *Die Verlorene Ehre der Katharina Blum*. She therefore had some understanding of what the film makers were trying to do in producing *Germany in Autumn*. She had taken notes and picked out the scenes which disturbed her, and tried to analyse why it had such an impact on her.

They sat on his settee with a bowl of cherries, notebooks in hand and watched it through again.

"It helped me understand the motivation behind the terrorist gangs, the difficulties of the second generation post-war, facing the horrors of the Nazi past and blaming their parents and grandparents," Doro explained.

"Vaterlösigkeit comes up several times, Schleyer the kidnapped ex-Nazi writing to his son, knowing he was probably about to die and the Greek father and son in the Antigone section, for some examples. Does it apply to us at all?"

Doro thought of her father. "I related well to my dad. He was an encourager. We had rows about high heels and mini-skirts, but he did love me."

"Mine did not understand me. He loved sports, hymns and reading about adventurous travel. I did like the travel books but not sport nor hymns. My brothers loved sports and bonded better with him."

"I had great solace from hymns through Richard. I like to go to a sung liturgy from time to time. I go to the cathedral for evensong when the choir is there."

"What disturbed you most about the film?" Adam looked down at his own notes.

"The frightening scenes, the threat of violence when the man on the run held a knife; the atmosphere of threat at the border when the guards were searching the cars."

"These scenes were placed next to other scenes with different character and a different agenda. It was confusing. That's what the directors wanted. I hated the Fassbinder scenes. He clearly planned to be as outrageous as possible; beating his lover, standing and sitting naked, taking drugs, throwing them down the toilet when he heard a police car. He wanted to shock, to disturb and to film while emotionally upset by the deaths in Stammheim. I'm not surprised that he and his lover committed suicide a few years later."

Doro asked again, "Why did we think this film was important to us?"

"The impact is real, even if we don't know why. It does describe what we were living in; the groups, the plans for revolution, the justification for violence, killing which leads to the dominating fear in the community."

She looked at her notes and Adam continued, "The impact of the film is greater because it is not polished, not edited in a coherent way. It is such a mix of fact and fiction, of conflicting emotions and confusion, hatred of the state and yet justification for killing innocent people. I think the most helpful and clear arguments came through Max Frisch and Horst Mahler and the Antigone clip."

"Did you read Mitscherlich?"

"Yes, I did. The outrageous Fassbinder made his mother mention the name in their discussion. She called him a person of authority."

"They wrote about the Fatherless Generation as early as 1963. Their key words were Vergangenheitsbewältigung and Trauerarbeit. Overcoming the past and mourning work."

"Frisch agreed that in trying to move forward after 1945, the generation of parents failed to do mourning work, a necessary prerequisite to being able to guide the next generation. He thought that the drive for economic success was uppermost in their minds."

"I suppose that is why so many Nazis with financial acumen were allowed to lead big companies."

"When that generation was about 20, they looked back in horror, in anger and in shame and saw the guilt of Nazism. They felt rage when they saw fascism still in the German state. This was illustrated by the extreme reaction to the demonstrations against the visit of the Shah and the Vietnam War, the My Lai massacre."

"You mentioned the lawyer, Mahler."

"That interview with him in prison. What did you think of that?"

Doro read her notes, "In 1945 fascist power was only partially broken. There was no anti-fascist revolution after the war. 1967 and 1977 were a deep incision in German political life."

"He mentioned the moral rigour of the revolutionaries which can lead to a presumptuous arrogance."

"Ah, yes, the prerequisite for overcoming scruples about killing people."

"The left-wing groups judged the moral corruption of the capitalist system and saw it as the embodiment of evil. That gave them the right to kill."

"I overcame my scruples about sex when I joined the commune. I had sexual relations against my scruples because I saw it was necessary in order to be trusted by the group." Adam was clearly uncomfortable and put a hand on her shoulder. She continued, "I understand how Ulrike Meinhof and the others could justify the killing; it was for the greater good of Germany."

"But Germany didn't want it. Fassbinder's mother, in spite of the unpleasantness of that scene, was clearly a representative of the ordinary person. Most ordinary Germans did not understand the aims of the terrorism; they lived in fear of it and just wanted it to stop. Tea, coffee?"

"Yes, please." She reread her notes while Adam made some drinks. "I'm having Red Bush Tea, want to try some?"

"OK." They sipped their tea. "I wrote about the Antigone sketch," she added.

"What about it?"

"I enjoyed the believable quality of the discussion, the clear depiction of the paranoia and the realism of their dilemma. The producers saw how the Sophocles story had some obvious parallels with the present situation in the '70s. And they all smoked too much!"

Adam smiled. "That behind the scenes look at the production of a TV program best revealed the political atmosphere of 1977. A perfectly well-known story which they thought could provoke violence. Antigone breaks the law by burying her brother disobeys the state and her father and pays with her life. Father treats the two brothers differently so the program is withdrawn from the TV schedules. Brilliant piece of scripting by Böll and Schlörndorf." Adam was still in interrogation mode.

"Anything else disturb you?"

"Plenty. The Schleyer funeral with the waving blue flags, the hundreds of black clad people in the church, the lavish post-funeral meal. Schleyer brought wealth to Germany and was treated as a hero. He had been Heydrich's right-hand man. I understood how the groups felt anger and outrage."

"Did it in any way make you aware of the importance of the work you were doing in the commune?"

"I'll need to think about it."

"Have we learned any more from watching?"

"To move forward, to heal, we need to acknowledge every aspect of the pain and horror of the past. We need to accept our responsibility or our guilt. We need to allow ourselves to grieve and to mourn. Trauerarbeit presupposes that there is a work we need to do to help us overcome."

"I need to hold you. May I?" She put down her notes and moved up and let him put his arms around her. She stopped herself holding him. It would have been so easy for her to lift her head up for a kiss but everything in her yelled 'No'. It was not a lack of forgiveness, it was deep, dark fear.

Chapter 13

"What's that music?" Adam stepped into her lounge when they next met again.

"Max Richter. Do you know him?"

"No. Music and I need an introduction. German?"

"Yes. I've only just discovered him. It's lovely and also disturbing in parts."

"So, I hear. Are you all ready for our meal with Lotte and Helga?"

"I am. Renate helped me choose a top to go with that lovely choker. People dress quite casually there, not dark suit and tie. I hope I didn't give you the wrong impression."

"Smart casual?"

"That's it. So, you have offered them your en suite? I am sure Lotte will want to talk to you."

"You think so? You see Dr Ford before then, I think."

"I always dread it but I also want and need her sessions."

Dorothea took her notebook with her for her next session. She poured out the changes and developments of the past few weeks.

"He fully understands what he did to you?"

"He's working at it. He hates himself and can't forgive himself. He's hoping I can forgive him."

"Can you?"

"I'm working at it. I fully understand his motivation. He thought only of the need to infiltrate. He made it worse for himself as he fell in love with me but he killed his feelings so that he went too far in the other direction."

"How do you react to all that?" Doro sat in silence trying to find words for her feelings. "Feelings rush through me. I feel the deep love for him that I felt when I first met him but I feel so frightened of his power over me. I find it hard to understand that he almost stalked me all my life and that he moved from London to be nearer to me when Edward died.

"However, I see the great effort he is making not to dominate me. He has not tried to make love to me. He asks if he can hold me, see me, and go out with me. All the while I know he wrestles with deep guilt."

"To me, that sounds like a huge healing step in both of you. His stalking, as you call it was his training, his skills, his way of life. What he knew and was familiar with, he put into action. His motivation was very unselfish love for you."

Dora felt happy and relieved by her words.

"We've been watching a film about the Baader Meinhof gang. We were involved with them for many years. We took notes and discussed it at some length and saw ways in which it resonated with our lives."

"That sounds brave to me."

"It was painful but we both felt we understood much more about people's motivations, the state's, the terrorist's and our own," she read her notes.

"To move forward, we need to acknowledge every aspect of our pain. We need to accept our responsibility and our guilt. We need to allow ourselves to grieve."

"I'm impressed, Dorothea. I think you have more to say."

"I've faced my anger over Rainer's abuse of me and I've admitted the pain of it, but I have also faced my own responsibility and guilt. He did not threaten me or force me, he persuaded, realising I had a crush on him. But I took the decision and I took the action. I was young and inexperienced but I had a taste for adventure and a strong desire to please this controller."

"You've covered a lot of ground." They chatted longer about Lotte and her visit. The doctor suggested that she cut her drugs by half but could take more if she had a crisis.

"Next time, think about your love relationship with Adam and what you want to do, if anything, about it."

"We've agreed that while I am on meds and while we end up crying whenever we share, we will not attempt to make love, but we will wait until we are on a stable base."

"You are both wise. Control in the short term won't harm you, but deadening, denying your real feelings, will cause harm. All the very best, Dorothea."

Helga and Lotte were picked up by Adam. He took them home for a drink and congratulated them on their lovely outfits; trouser suits, a sparkly gold for Lotte and sparkly wine colour for Helga.

"Love the painting!" said Helga.

"We've called it 'Hope' but it was inspired by a German artist and has another title." He told her about Fircroft and the resident artist. They picked up Doro who delighted them all with her outfit. She had chosen loose black trousers and a wine-coloured silk top. She wore pearl earrings to match the choker.

"We match!" said Helga, turning around in her sparkling red top. "You look wonderful," said Adam softly, kissing her cheek.

"It's a gift from Adam, from the Fircroft exhibition," she told them when they admired the choker.

They chose to sit inside in the rooftop restaurant in case it grew chilly.

Their table was right next to the window with splendid views over the town, the roof top garden and the brave customers outside.

"They've got heaters and window shutters," Helga pointed out.

"Tell us about the show last night," asked Adam.

"So good and absolutely hilarious. You might enjoy it but I suspect your tastes lie elsewhere," Lotte smiled.

"I do love music. Nearly thirty years married to a musician, I learned so many pieces I was ignorant of, and Edward could play so well too."

"I am a barbarian. My father's Methodist hymns put me off but my mother's love of Beethoven and Bach gave me a little taster. I want to learn to appreciate music more."

"You've influenced this man, Doro. He never opens up like that!" said Lotte.

The starters and wine arrived. Presentation was the strong point in this Thai cuisine; flowers made of carrots, small dishes, works of art with prawns, meats and vegetables.

"I can have a little wine, I'm on half dose." Doro smiled. Helga drank copiously and began getting the giggles. The noodles were long, wound around each other in a delicious sauce but difficult to eat with spoon and fork. That caused more giggles. Lotte poured her some sparkling water.

"Dilute it," she said, laughing as well.

Helga was calmer after the main dishes arrived and took photos of them all. An attentive waitress offered to take photos of them all together. Helga showed them. "You two clearly love each other dearly," she said and saw how they had looked at each other in one shot with a look of love. Adam and Doro smiled at each other again.

"They do," Lotte said, "they have baggage like we did, stresses, horrors even. I told Doro, didn't I? They might end up like us, we are a couple but we have our own quiet space."

"Consider it, my dears; it could be a way forward for you." Adam took Doro's hand and held it for a while.

"Who knows? We are first dealing with our past, waiting until the tears stop flowing." He kissed her hand and let it go. "Actually, I have forgotten to tell her something. Sorry, but can we just walk to the lounge area for a moment while we wait for dessert?"

"You may," Helga replied. "Not sure I have room for a dessert."

They studied the menu. There were sorbets, ice creams and liqueur coffees. "No, liqueur, darling," Lotte said to Helga.

"One sorbet scoop for me," Doro said. "And me," Lotte added.

"And me," Helga chipped in.

"And I'd like a liqueur coffee," chose Adam. He got up and led Doro to the lovely armchair lounge near the entrance.

"I'm so sorry; I forgot to tell you that I bought a gift for Lotte at Fircroft and they gift wrapped it for me."

"That's a lovely idea. I have a card to give her. What is it?"

"One of those enamel pendants."

"That will go well with her usual jumpers. Well done, dear Adam." She kissed him lightly. "I wonder why you forgot to tell me."

"Habit of an isolated lifetime. I'm learning to love." They walked back hand in hand. Desserts arrived.

"It's been so lovely, Adam and Doro. I feel very spoilt."

"Lotte, we owe you our lives. We want to present you with a gift." He drew a colourful pouch out of his pocket and Doro pulled the card from her bag. They both hugged Lotte. She was so surprised and smiled with tears in her eyes.

"Open it, darling," said Helga. She drew out the pendant on a thick silver chain. It had a mix of colours in shiny enamel. She took in a deep breath.

94

"It's gorgeous!"

"It will go with so many of your tops," Helga added.

"I'll read your beautiful card when I am alone. Thank you both, thank you very much." Adam drove Doro home and got out of the car.

"I've got things to say. Can we meet tomorrow?"

"Pick me up to see them off at the station, and then we can talk somewhere."

"Newlands Corner?" She nodded. The four kissed good night.

"I'll see you off in the morning. Thanks for the films, they have helped us. Two to go."

At the station Lotte asked Adam and Doro to consider coming to London for a concert. "You can stay the night. One of you with each of us." Lotte laughed.

"Thanks, great idea," Doro said. Adam thanked her too and said he would love that.

He drove through town around the one-way system and up to the A25 to Newlands Corner. They had a second breakfast coffee in the cafe at the top of the hill.

"We'll find a bench outside and I will tell you some of my thoughts. How is it going with Dr Ford?"

"Very well. She is really encouraged and impressed by both of us."

"She is?" He smiled.

"There are still things she wants to look at. I get my homework."

The old looking bench was backed by bushes and looked out over the farms below. He took her hands in his.

"I really want to listen to some music. Will you choose a concert for us in London and can I come and listen to some in your house sometimes?"

"Yes, dear Adam, of course you can." She took one hand back and touched his face gently. "You once said that I shouldn't feel rejected by you. I'm saying the same to you. Don't feel rejected by me. I love you. Please continue to hold back. You have things to work through and I have areas to work on."

"That's OK, dear Thea. I am preparing myself for a very negative reaction to what I want to say." Their hands remained joined.

"Wasn't it lovely what Helga said? I know she was a bit drunk but she saw that we loved each other."

"It was lovely. What Lotte said was also good, our own quiet space. Could work."

"I've been writing down our thoughts, notes on the film, things we concluded. I've been thinking a lot about the facing up to the past, facing fears and responsibilities and about mourning. I am aware that we must not run away from doing this. I had a good think back into the '60s and '70s and I had a thought, an idea, but it could be a bad idea."

Doro swallowed. What was he going to say that cost him so much?

"Talk to me about Aachen, not the commune, the city."

"Before I do, I want to tell you something. I've been hurt and angry and it would be easy to blame you and cast you in the role of dominator and destroyer. No way can I do that. I was young and influenced by your charm but I decided. It was my decision to go, to have an adventure. I made the decision to have sex with Manfred. I take my own responsibility. I am working through the fears I have been left with. Now, back to Aachen."

Adam was taken aback. Her words cut right into his plan to talk about Aachen.

"Doro, I doubt that I will ever be able to accept that. Just talk to me about Aachen the city."

"The myth, a history lesson, a tourist description?"

"What you felt and feel about it."

"It was a beautiful city. I saw only a little of its beauties. I always felt sad that I was not able to visit and get to know it, to enjoy the cathedral and the villages. I got used to focusing only on the commune. Tourism was a bourgeois thing to do! It's at a crossroads, borders with Holland and Belgium. Its idyllic beauty contrasts with the evil being planned there."

"I want you to listen, but don't make a decisive response. Think it through. I believe it would be a step to healing if you spent a few days in Aachen." She gulped and took in a deep breath.

"My insides scream 'Never' but my heart would love to see it again. But I need to deal with my fears. I will think it through."

"That's all I ask. I will contact the London office and find out the present danger level, if I would be allowed to go, if you would be allowed to go. Lots to think about but I can see that being there could be, might be, another step to healing."

"I would love to be able to think of Aachen with pleasure and appreciation. When we were called to the office, RAF gang members had been seen in Aachen and Cologne. That could prevent such a visit."

"I need to find out. While I do, just ask yourself if you think you could go there. Talk it over with Dr Ford Lloyd."

"Come back and listen to some music."

"Good idea." They were both quite tired; inner work can be exhausting. They walked back along the slope, loving the view stretched ahead of them, gradated colours of tree lines, hill tops fading in the distance. Dog walkers were beginning to arrive. Happy hounds rushed past them.

"I do love dogs, but I was hoping to travel before, before…"

"I ruined your retirement."

"Well, you could look after him while I travel." Doro smiled.

"But I'd like to travel with you, who would look after him then?"

"Nice dreams, Adam. I hope some of them come true."

At home she looked at her CDs. She was not sure what to play to help him the most. She put on Eric Whitacre to start with; *Lux Arumque, Sleep* and *When David Heard*. She introduced him to Karl Jenkin's *Mass for Peace* by playing the Benedictus, then she put on some Bach recorded by Richard.

"Thank you. Could I take a couple home with me?"

He left with the CDs saying he would give her a break from him unless she rang and then they would see some of Stammheim again, paying special attention to the arguments between the judges and the gang members.

"Just one more after that, the film version of Böll's book, *Die Verlorene Ehre der Katharina Blum*. We can return them to Lotte when we go to the concert in London."

Doro was beginning to accept that she could make plans to include Adam. They were smiling and laughing more in spite of their caution and uncertainty. Thinking of Aachen was disturbing. She wished she could short circuit her emotions and just be there looking at the hill of the Devil's Sand. She re-read the myth about Charlemagne and did have a yearning to see the cathedral door with the Devil's thumbs and the hill, the Lousberg.

"That was a threatened evil and destruction and it did not succeed. Rather like the RAF threats." She wondered what the music would do for Adam.

At the end of the week, she prepared a meal for Adam for after they had finished watching the film by Reinhard Hauff. He had been awarded a prize for the film but it was controversial. He had used as much of the trial report for the transcript as he was allowed to see. He had shown shots of the real security prison where Baader, Meinhof, Ensslin and Raspe were being held. Doro and Adam found that they did not take so many notes. There was long, agitated, shouted arguments between the judges and the gang members. The trial had dragged on for over two years. Some witnesses were brought to speak of the bomb atrocities at the trial.

News footage was shown in black and white. The accused constantly accused the judges in their turn; they accused the authorities of treating them badly, denying their rights, keeping them isolated and beating them. It was uncomfortable viewing.

Doro served up a glass of white wine with a fish dish.

"They were arguing from two different value systems. Did they really shout torrents of abuse at the judges and speak so quickly and with such fierce anger?" Adam asked.

"There was no meeting of minds, no agreement, no way of persuading the gang members. They were absolutely convinced that they were right, like Horst Mahler's comments in the last film. This one was not so relevant to our own situation but it illustrates well the mindset of the revolutionaries."

"It was important for them to be infiltrated," Adam said. Doro took their plates and topped up the wine.

"How was the music?"

"I'm learning to listen. I loved the Bach. My mother used to play that. I feel quite challenged by Jenkins, Whitacre and Richter, but there are sections I really enjoy. I am in London next week; I'll look up a concert."

Chapter 14

Adam needed a haircut and went to the barber he had tried in Godalming. He usually walked into town from his house and he strolled thinking of how very beautiful Dorothea had looked in the choker and wine-red blouse. He was longing to express his love for her, to kiss and caress her. He felt they had truly begun to clear the air and hoped that would both heal in a deep way and be able to have a normal love relationship.

"I think she is fed up with me. I can't do anything right." A customer was near the door talking with the barber trimming his hair. Adam was surprised to hear a very personal conversation as he sat waiting in a chair.

"Morning, sir, trim? Special night out?"

"Had it, thanks, just normal grooming."

"Who gave you that lovely thick hair?"

"Mother, long, dark hair she had."

"You're lucky. Most men have thinning hair by the time they go grey."

"I hate my job but at my age I'm scared to try and change." Came the customer's voice again.

"Are you depressed, John?"

"S'pose I am. Hitting the beer a bit."

"Oh, John, don't go down that path. Your wife will not be happy. Can you talk it over?"

"Never tried."

"It's worth it. Tell her about your job and see if she has any ideas. Cut down on the beer. Got any mates to chat to?"

"Not serious chat. We all mess around in the pub."

"How's that?" the barber held up a mirror to John.

"Fine, thanks, Greg. See you again." Adam was struck by how John reacted. He was actually helped and advised by a barber. He was really struck by that snippet of conversation. He remembered when he had needed to talk and taken the route to seeing a counsellor through the Department Office. He had been seen by Dr Ford Lloyd after he had been shot.

He was able to tell her about the woman he loved and the mess he was in. He told her that the woman in question was about to get married. Dr Ford worked as a specialist for damaged agents.

"That's what men need, a relaxed, quiet place to chat to a man or woman about their problems. We're so bad at doing that." Adam was thinking.

He paid for his haircut and spoke to the barber next to him.

"Sorry, I could not help overhearing." He went on to thank him for the way he had helped his customer.

"They all pour it out in here," said Greg.

Adam replied, "Men don't usually talk, do they? Do we?"

"There is an organisation where we can get some training. Someone realised the importance of barber chat and set up a program."

"I'm very pleased to hear that. I'm a psychologist and see the value. Well done! Keep it up."

Greg shone and straightened his shoulders and smiled. "Thank you, sir."

A project began to form in his mind. If he and Dorothea could be together, marry or at least be partners, he could use his house as a clinic. He planned to talk to Ralph and Dr Ford.

There would no doubt be red-tape, rules to adhere to, health and safety regulations, and police checks. He felt so excited and could not wait to talk to Doro.

Kisses, caresses and talks about clinics. Not just yet, he told himself.

"We have a film to see and Aachen to arrange." He began to write up a plan of action for his project. He would need two or three qualified psychiatrists in the team. There would be limits to what he offered; no PTS of military personal. He would focus on damaged agents. Then there would be help for local men at much reduced prices.

Adam spent a day in London and walked to Russell Square and sat reflecting on the past sitting on a bench. Then he walked to the office to meet Ralph and Martin.

First, he mentioned his project of setting up a clinic in Surrey for broken and damaged agents. Funds would be needed to run a team of qualified psychiatric counsellors. He would also arrange a separate program for local men with reduced fees.

"You're not wasting your retirement!" Next, he broached the subject of Aachen.

"Dr Ford emphasises the importance of facing the nightmare and revisiting the venues if possible. I feel that Dorothea would benefit from that if she agrees to go, and she has not yet done so."

"OK, it's like this. Jürgen was Manfred's right-hand man. He escaped arrest and he lives in a different area of Aachen. Bruno is out of prison and is elderly but he goes to see him. Bruno still lives in Cologne and some other elderly agents visit him. Both houses are being watched. I have a young undercover chap in the same block as Bruno. No sign of literature, meetings, packages or weapons. No contact with the released RAF woman. Our man has befriended Bruno, kept it simple, invited him for a drink. No sign of anything political at all."

"That's good to hear. What do you think? Can I go there with Dorothea?"

"We've had a team meeting," Martin added. "We'll give you the Aachen address, not for you to go there, but for you to avoid. Don't even walk past the house or down the street at all. If you stay in a hotel and do the tourist bit mainly outside the town and of course visit the important parts of town on very few occasions and sign to say so, then OK. Tell us when and where."

Adam smiled. "Thanks so much. How are you both?"

"Well, thanks but busy with the opposition, the neo-Nazis in the old East, Dresden, Halle and Leipzig."

"So sorry. I'm glad to be out of it. All the very best. I might bring Dorothea on my next visit. She's recovering but is still fragile."

"Are you…are you, you know?" Ralph asked awkwardly.

"No, we are not." He smiled and left and felt rather light headed to be out and to have permission.

"Walkies?" Adam phoned Doro. "A new area?"

"OK, where?"

"From mine." He drove over and found her relaxed and smiling. "Are you feeling fit?"

"Why? Hills?" He grimaced.

"Exactly." They drove to the car park at the base of St Martha's Hill. "It's the Pilgrim's Way, from Winchester to Canterbury."

"Chaucer?"

"The Shere church was also on the way. This has great views. I love space, air and vistas."

"You need them, my love."

They walked up the sandy path, stepping over winding roots, seeing the ferns, the variety of trees and the many other paths on the way up.

"You can see this church from my bedroom. It's blocked by the garage and trees from below." They stood at the top by the short stone wall around the church yard and cemetery. There was a 360-degree view.

"Dorothea this is fantastic." He took some photos on his phone and he took one of her too, smiling at him. He sat her on a bench and told her about his project, the barber and the use of his home.

"I think I could only set it up if you and I have a stable relationship, perhaps like Lotte and Helga of perhaps if we marry."

"That's our hope, isn't it? We do love each other. I'm not ready yet."

"I realise that but we can think, plan and have dreams."

"Yes, dearest Adam. I'll talk to Dr Ford about it and about Aachen. Do we know where that is at?" He told her of his visit.

"I'm so glad you get on with Dr Ford. She saw me in 1978 for some months. I felt she would be good for you and was pleased she agreed. She's retired really but takes on the odd case, especially if it is an agent."

Doro must have looked shocked.

"Don't worry, please don't worry. She promised total discretion."

"I always feel frightened when I learn of your influence, your control over my life."

"Dearest, you needed help and she is the best there is."

"She was very hard on you," She admitted.

"She was hard on me in 78, hard indeed. She told me I had abused you. I needed to hear it."

"How much did she know in 78?" she asked beginning to let tears fall.

"She knew I had to give up hope of any relationship with you forever."

"She knows differently now!"

"Does she?"

"You are my topic next session."

"I am?"

"Well, she's impressed with both of us so far."

"That's good. Now, Aachen?"

"I'm split in two." He explained the intelligence from the watchers.

"We have to sign a contract. We have permission to go as long as we go nowhere near the flat under surveillance and that we spend as much time as possible outside the town centre."

"Are we likely to see Jürgen or Bruno in a shop or a bus?"

"Ralph wants us to sight-see out of town but it could happen." He took a good look at her.

"Could he recognise your 28-year-old self?"

"I don't want to dye my hair. I could wear a wig."

"Quite an idea. You are not grey yet so a grey wig would change you. We'll ask at the office."

"A wig. How funny. Where do we stay?"

"Edge of town hotel. We will need to decide if we are a couple by then. Too hard to be together in a room or in a bed and NOT be a couple. Or we hire two rooms."

"Adam, Adam, Adam," she whispered and wept again. He hugged her, wiped her tears, stroked her hair.

"When you cry as we share, it delays our decision but it doesn't matter. This is worth your tears. We'll fix a time to go in a few months, perhaps for the Christmas markets."

"Did I say I would go?"

"Sorry. When do you want to decide?"

"After my next session with your expert spy psycho." She sat up and smiled and put her arms around him.

"Almost forgot, Royal Festival Hall, *Pathétique* by Tchaikovsky in three weeks' time."

"Wonderful. You don't know it?"

"Not at all. Hymns were the main music in my childhood until my mother played me some in my German lessons. The others showed no aptitude for languages but I got A in German A level."

"What about those hymns?"

"I enjoyed poetry but they were Victorian, romantic kitsch, like doggerel. Father was in the choir for many years when I was young. Doro, I'm really looking forward to you meeting Russell in Greece. The others are closer. Will you tell me when you feel up to meeting Rosamund, half an hour away and Steven, an hour away?"

"Thank you, Adam, not long, I think. I'd love to meet them. In many ways you are like a stranger I'm getting to know. Could I invite Renate to see the Böll film?"

"Of course, bring her to mine."

They stood by the south facing wall and looked down at the Tillingbourne Valley. She pointed out the direction of her house.

"See that tall dark building right opposite in the trees? It's a Benedictine Abbey. They sing in Latin, no Victorian simplistic doggerel. You must come some time."

"I did Latin. That's interesting. I think we had to for entrance to Oxford in those days."

"Where were you? I was in Marsden."

"Christ Church."

"That's where I went on Sundays for my cover story. You know that of course."

"Of course, my love. I had to stop myself dreaming of you sitting in my pew next to me!" She laughed aloud and they walked off hand in hand.

Lotte and Helga were delighted to go to the concert with them. "It's so sad, so heartbreaking," said Lotte.

"He doesn't know it at all. I've said nothing to him. He is so clever and knowledgeable but not in musical matters."

The date was fixed. Lotte was going to host Rainer and while Doro would stay with Helga. Lotte and Rainer, or Adam had a lot to talk about. She was aware of the intelligence on Aachen.

Dr Ford's session came two days before.

"We do love each other and I do want to be a couple with him but I have my very deep fears."

"Can you identify them?" She began to tremble.

"Meeting you has made me look back and face what I had repressed. I was devastated when my parents died. I felt so alone. Then dear Grandma got ill. I had sleepless nights worrying about my identity; who I would be when I had no one."

"How did you handle your grief?"

"I studied hard and was recruited soon afterwards so I put all my energy into that. When I hurt, I thought of the people who had lost loved ones because of the Baader Meinhof gang. I also felt sad for the gang members, hurting, disturbed, intelligent and gifted. What a waste. Then when Edward committed suicide just like some of those terrorists, I was devastated all over again. My biggest fear is loving Adam and then losing him." Doro poured it all out like Ensslin at her trial, non-stop rapid speech.

"Bit at a time. At school, any help for you?"

"The school counsellor saw me but I would not let myself cry. She was kind and gave me some guidelines. The teachers were fantastic."

"What did you do when you were alone?"

"I sold grandma's house and bought a flat in London ready for my secret work."

"Close friends?"

"No. A few mates to go out with, play sport, go to clubs but none to share with. They did care for me, though."

"Talk me through Edward's life." Dora described her super, wonderful, brilliant son. She described the unusually close relationship with his father. She recalled the Vaterlose Gesellschaft, the father and son theme in the films and books about the RAF. She told of his grief to see his father suffer gruelling chemotherapy and then die. She quoted his suicide note.

"He died of his fears; his fears of the same suffering overwhelmed him."

"I am sorry. Do not let your fears do the same to you. List them, face them."

"A new fear, apart from loving and losing again as I have all my life, is Aachen."

"Why do you want to go again?"

"I want to redeem the beauty of the town from the evil being plotted. I loved the town and the surrounding areas."

"What are your fears?"

"Feeling unable to cope when I see it again. Frightened of being recognised by an elderly RAF member." She described the plans being made to protect her and the ongoing surveillance.

"A wig?" She smiled. "They have some good ones in the Department."

"Will it be good or bad to go?"

"You are the love of his life. I don't like that overused phrase, but this time it's true. He will protect you and help you through. It's his idea that it will help you. I think it will be good for you. Prepare yourself. Write your thoughts down even."

"Doctor, he told me you had treated him in 1978. That caused more fear in me but I have learned to trust him and his motivation. Thank you so much for seeing me."

"We need to find some techniques for overcoming your fear of loss. It's good that you can fight the other fears with trust. That's so important. Let's stop the meds before your trip to Aachen, two months before. See me just before you go. Tell me what fears are bothering you then. I believe some physical exercise will help, yoga, aerobics or Pilates. Look for a class." They hugged at the door.

"Adam will want to tell you about his new project soon." Doro waved. *Perhaps he has already*, she thought.

Chapter 15

Renate came to supper and watched the film with them. She greatly admired Adam's house and garden, the art works, the painting and the tree.

"What a peaceful place to sit, a bench by the river. You deserve it, Rainer...I mean Adam."

"We've been seeing some of Lotte's films about the time when Doro was working in Germany. Tonight, it is a film version of the book by Heinrich Böll."

"I read it years ago. I can't remember much but I do remember he was often in trouble with the authorities."

"Was your family impacted much by the RAF?"

"They were afraid like everyone else. You never knew where the next explosion would be. No actual personal impact. I had read Max Frisch and seen a film version of *Homo Faber*, called *Voyager*. It moved and impressed me so I listened to a news item where Max Frisch warned Germans to consider the Nazi past and make sure they taught their children to value family and traditions over and above commercial prosperity."

"Did you see *Germany in Autumn*?"

"No, but I read Aust's book on the Baader Meinhof Complex. Thanks for inviting me, I need reminding of my German roots."

"That news item on that Frisch speech is in that film."

They watched *Die Verlorene Ehre der Katharina Blum*. It was a protest book by Böll showing the evil power of the Press. In this story the Press destroyed the honour, the life and the future of Katharina Blum.

"If I'd met that reporter, Tötges, I'd have shot him myself," Renate said.

"Böll wrote the script with Volker Schlöndorf for the Antigone scene in *Germany in Autumn*. This film was a clever, intellectual comment on the gutter Press," Adam said, pouring out some wine.

Doro was still in a rather stunned state.

"1975, before the famous events of Autumn 77. Anarchy was the main enemy. Marxist terrorists are not mentioned in the film." She held back because she did not want to reveal more of their past to Renate.

"I'm glad that's all over," Renate said as she kissed them goodbye. "Adam, that was amazing. How come the commune was never caught?"

"MI6 did not give all the names to the German anti-terror police for all those years because Lotte, Gerd and you got such important intelligence. They were waiting for the right time to pull out the agents and blow the groups."

"The terrorists were ruthless killers but in Böll's opinion, the Press was just as evil. They destroyed Katharina's life. In reality, they did just that to any suspects, guilty or not, to sell papers on the backs of the fears of terror in most of society."

Doro and Adam went by train to Waterloo and decided to walk along the embankment before meeting Lotte and Helga. They did not speak much but just enjoyed being in London, seeing the Thames and being quiet and peaceful together. It was mild and dry, if not really sunny that day. They each had an overnight bag for their stay. Dora just relished being relaxed with Adam, browsing the bookshop, wandering around the little shops. It felt like normal life for normal people. Lotte and Helga arrived and smiled when they sensed the relaxed atmosphere between them.

"We are feeding you but do you want a snack or a drink," Helga asked.

"A drink perhaps." Doro hugged them both. Lotte opened her jacket to show the new pendant.

"Looks so lovely. Good colour choice for your jumper," Adam said.

"And you've had a smart haircut!" said Lotte.

"I'll talk to you about that tonight," He responded. "You want to talk about a haircut?" They all laughed.

Adam was very moved by the music. He was breathless at times, almost tearful. Doro took his hand. No one spoke. At the end he applauded with everyone else but soon said, "Powerful. I have to be over 60 before I experience such power. I've missed out."

"So sad. So moving. 'Pathétique' indeed."

"I begin to be aware of the healing power of music and I've shut it out of my life until now." They went to Helga's flat for supper and chatted happily.

"How do you want to meet up tomorrow?" asked Lotte.

"It's walking distance," Helga pointed out.

"I'll come here from Lotte's, OK?" Adam suggested a time and made sure he understood her route. Doro was looking forward to talking with Helga. Lotte and Adam went to the door. He turned to Doro as Lotte went down the stairs.

"Goodnight, see you in the morning." He hugged her and so naturally they kissed, a real, loving, long kiss. "Sleep well." He touched her cheek and left to join Lotte.

Doro was feeling very happy as she spent time with Helga. "Do tell me about your family in Germany," she asked.

Helga said she was still in touch with her brother and sister who had accepted her gay relationship. At university her parents had supported her studies but not her lesbian friendships. They were very traditional and had been deeply affected by the war and by the erection of the Berlin Wall in 1961. Christina and Lotte and Helga helped with the tunnels. They went in to help with the collapses and to help people out if they were stuck. There were several tunnels, several helpers and several spies working for the Stasi. In those early days of the wall, as it became more solid, higher and better guarded, Lotte climbed through to pull out a mother and child. There were no mother and child, instead a border guard started to drag her. She put up a fight and he shot her. He left her and returned to the East but she managed to crawl back as soil fell, but she died near the mouth and was found there.

Christina contacted Lotte's parents and helped with the funeral. She decided to change her name to Lotte when she joined the secret services.

"She had been so brave. I was so surprised to find her in London. She has been so faithful and told me hardly anything about her work, total integrity."

Doro told Helga how they had worked together and that Lotte had saved her life. "Do you know if she ever had any support?"

"I don't know. Rainer gave us our rules. I know he looked out for her."

"I am so glad you found each other and that you have made a life together. It's just wonderful!" Helga smiled.

"We just might live together all the time when we come to old age ailments, and our last days together."

Lotte showed Adam his bedroom for the night but knew he wanted to talk so she did not put on her nightclothes, but opened the whiskey, poured them both a drink and sat to listen to what he wanted to say.

As he explained his barber experience and his project for a clinic, she was pleasantly surprised. He asked her who she had seen when she needed help. He remembered how she had tried so hard to get the details of a firebomb attack in the early '80s. Bruno had called in extra support from Düsseldorf and Cologne to get the car bomb into the airbase. The actual venue turned out to be a Department Store. Lotte had packed in the explosives. The Press next day showed atrocious pictures of dead children. Lotte wondered why they had lied and felt overwhelmed with guilt and horror. She was in danger of a breakdown. Rainer helped her give reasons why she had to return to the UK for a while. Lotte had seen Dr Ford Lloyd.

"She was great but I was transferred to a male doctor, I'm not sure why."

"I discussed my project with her a couple of weeks ago and she was very positive. Doro has really benefitted from her help. She's retired but comes back to see an agent from time to time. I think in the early '80s she had her own problems. One of her parents in Wales died after a long time suffering with dementia."

"Adam, your idea is really inspiring. Does Doro agree?"

"Yes, but she is dealing with fear issues."

"She has lost everyone she loved. She's probably afraid of losing you." Adam was quiet for a while. He had not considered that.

"We are probably going to make a holiday trip to Aachen in December. We've had it cleared with certain restrictions. I feel that for deep healing, Doro needs to see Aachen for the lovely town that it is."

"That's a shock. I'd need to think about that."

"Do you know the Aachen myth about the Devil and the cathedral?"

"I did read it. I think I showed Doro the statue of the old lady who fooled the Devil and saved the town."

"It means a lot to her. She feels the evil being planned by the RAF was prevented from destroying the city. She loves the mountain."

"We went there together!"

"She's going to have a disguise, a wig. Jürgen is still there and he sees Bruno, two old men meeting up but being watched."

"Could it do her more harm than good?"

"I think the risk of carrying the fear with her and the dread of the name of a place she loved is greater than that of either meeting Jürgen or of suffering a recurrence of her breakdown."

"I hope you are right. I wish you well. If you go, research Monschau, Kornelimünster, Maria Lach and the Eifel. Will you have a car?"

"Thanks, Lotte, I'll get a hire car and I'll look up those places. We will only be there a week." He jotted down the names.

"Better get some sleep. Wigs tomorrow."

Doro felt quite light-hearted as she and Adam caught a bus to Trafalgar Square. They walked to the office and greeted Ralph.

"It's good to see you looking so much better, Diane, welcome back to the secret world. Julia here will take you to the disguises room but first, here are your papers and a declaration to sign. Dr Adam Chamberlain, you are Dr Paul Baker and Diane, you are Mrs Caroline Baker. Your hotel has been paid for through us but you can use your normal Credit card for shops."

"Car hire?" Adam asked. "Oh, dear, use taxis."

"I can hire one online and use my normal passport for ID once in Germany."

"As you like."

"Thank you, Julia, I'll come now."

The two ladies left the room. Julia opened what looked like a stock cupboard; shelves with rows of head wearing wigs, male and female, boxes of toupees, moustaches, beards, boxes of glasses were before her.

"Do you wear glasses?" asked Julia.

"For close work, reading, plain glass will do for walking around. The disguise is only for central town. I can be me outside in the villages." They moved to the grey wigs.

"You still have light brown hair so dark grey would be best with an eyebrow pencil."

"That long wig with a clip to hold it back."

"Possible problems at the nape if it is clipped."

"OK, shoulder length grey and no clips. That's OK, isn't it?"

"Very good. Doesn't flatter you. Let's find some glasses."

Julia pulled out a box with shallow drawers. She took out a slightly tinted pair with black rims. Doro looked in the mirror and laughed.

"I look like a crazy scientist. Have you got gold or silver frames plus the tint?"

Julia closed the drawer and opened another. "Try silver." They looked acceptable but the arms were rather loose.

"I've got tools." Julia opened another drawer and found the tiny screw driver. She dexterously bent and tightened the arms.

"What about my Mrs Barker photo? No glasses?"

"You have to take them off anyway at passport control. They can be your new distance glasses."

They returned to the office, laughing to see Adam's reaction.

"Is she studious enough to accompany a doctor?" Julia asked him.

They signed the declaration and took the street maps with the banned areas clearly marked. "I'd need a wig if we went to Cologne. I was never seen in Aachen." Adam laughed, packing the papers into his bag. They packed the wig and glasses and walked away to Russell Square.

On the bench she turned to him. "Doctor, I never realised."

"I did a doctorate in research on Jung and his influence on more recent psychologists."

"Mrs Barker?"

"Sorry. If by then you are not at ease sleeping with me you can have a sleeping disorder, carry an oxygen box and ask for another room of your own."

"You are a careful planner." She smiled.

"Doro, I have not had sex, made love for decades."

"It's been a while for me too."

"Well, I am a bit worried that I won't be able to, to, you know what I mean."

"Yes, my love."

"I've been to see my GP in London. I have not yet signed on in Godalming. He's offered me the blue pill and other aids, but I wanted to tell you so you don't think I am fooling you, or disappointing you."

She put her arms around his neck and kissed him, like the first time, the night before, deep, prolonged, loving, passionate.

"Adam, I love you, the real you, the whole you. It would not be surprising if you had problems. We knew it would not be easy. We'll work it out together. I'm glad we still have some weeks before we go. I have fears too."

"You recall the Devil's Sandbags story?" letting him go but holding his hand.

"I do."

"I believe that being in Aachen together will be a closure; good overcoming evil. If we succeed in making love in Aachen, it will be like undoing my past. I lost my virginity to Manfred there. He took me often but he asked me until the rape. All that can be conquered."

"And if I can't?"

"Your loving efforts, your kisses, your caresses will still be healing." He took her head in his hands and kissed her gently.

"Dr Ford advised me to do some regular exercise. I am thinking of yoga or aerobics. Don't you think it would be good for you too? There's a leisure centre in Godalming near the park, near the lake we walked around."

"I like swimming. There's bound to be a swimming club sometime."

"I think we need to push ourselves hard physically. We live too much in our heads. What did the concert do for you?"

"I loved it, the way the music bypassed thoughts and touched emotions." She smiled. "Come to some more music. Do you know there is a Benedictine Abbey in Chilworth?

"There's a public Mass at 10.00 am on Sundays where the monks chant Gregorian chants and the liturgy. I took myself there and it reminded me of Christ Church and Marsden Evensong."

"I will gladly come with you, my love."

"And I go to the cathedral sometimes for Evensong."

"Right. Are you turning me into a religious man?"

"I'm not religious but I have a spiritual life. There is a creator spirit behind the universe. I feel a presence and I feel a care and love. I don't go along with all the Bible doctrines but I love parts of it, the Psalms and the Gospels, especially John. Other parts, I hate."

"I suppose I have the same concept of a creator spirit and a power of good in the universe, but the suffering of my mother's people is always inside me and I cannot let myself spend time on a God of justice, punishment or judgement."

"Which one first?"

"Abbey."

On Sunday, they drove up a narrow, winding lane and turned into the Abbey car park. Adam was delighted by the beautiful flint building in wide grounds. In the distance, beehives were spaced out under the trees.

"They make honey and waxy creams. They're on sale inside. When we came here, it was a Franciscan Friary, a parish with a very full church and lots of activities. It's a cold, Victorian building and as no new monks were coming, it was too much for a few elderly Friars. It was a sad day when it closed. When the Benedictines bought it, people were relieved that as a listed building, it had not been turned into a hotel or leisure centre. It is a monastery and no longer an open parish, but the public are welcome to most of the services."

They sat in a pew and enjoyed the organ music. Strains of Bach filled the church. Adam looked at the shiny wooden floor and the red carpet on steps up to the altar. A row of tall candles was being lit. The green curtain over the host contrasted with the red and with the pale cream-grey stone of the walls. On the left side were a series of small chapels where a few people chose to sit. Most people sat on the polished but ancient pews with drop-down kneelers. At the front on the left was a statue of Mary and on the right a statue of a saint with lilies and a child in his arms. In front of both was a bank of flickering tea-lights.

Both statues had a vase of pink and white flowers, roses and lilies. The whole church was well lit by ceiling clusters and by high, clear windows. The congregation stood up as the priests and monks filed in. Once they were out of sight in the choir stalls, they opened with a melodious, slow chant. Adam looked around to see when to stand, when to sit and when to kneel. Adam so appreciated the slowness, the peace and the beauty of the whole Mass. At the end the organist played a lively, loud postlude to send everyone home. They sat until it had finished and then met the Abbot and some priests at the door. They shook hands.

"There was a line in the Mass, 'and my soul shall be healed', that's what we need, to heal our souls." He was probably addressing Doro and himself but he had included one of the priests, who responded, sensing his seriousness.

"We are available to speak to you if ever you would like to talk."

"Thank you."

"We have a website, St Augustine's Abbey."

"That's kind of you; I may consider that in the future." Adam smiled graciously.

"Welcome, madam, I've seen you here before."

"Yes, I love coming. It really does me good."

"This is Dorothea and I am Adam."

"Gift of God and the first man, good combination! God bless, have a lovely day."

Chapter 16

In the next few weeks Adam and Doro both took up exercise. She tried yoga and he started with swimming, lengths of breast stroke and over arm strokes. He tried to stretch himself, feel the pressure, the pain even. Doro had never tried yoga but liked the slow start, the stillness before the different positions and the stretching.

"Did you play tennis when you were young?"

"Yes, but not after Oxford."

"We could try that or badminton or squash. I did none of them but I feel the need to move, to run, to jump."

"There are lots of runners in the park. We could begin by joining them." She smiled at him and took his hand.

"Running with you. So odd. I don't believe my life!" He took her head again and kissed her lips and then her neck over and over again. She made no objection and ran her fingers through his hair.

"Getting into practice," he said and held her close, caressing her back. He let her go. "Lunch?" he asked.

"OK." She did not feel hungry. She was moved and a little disturbed to find her own desire for him growing.

One Sunday they went to the cathedral for Evensong.

"So many lovely views of Guildford." Adam walked to the hillside and looked over the town.

"What do you think of when you think of a cathedral?"

"Darkness, stained glass, statues."

"Think again." She walked up the steps and showed him the angels etched into the giant glass doors. Inside the lightness and brightness surprised him and so did the size.

115

"No pews, comfy chairs!" They were welcomed with an Order of Service. "Acoustics are not wonderful at the back. Let's go to the first 20 rows of chairs."

"Lovely window." He looked up at the round window above the long curtain behind the altar. The large white dove in a blue background depicted the Holy Spirit. It was charming and impressive with the colour combinations.

There was a hush as the choir processed in and took their places on the light wood stalls. Men and women, boys and girls all wore rust-coloured robes. The choir was of a very high standard and reminded him of Christ Church and Marsden choirs.

Adam was impressed and moved by the whole of evensong. The readings were delivered with clarity and conviction. Prayers were read in the same way. The congregation around him joined in with strong voices. He felt rather lost and out of place but he loved listening. After the service they visited the Garden of Remembrance for Children.

"Edward was an adult but I still feel his presence when I come here."

They walked around the outside of the whole building as darkness began to fall. The angel on the top was lit up.

"That angel. It looks familiar. Where would I have seen it?"

"The Omen, horror film. The scene of the father with a knife and the boy with the devil inside, that was filmed here."

"I vaguely remember."

"The devil didn't win here either!"

"Then, my love, will you come to Woking and meet my sister?"

"Are you sure?"

"Yes. She'll love you and you will like her and her daughter."

"Not her husband?"

"Gordon is quiet and withdrawn. He does not say much."

"A first present, a first kiss and a first family visit." He smiled as they walked back to the car.

"No smart gear, casual, jeans if you like," he told her.

One evening they drove through Guildford to Woking and turned off before the town Centre to wind their way through Goldsworth Park. Doro looked lovely in black trousers and a pretty broderie anglaise blouse. Rosamund appeared to be about Doro's age with thick but lighter brown hair. She smiled and chatted a lot.

"I am so pleased that my little brother has a lady in his life at last. I am so pleased to meet you, Dorothea. How did you two meet?"

They had rehearsed their answers to the inevitable questions. "German Department of the Foreign Office."

"Have you both retired?"

"I did some teaching in schools but I have retired now."

"You are a widow?"

"Yes, my husband was an organist and we had one son and one daughter. They both tragically died young."

"So sorry, you must have been through hell." Doro nodded and sat in the armchair. Adam and Rosamund hugged.

"How are you?" she asked.

"All the better for seeing you and bringing Dorothea."

"It's a pretty name," Rosamund replied.

"And you are Shakespearian."

"I was teased at school because of that. I haven't been in touch with Shakespeare for a long time."

"Nor have I." The lounge door opened and a grey-haired man came in carrying the paper. "Meet Gordon, my husband."

"Pleased to meet you," Doro said.

"Crossword or Sudoku?" asked Adam.

"Crossword. Can't do the Sudoku today. What's your name?"

"Dorothea."

"Do you know German too?"

"Yes, I speak German and have some German friends."

"Terrible nation. Nazis and Stasi and terrorists and now they run Europe as if they won the war!"

"There are also a lot of lovely people in Germany too," Doro added.

"We're going there soon, just before Christmas," Adam added quickly. "There are fantastic Christmas markets. Our mum told us about them."

Gordon took a seat in the other armchair and put his head in his paper.

"Potato pie, your favourite," Rosamund said to Gordon. "Is Shirley joining us?" She came in at that very moment.

"Hi, you must be Dorothea. I'm Shirley, welcome."

"Are you in social work too?" asked Doro.

"Children and families. Often rather heartbreaking and tough. I liaise with family courts."

"That sounds very difficult. I had minimal dealings with them when I was a teacher in London."

"Did you see kids taken away from their parents?"

"Mine were older, secondary age but I saw a 15-year-old have her son taken from her and adopted. She had no rights to see him."

"Life is often so tragic. I see deprived children left with inadequate, drunk parents and others taken from their parents who could cope with more support."

"How do you unwind?"

"I date online, meet guys in pubs or clubs. I like dancing, clubbing, cooking and Netflix."

"Clubbing was before my time." Doro laughed.

"My ex liked clubbing, hip hop and beat box. He had an eye for bopping girls!"

"Sorry, Shirley. I hope you find another partner."

"Friends, dates, yes. Marriage again? No way, not yet!"

"Come and get it!" Rosamund called from the kitchen. Adam took Doro's hand and led her to the kitchen-diner.

"You've made such an effort. Thank you so much," Doro said.

"When are you going to Greece, Ros?" asked Adam.

"Early spring, end of April. You must take Dorothea. Russell won't believe you have such a lovely girlfriend." Adam put his arm around Doro.

"Come on love-birds, sit here," Shirley said. "It's a pity you did not meet years ago; you're made for each other." They both had a little laugh. Rosamund brought in a German looking potato pie and served up huge portions.

"There's cheese and egg. Mum's recipe."

"Did your mum tell you much about her country and family?"

She took us to her village and showed us the concentration camp where her family died. It was unbearable. Only Adam picked up the language. It's funny, at school Shirley did French and Spanish and would not touch German."

"What about synagogue and Jewish things?"

"She did take us sometimes. None of us went regularly. It was a Reformed synagogue, less strict than the usual ones, but it was so alien after the school assemblies," Ros explained.

118

Doro noticed that Adam made a real effort to relate to Shirley, to listen to her stories from work or about her latest date. It warmed her heart to begin to see another side of him.

Shirley had made wonderful desserts like Eton Mess, decorated with raspberries.

As they left, picking up their coats, Doro heard Shirley say to Ros, "Wow, he's smitten! About time!"

"Thank you so much. It is lovely to meet Adam's family. I have none at all so I always enjoy being with other families."

"You're most welcome. See you again soon, I hope."

"I hope you will come to my house for a meal, perhaps a weekend lunch. Not Cordon bleu but I do cook."

"Great," said Rosamund. "Brighton next?"

"Probably, then Germany and Greece in the New Year."

"Thank you, my love for making this evening so special." He kissed her and they did not let go. They had progressed a few steps and indulged in the 'heavy petting' for which teenagers were renowned.

Their touches became more intimate removing some clothing to access skin. "I am very inexperienced," said Adam, "I will need you to teach me."

"I don't expect you have ever thought about how to bring pleasure to a woman."

"You are right. I need to learn; will you teach me?"

"Yes, my love. Now, you mentioned Brighton and Greece, your two brothers. You would like to take me."

"I would. I love you so much I want to show you off. As you saw, Ros and Shirley could not believe I had a lady in my life, and such a beautiful lady."

"We won't stop if you don't go." Doro let go of him.

"I am going to the Abbey and asking to speak to a priest."

"Are you? I hope it helps you, my love."

"And my soul shall be healed," Repeated Adam. He had found the website and the phone number. He did not know who had spoken to him, so he asked if he could come and talk to a priest, telling the man on the phone of his recent visit.

"You were here with Mrs Harlow, weren't you?"

"Yes, I am Adam Chamberlain."

"Can you drive here one afternoon?"

"Yes, 2.30 a good time? Next Monday?"

Adam met Fr Tony at the front and was led through a side door to a small room with armchairs and a coffee table.

"How can I help?"

"That line of the liturgy, 'and my soul shall be healed'. I need my soul to be healed. Are you able to keep secret from your brother monks the things that I share with you?"

"As in the confessional, it will not leave this room."

"Thank you. That's important, I'm afraid because all my life I have worked in the Intelligence Services. I have more or less retired but I am just tying up some loose ends. I am afraid I have never been a church goer. My mother was Jewish but I am very ignorant of theology, the Bible and so on."

"What did you study?"

"I am a Doctor of Psychology and Psychiatry by profession."

"What is troubling you?"

"The immoral things I had to do in my work. I worked in the German Department and liaised with the German anti-terror police. It was important work but I am not sure that the end always justifies the means. I now hate what I did, and I need to deal with my guilt."

"We all need our souls to be healed, whatever we have done. Do you wish to talk about what you did?"

"I have done that of course with the trained counsellors provided by the Service. Many secret agents turn to drink or drugs. I didn't do that but I have caused some agents under my control great harm and distress. I am working on healing for me and one of my agents right now. I often weep and suffer fear."

"Do you have any beliefs?"

"In a benevolent Creator Spirit, yes."

"Do you pray?"

"In desperate times."

"What do you want to happen for you?"

"I want to know that my soul is healed. What's that line all about?"

"I am not worthy that you should enter under my roof, but only say the word and my soul shall be healed. You are inviting the Lord Jesus Christ to come into your life and you ask Him to 'say the word', to say forgiveness over you, to tell you your sin has gone and you are clean. Worship is about knowing that a good, loving and powerful God has enabled you to be forgiven."

"I feel very stirred and moved when I attend a Mass, hear the singing and the music. It's a new experience for me in my old age."

"You are being touched by the love of God. He wants to heal you and give you peace and happiness."

"I have been given a great gift. One of the agents I nearly destroyed loves me and is helping me heal up from my guilt."

"That's a blessing. Can you explain more? I'm finding hard to understand. It's a foreign world to me."

"In my role I had to lie, teach others to lie, handle weapons, make sure some enemies were killed. I was not an assassin but I had to order assassinations. I had to seduce women agents, get them to be promiscuous, all to prevent terror attacks in Germany. Lying, seducing, betraying – all par for the course. I worked with very brave, dedicated people. In old age we look back in horror."

"I feel very privileged that you have shared this with me. Your need of healing is no different to anyone else. I hope I can help you. I would like to say a prayer for you today and hope you are willing to come again. I have some things you should read which might introduce you to a more personal love of God for you. He will heal your soul. Give time to God and seek Him. Pray, not out of desperation but for some specific needs. You mentioned that music ministers to you. Listen to some with attention, meditate and pray with the music." Father Tony stood up, made the sign of the cross and put a hand on Adam's head. After a little silence, he prayed for grace, love and peace and forgiveness to fill his heart and mind and soul. Adam had to wipe his tears and thanked him.

"I'd like to come back. I am going on holiday soon and on some family trips. Would end of the year be acceptable?"

"Adam, I believe God is working in your life. Give me a ring after Christmas."

"I will, thank you very much."

Adam felt deep peace, relief and hope. He went home and put on one of Doro's CDs and sat staring at his painting for a long time. He had looked up the places mentioned by Lotte and made a rough timetable, leaving Sunday free for Mass at the cathedral. He felt he should see his brother in Brighton before they left.

"Would you do a day-trip to Brighton with me? Meet Steven and Ellie?"

"I have my date with Dr Ford tomorrow."

"Thursday?"

He would pick her up at 9.30 am but he wanted to tell her about his talk with Fr Tony. "Are you free to come around to me now?"

She noticed that his eyes were red as he opened the door and that he had been weeping. He explained about the confessional and that all he had talked about remained confidential. He explained how he had poured out his guilt and need for forgiveness and peace.

"I gave no names. I told him of my greatest blessing being an agent who loved me. I wanted to share it with you as it gave me hope."

She held him against her, feeling her heart pounding and aware of his own heart thumping. They had a few kisses and cuddles.

"The best laid plans! Do you want to make love now? Come on my love." She led him to the bedroom. They both wept as they touched so gently and then again as he reached the climax he had feared would never come.

"I love you, Adam. There you are; success."

"I love you, Thea, I love you."

"We can try again in Aachen, if you wish."

"Can I wait till then?"

"We have time, four days to go." They lay side by side for a while and then showered. She reluctantly drove home.

Dr Ford asked her how she felt about the Aachen trip. She laughingly told her about the wig and glasses and then explained that she was looking forward to going and to overcoming her fears. She told her about their efforts at exercise and about visiting his brother and sister.

"So, you are off the medication. Keep them in case there is a future crisis. I have some breathing techniques for you here for when fears rise up."

"Dr Ford, some lovely things have happened. Adam's been to hear a concert in London, been to two church services and spoken with a priest. He is feeling full of hope as he battles with his guilt." They arranged to meet in the New Year.

On Thursday they drove to Brighton.

"I haven't been here for years," said Doro as the pier appeared in front of them. "They live near the marina and they have sea views."

They pulled in to a tall, narrow terraced house with a double-parking space. Ellie answered the door and hugged Adam.

"Hello, Dorothea, glad to meet you. Welcome! I had a full report from Rosamund." She gave her a hug. Ellie was slim and lively with blond hair. Steven arrived down the corridor. He was so like Adam, thick silver hair, slim and trim.

"Welcome, Dorothea." He took them up the stairs to the living room and Doro looked at the photos on the wall. Steven showed her his son Conor with Chantal and their daughter Melanie, then his two daughters, Michaela with Carl and their daughter Courtney and finally, Ashleigh and Dave with their little ones, Dora and Mai.

"They all live quite near you? That's lovely."

"Yes, four grandchildren and all here at Christmas! Help."

"You love it!"

"Most of the time," Steven laughed.

They explored the house on four floors. Downstairs on the ground floor was the entrance hall and a store room with stairs down to the back garden. On the first floor was the large living room with a great bay window overlooking the sea. On the third floor was the kitchen and dining room with all the bedrooms on the fourth floor, under the attic.

"Where do you live, Dorothea?"

"Chilworth, not far from Adam."

"Are you retired too?"

"Yes, I was a teacher."

"So were we. Ellie still goes in to hear children read but I am putting my feet up."

"Feet up, he calls it. He is writing text books and story books for children in his den in the attic."

"Sounds like a romantic set up." Doro smiled.

"What are you doing with my baby brother?" Steven gave her a reassuring smile.

"Well, we are going to Germany in a few days, for a holiday."

Our mother tried to teach us German but Adam was the only one to take it up. He is the brains of the Chamberlain clan. A doctor and a fluent German speaker in the Foreign Office! None of us carried on our studies so far. Come and see the garden."

They walked down the back steps to a beautiful garden with shrubs and a wrought iron set of table and chairs.

"Come for our famous BBQ in the summer," Ellie said.

"I'd love to meet your grandchildren. I have no family so I am lucky to meet Adam's. I had a son but he died at 23, not long after his father died."

"How tragic. Have you got over it?"

"I'll never get over it completely. I think of him often. I have been making a new life for myself and then I met Adam."

"You seem very suited. Where are you going on holiday?"

"Aachen area for the Christmas markets."

"I prefer Stollen to Christmas cake, I'll bring you some and some bits and pieces from the markets," Adam joined in.

"Come up for some lunch. We are having a buffet. Help yourselves."

There was an inviting display of canapés and vol-au-vents and mini rolls on the dining room table.

"Shall I get you a selection?" Adam asked Doro as she accepted a glass of red wine. "Please." He leant over her and kissed her as he put a plate in front of her. She was surprised but took his hand and smiled up at him.

"Dorothea, you have transformed my brother. I have never seen him in love before." She did not know what to say. She smiled at Steven and at Adam.

"He's transformed me too," she added.

The two brothers talked as the four of them walked along the Downs above the town. Ellie and Doro swopped school stories. Ellie asked her about her husband and son. She also told her about Marianna but did not want to mention cancer and suicide at this stage.

"Is he taking you to Greece to meet Russell?"

"I think so, next year." Adam came and joined them and took Doro's hand.

"It has been lovely to see you both." Adam said to Ellie. "Thanks for such a lovely lunch. I hope you survive Christmas."

"And we hope you have a good time in Germany." Adam drove home smiling. "They loved you too! We'll get a taxi to the airport. Don't forget to pack the wig!" He laughed. He drove up to her home and she did not get out straight away. She touched his arm. "Stay," she said. "Or did you want to wait?"

"What do you think?" As they caressed and kissed, Doro said, "Let me love you. You need to learn to receive love too."

"Slowly. Take it slowly." She kissed him everywhere. "This is so new to us. I love you, Adam Chamberlain."

"I can't believe it. Am I doing okay for you?"

"It gets better." Showering and soaping was becoming their new ritual. They spent their first whole night together and slept well, refreshed to make their flight to Aachen.

"I'm going home to pack. Taxi comes at ten. We can sleep in the plane."

"The flight is not that long!"

Chapter 17

The plane approached Koln/Bonn airport. They had dozed a little. Doro had been on this flight three times a year for ten years until 1979. She looked out of the window; the sights of the vehicles and the signs on the airport buildings made her heart beat. She began to struggle for breath. From somewhere inside a sense of panic was rising. She tried to do one of the breathing exercises Dr Ford had given her.

"Sit for a bit. Let others off," Adam whispered. The deep breathing and counting helped and she eventually walked off the plane, through the plastic tunnel and into the Arrivals area. The smells, the sounds, the sights of Koln/Bonn made her head spin a little but she kept going. Their fake passports caused them no trouble.

Doro could not wait to take off the wig and glasses, but she could not do that until they reached the hotel. She needed to wear it in the town centre only. Adam looked at the map he had been given and saw that the old commune and the address of Jürgen were very close. He had asked for a luxury hotel on the outskirts of town near the Lousberg on the opposite side of town.

"How are you doing?"

"Bit shaky." Tears were in her eyes. He stood and held her.

"You are going to beat it, to overcome. You will be calm and peaceful. Keep up the deep breathing." He pushed their luggage to the 'car hire' desk, holding her still as she held on to the trolley. He had booked in his own name and with his own passport so he opened the satchel to pull out the documents. Doro focused on scanning around the airport, so familiar to her but now so upgraded and modernised; it was clean and shiny with luxury shops. Adam took his car keys and took her over to a sparkling shop. He sniffed the tester bottles.

"I'm getting you some perfume, my dearest love." He let her sniff. "Good choice?"

"Fantastic!" He put the bottle of Opium in her bag.

"Thank you, my love." She kissed him. He collected their car and used the GPS to find the way. Lousberg loomed before them. She removed her wig and glasses and packed them in the bag. He drove up the hill to the most Germanic looking hotel with carved wooden shutters and balconies. Small green and yellow shrubs grew in the window boxes.

"It's picturesque, charming and historic." They had to use their false passports but they agreed that Doro could safely be in the hotel without her wig. She pulled her hair back with a clip in case she was challenged.

"Your suite is on the first floor, overlooking the Lousberg. Welcome Dr and Mrs Baker."

"I'm pleased to see the Devil's Sand." Doro smiled.

"You know the myth?"

"Yes."

"You must see the beautiful statue of the old woman and the devil. Here's a map."

"Thank you so much."

They found their suite and were amazed at its size. The bed was king sized, the lounge area had a giant television screen and a drinks refrigerator. There was a table and four chairs so they could invite friends. The bathroom was magnificent, a wet room with a bath, a shower and a basin. Dorothea had never seen anything like it. She was still unsure of herself but this was another world, not her Aachen world of the 1970s. They unpacked, explored the hotel and scanned the menu.

"We must have Sauerkraut, local specialty," Adam said. They sat at the table and unfolded maps and brochures.

"We're tired. Tomorrow we'll go to Maria Lach and have a boat trip. Rest this evening, eat in our room perhaps? Next day we could do the town centre and you can show me the parts you love. Doro passed him a flyer from the table.

"Poulenc Gloria in the Cathedral! Oh, yes, please do that on Wednesday. The hotel was able to book tickets for them.

"Can we go up the Lousberg before supper? We can have a drink in the revolving restaurant." Adam felt so pleased that she was relaxing and not building up to an emotional crisis. They drove up the winding road and parked at the restaurant. Adam took photos of the view from the top. They spotted the spa, the cathedral and the Town Hall. It was a spectacular panorama. In the distance was a long, straight road a rising hill leading out of town to Stollberg, Kornelimünster and Monschau.

"We are going up there one day." He pointed to it.

"I feel I am on honeymoon." She smiled.

"I'd like a creamy coffee up there." He looked at the top revolving slowly. Doro chose a Hagebuttentee, a Rosehip tea.

"For old time's sake. We lived on that!" She sipped with her eyes closed and could see herself in the commune.

"Printen. You must have one."

"What's that?" She told him about the spicy, ginger specialty biscuits from Aachen and asked for some in the restaurant.

"Mmm! Delicious." Adam bit into the firm brown biscuit with a soft, bendy interior. "There's a special shop in town. More than one. Take some home to your nephews and nieces."

"It really is an idyllic town." Adam looked out over the views.

"It has honoured its Jews killed in the holocaust. Each known resident has a gold tile with their name engraved on it and sunk into the pavement in front of the house they lived in. That long road up leads to Brand, a village outside the town. One German resident researched the Jews of Brand, had a memorial built to them outside the church. He found a survivor who lived in America. He travelled there and brought him back to Brand and held a memorial celebration for him. It was all reported in the local paper. I could not talk about it in the commune because they were so anti-Zionist."

"Well remembered. What a story!"

"The commune was anti-Zionist and antisemitic. All Jews were seen as potential Zionists."

They were so tired and needed to sleep, so they ordered some soup and a snack to eat in their room. They had agreed on an early night but she did not want to deprive him of lovemaking on their first night in such a huge bed. She put on a therapist's hat and gave him some techniques to help him. She made sure she boosted his confidence by showing her appreciation of his efforts. They slept peacefully and were awoken by the winter sun streaming through the balcony widow.

Doro rose and showered and dressed. She stood looking through the balcony doors as Adam prepared himself. It was cold. They went down for a very German breakfast; dark rye bread, cheese and hams, jam and Quark with bread rolls and different slices of other types of bread. They drank a lot of black coffee.

"Off we go to the lake." Adam smiled, kissed her and put on a warm coat. She had scarf and gloves and a winter coat.

He had worked out a route into the Eifel mountains. Distant hills had a snowy top but it was neither freezing nor snowy in Aachen. Wooden chalets nestled in valleys; thick woodland grew on the slopes. A few cattle and horses munched grass. It was a tourist idyll without the tourists. Some villages had very high hedges, originally planned to protect houses and gardens from the high winds. Hedges about 20-foot-high had holes cut into them for doors and windows. They saw a sign to Krippana, an exhibition of various Nativity scenes. They decided to visit the large barns containing the display. Inventive, inspired and charming, the cribs were both ancient and modern.

"What a wonderful idea!" Doro exclaimed. Adam asked if he could take photos. "Next year's Christmas cards? Do send them in an email to Lotte."

The lake stretched for miles before them. Doro could imagine the scene in the summer, the families picnicking, the swimmers, the beaches. The white boat was large with flags fluttering on the top. They sat on the deck as they wanted to get the most from the cruise. Grey cloud broke to reveal patches of blue sky with fluffy white clouds moving quickly across the sky. There were stops at some villages but they decided to stay put to admire the beauty all around.

A little girl ran around the deck. Her mother was chasing her. She ran up to their seats and put her hands on Dora's knees and smiled up at them.

"Marianna, komm zurück!" a shrill voice yelled. Doro's heart jumped and she held the girl's hands.

"Du heisst Marianna?" she asked, smiling down at her. Adam remembered her daughter, Marianna, who had died within weeks of her birth. He took one hand of the child and put his arm around Doro. By then the mother had reached them.

"Tut mir Leid," the mother stuttered. She apologised over and over.

"Meine Tochter war auch eine Marianna." She handed her to her mother who picked her up, told her how dangerous it was to run on the deck and she could fall into the water.

"Look at the birds," shouted Doro in German to the kicking child.

She leant her head on Adam who whispered, "I'm sorry. I know about your daughter who died and that she was called Marianna. How did Edward cope?"

"He was only two but he remembered his baby sister for a long time afterwards."

"My dearest Dorothea, you have had more suffering than most. I hope I can give you some happy years."

"Thank you, my love. You have made a good start. I'd like to ask your priest if there could be a reason for all that happened to me. I lost everyone I loved from 17 to 55."

"You can come with me next time, if you like."

"Not next time, that is for you, it's your time, your soul. A little later, I'd like that." He kissed her lips and their hands were gripped until the end of the cruise.

"Marianna was Richard's grandmother. He was so upset to lose our daughter but I never got pregnant again although I longed for another baby."

"I'd be a bad father like I am a bad husband," Adam said softly.

"I don't believe it. You'd love your child like you love me. I wish we could have a child but we shall have your great nieces and nephews instead. We shall help broken people in your clinic."

"Dorothea Chamberlain, one day, I hope. Thea, I do love you so deeply." Back in the hotel, Oche Stube, Adam sat her down to talk to her.

"Tomorrow could be painful for you, my darling. Wig and glasses, but we'll concentrate on the positives, all the amazing places and the fact that you got out; evil did not win. Where do you want to go?"

"The cocktail bar, if it is still there, the spa square, the central street fountains, the Town Hall, the cathedral and the Roman museum? The Printen shops are in the central, narrow streets."

"Shall we save the cathedral for Wednesday? We can visit it and then have a drink before the concert."

"Good idea. Sauerkraut this evening? It's filling but we did not have lunch today."

"On Thursday we go to Monschau and Kornelimünster."

"Lotte used to tell me about them but I was never there long enough to have much free time. Too busy on the printing press, packing explosives and being at Manfred's beck and call." Adam winced and closed his eyes.

"It's okay, my love. It was just reality but I am healing up now. You are helping me heal."

"My soul shall be healed," he whispered and they kissed each other for several minutes.

They sat in the restaurant near a window and when the sauerkraut arrived, they stared at the ten-inch-high pile of white cabbage with chops and sausages poking out of it. A big bowl of mustard was placed in the middle of the table with two large glasses of lager.

"We'll never eat all that!" When the waiter next approached, Doro asked him what happened to the leftover food.

"We have a system; many Vietnamese work here and they can take what they like. We also have a charity which comes to collect food for the homeless, out of date food and some leftovers."

"Well done. Congratulations."

He gave them a hot plate each and some serving spoons. "Shall I serve you?"

"No, thank you." They smiled. They served themselves with a chop and one each of the sausages, frankfurters and Bratwurst as well as a few boiled potatoes and a pile of sauerkraut. She had eaten some on the commune but this was made with peppercorns and spice. It was delicious. They did not want a desert and asked for coffee in their room.

"Oche is the old dialect name for Aachen and you usually see it with a picture of a hand with a crooked little finger, a traditional greeting between the folk of Aachen." She pointed to a plaque on the wall. They sat by the balcony looking at the winking lights outside. Her nerves began to bother her.

"Edward and Marianna, God look after you in heaven. So strange about that little girl today."

"She's a handful for her mother. You will always wonder what Marianna would be like and what kind of man Edward would have become. I'm sad for you, my love, you are trembling. Try the breathing again." He put his hand on her chest and felt her rapid heartbeat.

"I'll find some music." He flicked through the channels until he came across a classical music channel. He let it run softly.

"You don't have to go. We can change the day or leave it out."

"I am not giving in, not giving up."

"You never did. I loved you for that in all those years." She let her tears fall while Adam held her gently.

"The music is lovely. Look at the names on the screen." Adam wiped her eyes and kissed her wet cheeks.

"Give me courage, Adam. Slowly, gently love me." He had learned the importance of touch, gentle, not desperate.

"That was the best yet. This is our special honeymoon."

He was panting a little. "We shall have another one when we get married."

"It won't beat this one. Wow! Is there some wine on our cabinet?"

"Red or white?"

"Red please, my love." She grabbed him before he got up and hugged him. "Don't you dare die before me, my wonderful love."

He held her and they sat with eyes closed.

"Aachen, I am ready for you." Adam poured himself a cool white wine and a red one for Doro.

Their sleep was sweet. They could hear rain falling outside. Adam checked his iPad. "It's due to stop mid-morning."

"We could start in the market; it is nearly all covered. There is rarely anything to resemble such markets in England. However, some German style markets had begun to come to the Southbank, selling hot Glühwein and sausages."

They bought some irresistible decorations for his sister and brother and their children. They walked through the narrow streets to the various fountains. The metal statues depicting local characters had moving parts, heads to twist, legs and arms to bend. Children loved moving them even in the cold water. They were all delightful and much photographed and seen on postcards. A dancing girl statue was outside the Printen shop so they bought their gift tins. Near the spa was an arcade with modern shops and the cocktail bar. They chose the most outrageous titles and sat drinking their blue and orange drinks.

"Shall we do the Roman museum before lunch?" Doro suggested.

"Have you brought your choker?"

"Yes, and the red top."

"Look at that dress." She had not even noticed the fashion shops. There in the window was a model wearing a close-fitting blue dress in a silky material.

"Perfect for you. Let's go in."

"A wedding dress?"

"Why not? Great idea. You ask for your size." It took a while for all the winter layers to be removed. She pulled it on and stood looking at her image. Hating the wig, she loved the dress. She put the wig back on and opened the curtain. Adam twirled her around.

"Will you marry me?" The shop assistant smiled.

"Yes, my dearest, I will." He kissed her.

"What a proposal!" said the assistant. "Congratulations! Madam, you look wonderful," she spoke in English.

"You asked her in English. Aren't you German?"

"English speakers of German," Doro answered. She put back all her warm clothes and they walked out with a big, shiny bag.

"Thank you, Adam. It's a wonderful gift. I'd be happy to get married in it."

"Museum?" he was smiling. They had to put their bags and heavy coats in a locker. They had their education about the town and Charlemagne as they walked around. It was light and bright and well set out. The gift shop was tempting but they could not carry that much home.

"Let's load up the car and find lunch."

"Do you want a snack and a main meal this evening?"

"I'd like to take you to a Turkish restaurant, something different and a light soup supper."

"That suits me." As they loaded the boot, they feared they might need another travel bag, or they would have to leave some clothes behind. Adam drew out a map.

"We have to avoid certain streets; we'll have to walk back through the narrow centre to reach the Turkish restaurant. Do you know it?"

"I saw some in town, cheap and full of men smoking. They won't be like that now."

"I saw it on a leaflet in our hotel. Should be more up-market than your old ones."

The waiters wore traditional dress; musicians in Turkish outfits played their cultural instruments in one corner. Smiling waiters showed them to a table. Doro asked Adam to choose as she was not familiar with the food. The starter was humus and the mains were a lamb dish with vegetables and rice. It was delicious.

"Is the Town Hall near the car park?"

"Not really because of our forbidden streets."

I'm exhausted. Could we do the Town Hall and the cathedral tomorrow?"

"Back for a rest. Of course." Adam was exhausted as well.

His emotions had surprised him. He had never felt this kind of happiness. It had its own tension and he too needed a rest. He acknowledged that this was healing for him. He told God how grateful he was.

They both needed to sleep and agreed to do just that. On Wednesday they felt refreshed and ready for a return to Aachen. First, they found the statue of the Devil with his Sandbags and the old lady who fooled him. Adam took several shots. They had a tour around the Town Hall and saw photos of the destruction of the town during the war. They booked a tour of the cathedral. Adam saw the massive door and the Devil's Thumbs, the wolf with its soul ripped out and then the throne where subjects had to crawl underneath to show their respect for the seated Charlemagne, and finally the huge tomb of Charlemagne. The guide pointed them all out and retold the myth. He then showed them the unusually tall stained-glass windows. They were the tallest in Europe. They had been removed and kept in a safe place before the bombing in the war. It was a strange shape for a cathedral. After the main entrance were pillars forming a circle for the main seating area.

This was below a vast, very high dome. Above the seating was a heavy metal circle with candles, held by a single chain from the top of the dome, linked to chains to each segment of the circle. People just had to stand and look up. The guide pointed out that the chain was very thick and did not get narrower to the sight as it reached the dome. He said that the original chain had been strong enough for the corona but from below, the top of the chain looked like cotton thread.

To reassure those walking underneath the chain was thickened by a decorative thick chain in light material.

"We can sit here or in the gallery. The choir is up on one side of the gallery. You can look up or look down."

"It would be good to see the choir but the acoustics under the dome are no doubt fantastic."

"We'll arrive early and see. I fancy Bratwurst and Kartoffelpuree," he spoke. "There's an old German restaurant opposite the Town Hall."

They walked back and found the tall, narrow restaurant. The decoration inside was peasant style with heavy wood carvings.

"I won't get into my blue dress after all this heavy food. I'll have to go running." Adam patted her tummy.

"Where would you like to get married?"

"I have nowhere definite in mind, but I would like a church wedding. God seems to be blessing us."

"I'm so pleased you said that. I am feeling grateful to God. I've got some prayers and reading from Fr Tony."

"I wonder if they do weddings at the Abbey?"

"We'll ask, sound them out or we could look for a smaller, local Anglican church.

"I've had a thought about our second honeymoon. Russell owns properties in Greece. He lives in a lovely house with a pool and next door is a block of luxury holiday apartments. We could go there, spend time with him and his family as well as have time to ourselves."

"That sounds like a very attractive idea! I look forward to meeting him. Would your family come to our wedding?" Doro wondered.

"Oh, yes, they would, all of them!" Adam assured her, referring to his large family,

They lingered over their meal, drank beer to match the menu and then lingered over coffee. Slowly they returned to the cathedral as the audience was beginning to gather. The gallery was very popular but they managed to find two seats together.

"I love Poulenc. The Gloria is my favourite. Interesting man, probably gay."

"One of my agents was gay, but like Lotte, he did not seek out young men, or girls. I hope he has found a partner now he has retired."

Doro stopped herself asking. There should be no contact with agents but now that the RAF had disbanded, the Department had allowed Lotte to have contact with Rainer and for them to contact Diane.

As the crowd gathered, it was noticeable that people did not wear formal clothes for such a concert. They wore their normal winter clothes. The choir arrived in ordinary clothes too, all black or grey. The organist and orchestra wore dark suits.

During the Gloria, Adam and Doro were in a kind of ecstasy. The lighting, the candles, the silence, the music reached their inmost being.

In the interval she went down the gallery steps to look over at the seats below. She went rigid, staring at a man getting up from his seat, talking to another man. She was trembling.

"It can't be! It can't be!" she called Adam.

"Look down there, second row on the right." Adam went white.

"A Marxist revolutionary in a church?" Doro watched them both as they stretched their legs but did not leave the row of chairs. She stared at the second man. Both were grey haired; one was stooping at the shoulders. They were relaxed and smiling together.

"My God, it's Gerd. Whatever is he doing here? He knows me and will recognise me!"

"The other man, I'm sure it is Jürgen, Manfred's number two."

They were both shaken.

"They won't recognise you in your wig. Jürgen never met me. Gerd, of course, communicated regularly. He must not see me, so at the end we will wait for them to leave and you can follow them and let me now when it is safe for me to come down and leave by another door."

"Oh, Adam, what a strange coincidence. Marianna was strange but this is amazing. When you talked of a gay agent, I thought of Gerd. I guessed he was gay 30 years ago."

"We'll have to report it, unless the watchers have seen them together already. Jürgen lives not far from here on the street that leads to the university. In the second half they held hands and tried not to shake. The beauty of the music brought them some calm. After the applause they went down again to the bottom of the gallery and watched the two men leave by a door.

"Where's that door go?"

"To the square near the little bird fountain."

"Right, go down and see if you can discover where they go and we will find another exit. Is there a back door?"

She was shaking as she went up to the top of the gallery and then down the steps to the ground floor. They seemed to linger by a bar but did not go in. It seemed to take ages. Adam was being invited to go down by the cathedral staff, wanting to clear up. He stood at the bottom looking at the various doors but could not see Doro. He began to shake too. Staying still was his best option. Doro watched the two old men who seemed to be turning back to the Cathedral. She re-entered and looked at their empty seats. Perhaps they had left

136

an umbrella. Adam saw her but she waved him away. He moved back to the literature stand and hoped the pillar would hide him. Doro saw the men re-enter and walk towards Adam. She froze and tried to make him go back to the seating area. He was not quite sure what she meant when suddenly a voice boomed out.

"Oh, my God!" and Gerd stood in front of him. Doro stood away watching. Gerd turned to Jürgen and spoke to him. Jürgen left the church. Doro watched him hurry away. She then stood behind another pillar and tried to hear the conversation.

"Rainer, whatever are you doing here?"

"Gerd, whatever are you doing here? I can't tell you but it is nothing to do with our work. I'm on holiday. I've retired. I have no agents."

"I've retired too. I've signed all the right papers but before I left for the UK, I had some conversations with Jürgen. It would be good to tell you. Can we talk?"

"Can you give me a few minutes? Can you wait right here?"

Adam went to the door and went out. Doro followed him out from the other side. "Dearest, I need to speak to Gerd. Can you take a taxi back to the hotel? Jürgen has gone home. Have your money and a key?"

"Yes. I will, I'm so shaky. I hope it all goes well." She walked towards the taxi rank by the market and found one to take her back. She managed to remove her wig as she sat at the back.

Adam and Gerd were being ushered out so the doors could be closed.

"I came back for some brochures for the next concerts and there you were with your thick hair, no longer black but totally recognisable."

Outside the Devil's thumbs, Gerd pointed to a bar where they could sit and talk. It was an amazing conversation.

"I'm here with permission, but I cannot explain why. It's to do with breakdowns and healing from the past."

"I signed everything but after all that time I decided I could come back to see Jürgen." Gerd had never betrayed other agents nor had he told him that he had been undercover, working for London. They both shared their misgivings as the bombs continued, as Manfred became mentally ill. They both suffered emotionally when they knew what Manfred had done to Diane. They remained a few more years after Diane had left and worked with Lotte. They then belonged to the new Cologne groups. During that time, Gerd and Jürgen

137

realised that they loved each other. Gerd had commitments in the UK but Jürgen could never go there. As the RAF officially renounced violence and Jürgen had moved to another flat, Gerd decided he could travel to see him on his own passport.

"You've been to his new flat?"

"Yes."

"Have any of the others been there. Has he told you?"

"Do I have to tell you that?" Gerd clearly did not know that he was being watched. "Has he seen any of the released RAF members?"

Gerd wanted to explain first what had happened to Jürgen.

He had become disheartened by all the ideas of revolution. He saw that it would never work. Innocent people would go on being killed. He became very depressed and felt that he had wasted his life. He had bombed and assassinated. He was tempted to take his own life. Jürgen had a breakdown but could not tell doctors why because he would have been arrested as a criminal. He got tablets and kept himself in isolation. Gerd had enabled the first Cologne group to be blown but he had supported Bruno so he still had important intelligence to give London.

Gerd made secret methods to keep in touch with Jürgen. Rather like Ralph had said, their observation showed old group members, lonely and ill keeping in touch with each other. Gerd told him his real name and address in England and came to see him often. Christmas was one of their times together. When Jürgen was in hospital, Gerd came to be with him. In desperation, the sick man walked into a Catholic church and poured out his heart to God. He was no longer a Marxist revolutionary; he went back to his mother's religion and attended Mass every Sunday and on several other days. He went to confession but did not tell the priest he had been a terrorist. He mentioned his Nazi father, his homosexuality, anything but killing and bombing. The prayers made him feel better but he wrestled with his conscience.

He talked through with Gerd: "If I confess, I will die in prison but that won't bring justice to the dead. Can I live with myself and have a relationship with you if I don't?"

He set himself to study German history and began to write a memoir. He had advanced cancer and did not have long to live. The cathedral concerts were his greatest joy.

"He has never met you, has he? He used to ask me what became of Diane." Adam was not going to tell him.

"What about the released RAF members? Some died; it was announced in the Press, but some are alive and have been meeting up with others."

"I think none of them are a danger. They are old and broken after a life in prison."

"Are you sure the London office doesn't know of your meetings with Jürgen?"

"How could they, unless I am being watched." Gerd had broken the law by meeting him without authorisation. Adam would be doing the same if he told Gerd that Jürgen was under surveillance. Ralph would already know that Gerd was visiting him. He did not name him to Adam but had mentioned 'lonely, old men meeting up'. However, he could not be sure that there was not another visitor of significance.

Adam had another try.

"Do you know if he sees Bauman or any of the RAF women let out a few years ago?"

"Not Bauman, but yes, some have found him but only Bruno visits him. I make sure I am not around when he comes. He is very frail now. Amazingly they have not suspected me or Lotte of being double agents."

"Gerd, I am not sure what to do about this coincidence. Would you like me to say anything to London?"

"Rainer, you've given them your life. Don't harm yourself. You could tell the new boss of our encounter and let them know that Jürgen is dying of cancer, is writing his memoirs and is of no danger to anyone. He is a catholic, not a Marxist now. I intend to look after him for the rest of his life and I will stay here with him when the end comes."

"Thank you, Gerd. You served us well for many years. It's a job of self-sacrifice and self-destruction! I can say that I am turning to God and finding happiness in my old age."

"A woman?" Adam nodded.

"All the very best, Rainer." They shook hands. Adam walked rapidly to his car and drove back to the hotel. Two or three hours had passed so he was sure that Doro would be anxious.

He found her sound asleep with the music program on the television playing. She looked calm and peaceful as he sat staring at her. He turned off

139

the music, crept around to clean his teeth and slipped in beside her, trying not to wake her. He could not sleep but lay there with the events of the day spinning around in his head.

What were the odds of him being recognised by the one agent who knew him? What were the odds of finding in a cathedral Mass a Marxist revolutionary who had turned to Christianity? What a strange life. He eventually slept knowing that the trip the next day would bring them pleasure and ease their emotional pain.

Doro awoke as the light came streaming in and was aware of the sleeping Adam on the far side of the bed. She did not want to wake him, but wondered how his talk with Gerd had gone. That evening she had stopped trembling and sat waiting for him, sipping some wine and listening to music. She could not focus on any TV programs. She fell asleep and slept well.

She watched her sleeping lover. She washed and dressed and rang down for breakfast in their room.

The knock on the door woke Adam.

"Thank you." She took the tray and put it on the table. She sat gently on the bed as Adam stirred. She bent over and kissed his eyes.

"Are you OK?" He managed a smile and reached out to her.

"Breakfast is here, no hurry." He sat up and saw how calm she was. She was not at all agitated and demanding to know what had happened.

"That was a shock," she said. "I hope there are no more to come." She passed him a cup of coffee.

"And how are you, my love?"

"Fine. I got through the hours of not knowing. I didn't feel Gerd was a threat to you as you had been his controller for so many years. I recalled what Ralph had said about old, lonely agents befriending each other. That's what they looked like."

"It's funny, they had come back to get brochures for the next concerts and came to the very place I was hiding!"

"Like it was meant to be!"

Adam showered and got dressed and had breakfast, telling Doro the details of their conversation and that Gerd had given him permission to tell Ralph. He assured her that he had not mentioned her name.

"It was a wonderful concert," he said. "We are going to Monschau which comes from the French Mont Joie. Joy for us today."

Chapter 18

Joy, how they needed joy. Doro knew that Jürgen had made and planted bombs and was an assassin and had killed several people.

She wanted to think of other things today. There was in Monschau a shop which sold Christmas things the whole year round. They probably had enough decorations already. They parked in a large car park by the river. It was in front of an outlet like a covered market but expensive glassware and ceramics were sold there, along with arts and crafts of all sorts and food of many kinds. From there they walked by the fast-flowing stream which babbled away over the rocks in the valley below. They crossed a bridge and walked into the centre of the village.

The approach roads had given views of the roof tops below and the ruined castle on a hill above. Now they walked on cobbled streets lined with ancient houses. One feature was the mustard shop where jars of all flavours of mustards were sold in many different sizes.

Further down the road was the factory with old mustard mills. Adam favoured the herby mustard while Doro preferred the honey-mustard mix. The mini pots with cork tops made lovely gifts.

Every corner of the village was charming, ancient, decorated doors, windows with check curtains and bright tie-backs. Every shop was an artistic spectacle. Near the Christmas shop was the famous Kafe Kaulard where every window and counter had displays of homemade cakes. Upstairs was a tea-room and restaurant with dramatic stained-glass windows.

"It is Mount Joy, like a little paradise," Doro said as they stood on the narrow bridge above the raging torrent beneath them.

"I am so glad Lotte told us about this place. What shall we take her?"

"Mustard, of course."

One beamed restaurant had a room which was overhanging the river. They decided to have a small lunch there to watch the water rushing over the rocks while they ate. She wanted to buy a gift for Adam but had little idea of what to get him. He wore no jewellery and she wondered if he would like a ring or a chain.

"Would you wear a ring?" she asked him.

"Yes, I think I would."

"How about a neck chain?"

"Probably not. Never tried."

"You don't wear a watch now; I'm looking for inspiration. You've given me lovely gifts and I want to find a gift for you."

He smiled and reached for her hand across the table. "A dog," he spoke.

"You'd like me to get you a dog? Before or after Greece?"

"That's a good point. We'll need to find someone as dog carer for our travels."

"I am very happy to get you a dog. It needs some planning. I would hate to leave him in a kennel, I'd prefer someone he knows and is happy with. What kind of dog would you like?"

"Spaniel size, not very big."

"I'll check out some breeds while we think about carers and travel."

"We can ask Rosamund and Steven. They might be interested."

"You'll be busy setting up your clinic soon."

"When we return the wig, I have an appointment with Ralph and the London clinic. I can't stop thinking about Gerd. Ralph will be in a difficult position. He is understanding about the needs of elderly agents but he will have direct access to a wanted criminal. What is he waiting for? Perhaps he is expecting other terrorists to turn up."

"How will Ralph react to your meeting with Gerd?"

"I dread to think."

"Let's think of other things in Monschau. It's such a beautiful place." They finished their lunch and walked by the river.

"We'll get a dog passport and bring him here for a holiday." Doro laughed. "One more look around the glass and ceramics?"

"Of course, and then we will go to Kornelimünster."

Near the glass displays were woodwork cribs and silhouettes of scenes with lights behind. They were attractive and unusual.

"We'll have to come back; we can't take anything else in our luggage. Such gorgeous designs."

Adam looked earnestly at her.

"I can't believe that I am going to marry you. You have agreed to marry me. We have begun a healing process that both of us thought was impossible. The Devil's Sandbags did not destroy Aachen and did not destroy us."

"We'll work at mending our lives, Adam. Let's talk to Fr Tony and ask about a wedding."

"They are Benedictines in Chilworth and in Kornelimünster there's a Benedictine Abbey too."

They left the half-timbered houses of the mediaeval centre of Monschau and drove through the Eifel towards Aachen. They turned off to another main square, also surrounded by half-timbered houses and ancient buildings with a beautiful, old architectural style. The grey walls of the Abbey towered over them after they had crossed the bridge over the Inde. In the tall, echoey Abbey, they walked around and then sat for a while to benefit from the silence. They felt at ease with each other in deep contemplation.

Outside in the cold, Adam started speaking about Gerd.

"I feel for him. He escaped detection, got the Cologne group arrested and was a faithful agent. Strange that he found love with a terrorist assassin and murderer. I shall ask if I can keep in touch with him so he is not all alone when Jürgen dies."

"You are showing compassion, Adam, just as you have for men in difficulties. I would be happy to have Gerd as a guest. I presume he has a home in London?"

"In normal circumstances I would go and see Jürgen now and talk with him, but nothing is normal. I dare not. The watchers are there and I signed to say I would not even go down that street."

"Well, you'll feel better if you do it through the right channels."

"Agents have such a hard time, don't they?"

"Lotte has done so well. You helped her keep Helga and they seem to have adjusted to normal life."

"Thank God! How would you like to spend the last day tomorrow?"

"I'm a bit nervous of the town centre in case Gerd is there. Somewhere with a view."

"We'll go back for supper and investigate the brochures."

In the hotel lounge the fire was burning with a sweet wood smell. Doro claimed an armchair at the fireside. Adam brought over the Glühwein.

"Are you OK?" he asked again.

"I suppose I'm quite disturbed after seeing Jürgen but it was rather comical after all our efforts to avoid him, Gerd went to the very place where you were hiding."

He passed the brochures down to her and drew up a rustic chair to join in the perusal. They saw the Eifel brochures with several more picturesque villages in the mountains. Another brochure showed an area called Hohe Venn on the Belgium border.

"We could use our own passports," Adam suggested.

This is what they decided on in the end, open air, cold air but wide-open spaces. After their hearty German soup, they went to their room for their final night.

"I am glad we came. It has helped me but also reminded me of the hellish times in the commune. Thank you for bringing me."

"We can comfort each other." The troubled lovers awoke to cold sunshine. The skies over the Hohe Venn were turquoise with white streaks of cloud. The tufts of grass undulated for miles around them. Several hardy people were out walking on the Venn. It was calming, refreshing and health giving.

"Where does Russell live?" They sat on one of the benches near the damp ditches.

"On a small island called Aegina. It's very beautiful without the commerce and traffic of the mainland. He is very pleased that we are getting married and so proud to have us for or honeymoon."

Adam told her about his family. Russell and Lesley were nearing 70 and their three children had been educated in England. All three had married and decided to stay on the island. When their own children came along, they all decided to stay. Sometimes they had to travel to the mainland for their work. Russell had a large coastal property and was still running the holiday flats he owned. All his children had managed to buy houses less than an hour away. He ran through their names and ages; Raymond and Gloria have Sara, 12, and Craig, 10; then Simon and Katy have Christopher, eight, and Paula and William have Vicky, six, and Vernon, four."

"Five grandchildren."

"More later; Paula wants a larger family. The grandchildren have all been to school in Greece and speak better Greek than their grandparents."

"So, we will be in a luxury holiday flat near the coast and near Russell."

"That's the plan. They will respect that this is our honeymoon and will give us time to ourselves. I think we should take two weeks so we can see all four families and still have some days to ourselves."

"Idyllic!"

"When we get back, we shall have churches, Intelligence Services, clinics and kennels to see."

"And Dr Ford Lloyd! I made it! I went to Aachen and have put the negative past behind me. I faced it, acknowledged it and overcame it. Thank you for thinking of it!"

"Have a rest for a few days when we get back. I can go to London to return your disguise when I talk to Ralph. You might like some time away from me."

"I will need to assimilate and meditate. I'll think of how we sat in Kornelimünster Abbey and heard the Poulenc in the cathedral. Seeing Gerd rather spoilt it for us."

"But the memory will linger and still bring joy."

Chapter 19

Dorothea sat alone in her quiet house. She realised that they had not discussed Christmas at all, other than getting a few gifts for family and friends. She invited Renate for lunch and told her about their wedding plans. Renate was very happy to see her friend find some happiness after her tragic losses.

"Of course, I'll come with you to buy some shoes." She looked at the stunning blue dress and the choker. Silver sandals were needed. They would hunt for them after Christmas.

Doro sat in Chilworth Abbey while Adam went to London. She had turned off her phone to be silent in the lovely church. She hoped Fr Tony could see them before Christmas. When she returned home, she was very surprised to see Adam's car outside. Why ever was he back so soon from London?

"Dorothea, I have some amazing news." They went in and sat in the lounge.

"After my talk with Gerd, he made the decision to tell Jürgen that he was a double agent, reporting on the RAF to London and thus to the German anti-terrorist police."

"I am so amazed. Why did he do that?"

"He could no longer live with a lie and betrayal as he faced Jürgen's death in the coming months. He had seen him reject his terrorist past, change his views and become a Christian."

"I see, putting things right before death."

"That's not all. Jürgen had been totally shocked. He had never guessed, but he was happy that his lover had not sympathised with terrorism and had betrayed the group to prevent more violence.

The next day he asked Gerd to accompany him to the police station. He told Gerd not to come in. He said he would be going in alone and would not come out. He said he deserved to pay the price for his evil actions. Now he was a Christian he could not lie any more. He had to give himself up."

Doro tried to take it in. What a turn around. What bravery by a killer?

"If Gerd had gone in, he would have been arrested as a suspect terrorist. He would eventually have been released after they had contacted the embassy but he would lose time for visiting his partner in prison.

"Jürgen had taken his fake ID and RAF membership documents, his own writings and plans of the US airbase attacks and his diary and memoir. At first, he had not been believed. He was seen as a stooped, old crackpot. One Officer on duty had more knowledge of the RAF than the others and took him seriously. He was placed in a cell while Superiors and the Intelligence Services were contacted.

"Gerd has left me some contact details and asked if he could meet me in London when he returns after Jürgen's death. He intends to stay in Germany until then, living in the flat."

"That was brave of Jürgen and you have your wish with Gerd. I wonder how long it will be before he dies?"

"I have a deep sense that this is the right thing to do. Hard on Gerd, but I reckon he agrees with the decision. I have not been to the clinic nor spoken with Ralph. I will have to make another appointment. Do you want to come with me and catch up with Lotte and Helga?"

"I'd love to. Did the wig find its shelf?"

"Yes, I just had to see you when I was given the news." She hugged and kissed him. "Good come out of bad." She was thinking aloud.

Doro received cards of congratulations from Rosamund and Steven. Adam had phone calls with endless questions he could not answer.

"Possibly in Chilworth Abbey, we haven't asked yet."

"An Abbey? You never cease to amaze me. Russell has invited us all to Greece for the Reception," Rosamund explained.

"That's generous of him but not terribly practical. We're having a honeymoon on his island."

"Adam, you have no idea how happy we are for you!" Adam was quite surprised at the joy in his family. He realised how much he had cut himself off from family love and normal life. He knew that this was his opportunity to get back into family life. He did not cease to be amazed that Dorothea had agreed to take him on.

He was pleased she would be with him when he discussed the clinic project with Ralph. Ralph agreed that there was room for more counselling services for agents. He had been in the field himself and was aware of the dangers and stresses.

"What do you see as your role?"

"Manager. I shall not be counselling. I need to recruit some experts like Dr Ford Lloyd. I shall ask her soon if she can introduce me to some colleagues and even help me interview them. I will give priority to agents but I shall also have sessions for local men who would not dream of going to a counsellor through the normal routes. I will liaise with the barbers' organisation. He had to explain how he had been inspired by the barber.

"Why don't you put your feet up, why take on such responsibility?"

"I won't even dignify that with an answer." Adam smiled at Ralph.

Doro ventured a comment, "We have both been helped by the clinic, especially by Dr Ford. We are in a position to start a project to help others. We have the room, the time and the motivation."

"We?"

"We're getting married. Forgot to mention it," Adam announced. Ralph opened his eyes wide.

"Rainer and Diane getting married. You would have needed our permission a few years ago."

"No, we use our real names and when Gerd returns, we shall use them with him. Jürgen gave himself up but he did not betray any of the others. He lived alone and some of the old members visited him but there was no political activity."

"We have knowledge of the other old members. We may give them up to the Germans if it brings us any advantage."

Adam was sad to see that justice played little part in the Department's decisions and he felt glad to be out of it.

"Ralph, Gerd sent his message to you. He told Jürgen that he had spied on him but now that he had found religion, he felt safe to tell him the truth and promise to see him through his illness and inevitable death. We owe him. He gave his whole life in sacrificial service. I want to befriend him when Jürgen dies."

"I see no reason why you cannot do that, Rainer. Go with my blessing. If London clinic is happy with your project, almost having a new branch in Surrey, then I will agree to the funding of any current agent. We have infiltrators in the neo-Nazi groups right now, often in the old East."

Doro kept quiet. She hated being in the office with Ralph and was longing to leave and go to the clinic. Adam sensed her discomfort. He had achieved what he wanted to, so affected an exit as soon as he could. Ralph saw them out.

"Congratulations, by the way. You deserve happiness together." They were both surprised by the human touch in Ralph and shook hands with him. Adam put his arm around Doro's shoulders as they walked to the clinic; the private clinic which doubled as an emergency counselling service for the victims of the secret services.

"Are you coping, love?"

"Just. I'm glad to be out."

They were given coffee with the new director of the Psychiatric Services, Dr Winston Bowden.

"I am pleased to meet you both. Dr Chamberlain, I have heard a lot about you. I am sorry that Dr Ford Lloyd is retiring. She will be greatly missed."

"Thanks so much for seeing us. Here are some photos of my property. I would use the lounge area as the consultation room. There's a toilet on the ground floor and a spare bedroom upstairs that counsellors could use for an overnight stay. We need advice on finding a team of counsellors. It would be on a sessional basis, mainly for agents but also for local men needing help. The MI6 funding would also cover some of the fees for these clients."

"Very philanthropic of you. Any ideas for names? How would you advertise?"

"Secret services would refer clients to us in conjunction with your clinic. We would advertise in local barber shops and GP surgeries. Have you heard of the training for barbers to become listeners and to refer men on if they think they are in distress?" He had not. This was not his world. Adam was pleased by his reception and Doro liked the new Director as well.

"I have some ideas but I haven't talked them over with Adam yet."

"Go ahead, love."

"The Sandbags Care Centre, with the logo of a statue in Aachen, depicting a myth about the town and cathedral being saved from the Devil's destruction."

"Well done. I'd love that!"

"For the barbers?" Winston was fascinated.

"Yes, the barber being spoken to could have some cards with 'Tell your barber, a listening service for men'. If the customers talk to the barber, they can then receive a leaflet about Sandbags. No pressure. Desperate men will end up coming."

"You have a good grasp of the issues," Winston said.

"You are brilliant!" Adam said. Dr Winston was pleased to cooperate with Adam and would send him some details of possible team members and would help with interviews.

"Great result," Adam said as they sat in an Indian restaurant waiting for Lotte.

"I didn't think we would be talking about advertising so soon. I have a file at home where I have been looking up how to make a logo from the bronzes."

He held her to him. "I am so grateful to you."

"Dear Adam, do you realise we haven't even mentioned Christmas and it is a few days away?"

"We'll have a quiet one and look at dogs." Lotte came in and greeted them affectionately.

"Chicken biryani," just what I need."

"Good to see you. Is Helga okay?"

"Fine, thanks. When's the big day?"

"Hopefully next spring. We haven't even asked the church yet."

They relaxed over the curry meal and Adam told Lotte the story of Gerd and Jürgen. She was very surprised.

"Jürgen was ruthless with Manfred. I find the conversion hard to believe."

"It's real." Adam explained how they had met him in the Cathedral at a Poulenc Mass. "It's a kind of justice, I suppose, but not for the dead families. Gerd was great. I'll be happy to see him again."

Christmas became top of the agenda. Doro wanted to go to the Abbey services but hoped they could speak to Fr Tony. Adam contacted him and was pleased that he did have time to talk.

He asked if he could bring Dorothea.

The three of them sat quietly in a small room. "I am very pleased to see you both."

"I was due to see you on my own, but our situation has developed somewhat."

"Were the readings and prayers meaningful to you, Adam?"

"Yes, they were, thank you. It's hard to know where to start. Dorothea and I have had to work hard on facing our pasts, on healing, on forgiving and on considering our future. Dorothea has suffered a great deal; in fact, she has lost everyone in her life in a tragic way so she wants to ask how that matches with a God of love. The universal mystery of suffering. I need to learn how to love, how to relate in a normal way to my family. I have spent my life in a very different environment."

"You are still wanting to experience your soul being healed?"

"It's begun, Father. We have both experienced some healing and we are working hard on sorting out our lives."

"Dorothea, do you want to add anything?"

"Churches and music have come to mean a great deal to us, a real factor in the healing process. I lost my parents in a car accident when I was 17. I had some traumas in my work and then I had a happy marriage but my husband died of cancer. I had lost our second baby with a heart defect, then my son killed himself when he was diagnosed with a melanoma not long after seeing his father suffer for some years before he died. He was afraid and could not face such suffering. Father Tony, I'm sure I cannot ask for answers but I am left with a sense of fear that I will lose Adam, a fear that more terrible things will happen to me. I need help to deal with fear."

"Dorothea, I am sorry for your suffering. Thank you for your honesty. It would be a privilege to accompany you on your spiritual journey. As Adam said, the universal mystery of suffering. Are you in a relationship together?"

"I am so sorry. I am not thinking straight. We are planning to get married in the New Year. We did want to ask you if we could get married here."

"Well, congratulations! We could talk about your wedding in the New Year when the Abbot is not so busy. Is that alright with you?"

They both nodded.

"We are thinking of springtime because my brother has invited us to Greece for our honeymoon. He has a house there."

"As you lead up to that time, do consider coming regularly to some services. Being in the atmosphere of worship brings hope, healing and peace. I think you would both benefit from finding a personal way of meditation, or contemplation or simply prayer."

"We are outside our usual experience. It's a new way of thinking for us," Dorothea spoke softly.

"I think you have both been through some deep suffering. Don't worry about lack of theology or ritual. Jesus is everywhere. Just sit with a lighted candle. He will be there with you. Listen to music with an open heart. He is with you. Walk in nature. He made it all. He is with you." There was a prolonged silence but no embarrassment, no uncomfortable feelings.

"Did you want to say anything else?"

"Just, thank you." She smiled.

"May I pray over you?"

"Please," Adam replied. Fr Tony stood up and put a hand on their heads. It was not a set, read prayer, he just poured out his prayer for blessing, peace and joy. They both got up with damp eyes.

"Can we talk after Christmas? We'd like to tell you our plans for supporting people with problems."

"I look forward to that. By then, I will have talked to the Abbot about your wedding."

Feeling moved yet happy, they drove to Doro's home. "We cannot talk about the agents, can we?"

"No, he doesn't need to know. We can find some terminology which does not betray our trust."

"I'm sure he will be happy with the barbers."

"Christmas dinner in a local pub? I've never done big family Christmases."

"My dearest, I'd rather cook for us, a simple Christmas meal and listen to music and watch TV and rest and relax."

"I would be happy with that, my love."

"When do we look at dogs?"

"Just research for now. Get one after our honeymoon and investigate carers for when we might travel."

Chapter 20

Christmas was a real time of rest for Adam and Dorothea. They attended the services at the Abbey and the carol service at the cathedral.

They went on many local walks to help them relax from all the tensions of the last few weeks. Lotte and Helga invited them to a New Year celebration in London during the first few days of January. They had been invited to see the New Year by Steven in Brighton. His three children and their families were coming for the party but lived near enough to return home.

The Christmas vigil took place just before midnight. There was a very full church with many cars in both car parks. They both loved the dramatic effects of a dark church becoming a magic land of light as candles were lit on stands all down the aisle and around the altar.

The harmonious chanting of the monks, out of sight in the choir, added a deep spiritual joy. It was well after one o'clock when they waited their turn to drive out down the steep, narrow drive to the road.

Adam stayed the night with Doro and in spite of the late hour, they made love in an atmosphere of peace. Doro was trusting her lover more as the weeks passed. She ran her fingers through his thick hair.

"To think that your hair has opened a door for a future project!" She played with his hair for some minutes.

"Leave some for me." They laughed and were more playful together. "Adam Chamberlain, I trust you and I love you with all my heart."

"Dorothea Harlow, shall we get some rings? I love you so very much."

"Rings? Matching wedding rings?"

"Why not?" She stayed the night with him on Boxing Day so they could walk into Godalming to visit a jeweller.

"I'm so inexperienced, aren't I, but your lovemaking teaches me so much and brings me such joy."

"I am glad you were not a James Bond agent!"

It was late morning by the time they reached the jewellers. Doro had struggled to remove her wedding ring which she had never taken off after Richard had died. They had their fingers measured and were shown a catalogue of possible matching wedding rings. They chose wide, silver rings with a word engraved on the outside, 'Truly blessed' and inside, the German equivalent, 'Gesegnet' as 'wirklich' proved too long. Trays of engagement rings were put on the counter.

"We have engagement rings made to fit with the wedding ring. May I show you?" Silver rings had stones which slotted and clipped onto the rim of the wedding ring.

"I love them." Doro looked at the variety of stones.

"Sapphire to match your dress?" Adam picked it out. It was so pretty, so sparkling, she could hardly believe it was happening. It was too big and spun around her finger.

"Madam, we can make it the right size and you can collect it with your wedding rings in 10–14 days' time."

"I wish you well to wear it," said the jeweller.

"My mother used to say that when my brother and sister got engaged?"

"Is she Jewish?"

"Yes, but she died many years ago."

"So am I, at least half-Jewish."

"Pity I can't wear it for New Year," Doro said.

"You can. I can change the size today and you can collect it tomorrow. The engraving takes longer."

They thanked him and went to buy some food and gifts for Steven's party. Doro rubbed cream into her fingers to prepare them for the new rings.

Brighton has its own beauties in the winter. The sky alone was like an artist's palate with streaks of different coloured clouds, some wintry sunshine but some brilliant sunsets.

Ellie had prepared them a bedroom with a double bed. They were amused but pleased. They unpacked and Doro looked at the walls and windows.

"Adam, love, look at the decor. We must work on your second bedroom and choose a lovely, attractive decor for when the patients or the doctors need to stay overnight. Adam could appreciate the light pastel shades, the blind which matched the wall paper and the single painting of sailing boats on a blue sea.

154

"Mine is plain but something restful like this would be ideal."

Steven and Adam chatted in the bay window while Doro helped Ellie prepare the food and the glasses and crockery.

"You have four grandchildren? How old?"

"From 15 to 2. Melanie is 15, Conor's daughter, then Michaela has Courtney who is three and Ashleigh has Dora, four, and Mai, two."

"How lovely."

"Wait till you see Russell's tribe. He has five."

"I've met Shirley."

"She's so good with her cousins."

"I hope to share them too. I have no one."

"Yes, I am sorry what you have been through. You're very welcome to share mine!" Conor, Chantal and their teenage daughter arrived first. Melanie was a pretty girl but dressed like a punk or a Goth; strange black top, torn black jeans. Her hair was coloured in three different colours. One side of her head was shaved and the other side was long so blue streaks covered her forehead and one ear. They greeted Uncle Adam and his fiancée. Chantal looked at her ring.

"So pleased to meet you. Gorgeous ring. Sort out my uncle please." Chantal smiled and gave her a kiss.

"Why does he need sorting out?"

"He needs a life. He's been like a hermit in the Foreign Office and needs some laughter and relaxation and pleasure."

"I'll work on it." She laughed and ruffled Adam's hair. A people carrier drove up and seven people emerged.

"Ah, here are my daughters, Michaela and Ashleigh." Two lovely young ladies gathered up their children and led them up the steps. The mothers were both blond with long hair and could have been taken for twins. Michaela wore and elegant beige trouser suit with a red blouse and Ashleigh wore a blue dress. Carl and Dave, their respective husbands wore casual jackets and carried bags and boxes up the steps.

"Where's your lovely fiancée, uncle?" called Michaela. Adam led Doro to the front door to meet them all. She had worn her silk outfit with the choker.

"Oh, Dorothea, how did he manage to catch someone as lovely as you?" She hugged Doro and kissed her cheeks. Ashleigh was holding her two-year-old.

155

"Pleased to meet you. This is Mia, Dora's gone in somewhere. Congratulations on capturing Uncle Adam and making him happy!"

Doro was stunned at the enthusiastic greetings. She went up to the lounge and saw Melanie with a small girl. She was wearing a pink jumpsuit and had a head of long blond curls. She was pulling at Melanie's jeans, putting her little fingers in the holes.

"Leave it," Melanie said.

"You've got blue hair," said Dora and went to touch it. Melanie pulled away and Dora gave up. She turned around and saw Dorothea sitting on an armchair. She came over to her and put her hands on Doro's knees and looked up at her. She had dark brown eyes instead of the blue that Doro was expecting. She smiled at Doro and stood there.

"What's your name?" Doro asked, holding her hands. "I'm Dora and I'm four." Doro's heart began to melt.

"I'm Dorothea. Do you want to call me Thea? Most people say Doro, rather like your name."

"Hello, Thea." She remained standing at her knees.

"I like your pink outfit, it suits you," Thea said and Dora shook her curls and smiled.

"Aren't you like a little angel?"

"Yes, I am." She shook her curls again. "Does your mummy brush those curls?"

"She hurts. Daddy brushes better but I can brush myself." Dorothea felt emotions she had not felt since Marianna was born.

"Do you want to sit with me?"

"I'll climb up." And she did.

"You're all shiny." Dora rubbed her silk trousers and touched her red silk blouse. Thea stared down at her, longing to touch her hair.

"Why are you here in our party?" asked the precocious four-year-old, realising she was a stranger.

"I am with your uncle Adam and we are getting married and I want you to be a bridesmaid, or my flower girl." It was out before she had thought it through. She planned to ask Michaela if Courtney and Dora could be flower girls. Adam came over and tousled the blond curls.

"You're sitting on my best girl." He smiled and looked at Thea.

156

"She's Thea," said Dora stretching up her arms to be picked up. The charming little girl put her arms around Adam's neck and kissed him on the cheek. Thea watched Adam handle the little girl so gently and lovingly.

"You've grown, Dora, how tall are you?"

"Don't know. Mummy measures me." He put her down and she climbed back onto Thea's lap. Adam took a photo of them.

"You look so good together."

"I'd like her as my flower girl with Courtney."

"What a lovely idea. We'll have to buy you and Courtney a special dress."

"I haven't met Courtney yet." Dora jumped down.

"I'll get her." She ran out of the room. Adam sat on the arm of the chair and could see she was deeply moved.

"She's absolutely beautiful and such a friendly little girl." Thea nodded. "I don't suppose you know Joan Baez songs?"

"The one in *Germany in Autumn*, the protest song? Lovely voice."

"She wrote a song called *Marie Flore* which I always loved. Joan was singing for a village in the south of France and was meeting dignitaries when a small girl came up to her, looked up at her and smiled. She was the daughter of one of them. All through the concert, the child kept near Joan and when she took her bow, the girl held her hand. Joan was filled with love for the girl who seemed to love her too. It was a magic moment for Joan, and she wrote the song *Marie Flore* for this child. That's how I feel. It was magic when she came and touched my knees and climbed on my lap." He leant down and kissed her.

Suddenly Dora rushed in holding Courtney.

"Here's Courtney." The girl smiled and said, "Hello." She had long, black hair and a pretty face.

"Hello, Courtney, I'm Thea. I am happy to meet you. I would like you to be a flower girl as my wedding."

"Flower girl," repeated Courtney. Ashleigh came and stood by Thea and her daughter. "Well, well, how unusual. You have a magic power, Thea. She never sits on laps like that."

"Ashleigh, I have a confession to make. As soon as I met your lovely Dora, I asked her to be a flower girl at our wedding. I am so sorry I did not ask you first. Very sorry, I could not resist this blond angel."

"Well, she's not always an angel, are you? But she'd love being a flower girl."

"I asked Courtney too, so I would just have the two small girls. Is that OK?"

"With me, yes. Do talk to Michaela."

"Where is she?"

"Not sure. She'll be here soon to call us to the dining room."

"I've dominated. I've behaved like Adam. I'm so sorry," Thea said as Adam smiled at her. Michaela arrived and picked up Courtney.

"You alright, love?" she said.

Thea called her over. "I am so sorry, I could not resist these two lovely girls. I have mentioned to them about being flower girls at our wedding before I asked the mothers. I am sorry. I got carried away. Will you let her be my flower girl?"

"Courtney can't say much yet. She has speech therapy. She repeats but does not say many words. I am sure she would love to carry the flowers and walk with Dora. Dora takes care of her. We'd have to practice with her so she understands. She's likely to run off with the flowers in the wrong direction."

"You are so kind. Thank you so much. We don't have a date yet. We hope to use the Benedictine Abbey in Chilworth but it's not yet fixed."

Dora was watching her talk and stroking the silk trousers. Thea smiled at her. "I'll come to Brighton and get the girls a special dress each."

"You'd do that? A special dress for my Courtney, fantastic!" Ellie came in with an old school bell and rang it heartily.

"Food!"

Ashleigh led Dora to the children's end of the table. Adam hugged Thea and said, "Thea, it's your new name from now on. Dora and Doro could get confused. What's more, it's such a pretty name."

"With your family, to start with." He bent over and kissed her on the lips and then went into the buffet. Thea felt challenged by Melanie who seemed to be near her uncle Carl. She wore that sulky, teenage expression.

"How do you relate to Melanie?" Thea asked Adam.

"Like relating to an alien. She'll grow out of it one day. She's rebelling against her dad. He hates punk and Goth and wants his little girl back." Thea moved over to Carl and Melanie.

"What a wonderful get together. I'm so grateful to be part of your family." Melanie half smiled and half scowled. Carl said how pleased he was that Adam was getting married at last and to such a lovely lady.

"We thought he must be gay," Melanie spoke.

"He was a workaholic," Thea explained.

"You're a widow, I think."

"Yes, I was married to a lovely man called Richard, a classical musician. We had two children but sadly they both died."

"How?" asked the unthinking Melanie.

"My little girl, Marianna had a heart defect and only lived a few weeks. My son saw his father suffer with cancer treatment and when he was diagnosed with a melanoma, a skin cancer, he had a massive panic and sadly took his own life."

Melanie went pale and silent. She touched Thea's shoulder and left her hand there. "Suicide? How?" Carl was angry.

"Mel, show some sensitivity. It's new year." Mel glared at him but kept her hand on Thea. "Sorry," she said softly.

"Melanie, one day I will explain to you. It's not the right time tonight."

"OK." She took her hand down and walked away to find Shirley.

Adam and Thea also found Rosamund and Shirley. "Haven't spoken to you yet. Are you all well?"

"Yes, thanks. Dad opted out, not a party person." They had a good look at the engagement ring.

"Did you like my flans?"

"Asparagus, broccoli, ham and cheese, all yours?"

"All mine."

"Loved them. Well done!"

At midnight they all took champagne into the garden and looked up at the moon and stars and cheered in the new year. Everyone tried to hug and kiss everyone else. Melanie came to Thea and gave her a generous, meaningful hug. Adam and Thea hugged each other for a long time.

"Our new start, my love."

"Happy new year, my beloved, Adam." After their kiss they reached out to others and Thea felt her hand being taken. Dora stood there giving her a look of love.

"Just like Marie Flore. Happy new year, Dora."

As they all split up to find their beds or their cars, Adam had a phone call. Russell had sent greetings on Skype as his siblings and relatives watched.

159

Adam guessed he was ringing to speak especially to him, but it was not Russell but Gerd.

"Happy new year, Rainer. Thanks for your message. Sorry to ring on this night. I needed to let you know that Jürgen has passed away. I'll be back in the UK in a few weeks."

"Gerd, thank you for telling me. As soon as you arrive in London, let me know. Come and stay with us for a while."

"Thanks, Rainer. Who is us?"

"I'm getting married to Diane, her real name is Dorothea, sometime in Spring."

"I am amazed. Congratulations, and see you soon."

In their room, Adam asked Thea to sit down. "I've had a call from Gerd. Jürgen has died."

She did some deep breathing and did not speak for a while.

"I invited him to stay with us when he gets back. It will not be for several weeks. He will have to be debriefed in Germany and London."

"I look forward to seeing him and hearing his story," Thea reassured him.

Chapter 21

It was a chilly day half way through January when Adam and Thea went to see Fr Tony at the Abbey. They had spent a lovely day in London the week before when Lotte and Helga celebrated the New Year with them over a German lunch. Both Lotte and Helga had cooked German food and a huge cake. Lotte was told about Jürgen's death and that Gerd was due back in the UK soon.

Even with a life of openness and truth, the past secret life could not be ignored. They had planned a story line for the priest to avoid going into the details of the undercover activities in Aachen. Thea would say that although she and Adam had met years before, they had not kept in touch after her retirement from the Foreign Office. Recently they had had to go over some of their past work. Coming after her tragic loss of her husband and son, this caused Dorothea to have a breakdown. In her recovery, she and Adam had fallen in love and decided to marry. Dorothea wanted to talk more about God and where he fitted into human suffering but they both wanted to ask about their wedding. They both felt nervous and did not enter the room full of confidence. Fr Tony greeted them with warmth and friendliness.

"Congratulations on your engagement. How do you wish to start today?"

"Feedback," said Adam, "Thank you for the prayers and readings. I have read them, spent time contemplating and Thea has helped introduce me to the healing qualities of music."

"That's a good start. How are things for you, Dorothea?"

"So much better. We are working on our spiritual healing together. I do see a very good counsellor but we do not deal with theology. We probably need to give some background knowledge before we ask you theological questions."

"So, my soul shall be healed. You began there, Adam. What healing were you looking for?"

He explained about the special tasks in the FO, which caused him to be isolated much of the time from his family and close friends but now he discovered that his family really seemed to love him and care for him.

"I had to take decisions in my work which I now regret. They caused harm to me and to others."

"Are you speaking to me in confidence because you are not permitted to speak of your work?"

"Quite so. Thank you for understanding."

"Dorothea, you have your own story. Let me say a prayer before you begin. Sharing like this is a holy time."

He lit a candle and placed it on the table between them and asked the Holy Spirit to come and lead and guide them and fill them with the presence of the love of God.

They sat in silence as the flame flickered brightly.

"I told you of the extraordinary suffering and loss in my life. It has left me frightened of harm and loss. I am very confused about God's role in my life, in the world and in the universe." Adam held her hand as she rehearsed the details of Edward's suicide and then he heard her say words he had never heard her say before.

"I have wondered if I am cursed, destined to be in pain, being punished in some way. Meeting Adam, loving him, being loved by him has been a joy and I am more hopeful inside now."

Fr Tony had tears running down his cheeks.

"All my compassion and care go out to you. Please don't worry. I cry when I watch the news on TV. Suffering moves me deeply and yours is truly terrible. I look at you, see the love between you, your beauty and inner strength and I bless God for how He has protected you. You don't do drugs; you don't turn to drink. You don't let out your anger and pain on others. You are kind and caring. I see that God has been with you."

"Well said, Father, you have summed her up well. I'm sure you cannot help us solve the mysteries of the universe in one sitting. We could deal with some practical issues and make some appointments to come and speak with you, if you are willing to guide us through the labyrinth of suffering." Fr Tony wiped his eyes.

"You make good points but we will look at your suffering in as much detail as you wish, perhaps slowly over some months."

"I've gone over it all with a counsellor. I think I want to know, if possible, to understand God's dealings. Tell me more about God. What IS He doing?"

"That's a good next step, getting to know more of God. Do you have a Bible? I suggest you read two passages before we meet for spiritual direction. In the Old Testament, get a modern translation, read the book of Job. In the New Testament read the beginning of the Gospel of John. Come to Mass and at home do some silent meditation. Here's a book about it. Short and sweet but life changing."

"Can I have some water, please?" Thea felt exhausted and had a dry throat.

"Adam, next door there's a little kitchen. Bring us all a glass of water." Adam found a large jug and three cups and brought them in. They had a little break while Dorothea was having a slight tremble. The priest opened a cupboard and pulled out a blanket and placed it around her shoulders. Adam leaned over to hold her.

"What are the practical things?"

"We would like to get married here if possible. What did the Abbot say?"

"He was happy to leave it to me to guide you through the spiritual steps and would be delighted for me to marry you in the Abbey. We'd have to avoid Easter."

"End of April, beginning of May?" Adam suggested.

"Thank you so much," Thea added as they checked a calendar and settled on the last Saturday in April.

"One more thing, it's about barbers." Adam laughed.

He told his story about his project to use his home as a clinic, not only for the rich, high flyers, but for local men in difficulties.

"The barbers and GPs would refer them and the private work would fund the sessions for local men. We are looking into all the legal requirements, and getting advice on getting the right staff team."

Fr Tony was opened mouthed. He took in a deep breath.

"What a couple you are! A new life together but putting the needs of others on the top of your agenda. You are both really blessed and it is a privilege to know you."

"Our rings have 'Truly blessed' and 'Gesegnet' engraved on them," Dorothea told him.

"Wirklich gesegnet," announced Fr Tony.

"Sprechen Sie Deutsch?"

"Another story. Jawohl. My father knew Bonhoeffer in the '30s and '40s."

"Dietrich Bonhoeffer, amazing man," Dorothea added.

They stood up and Fr Tony hugged Adam, a real bear hug, and then Dorothea. "In about two to three weeks?" asked Adam.

Adam drove them home to her house.

"I think you should lie down in a warm bed for a while and have a rest."

"Why do I get so shaky? Please don't leave me yet."

He tucked her up in bed and hoped she would sleep. In the lounge he put on some music and sat with his eyes closed, feeling happy but drained. His phone beeped and he saw he had a text from Gerd.

"Ralph gave me your number. Love to see you. Need to go to Leeds to sort out house. How about end February?"

He was glad it was not sooner. He needed a rest too. They both rested for several days and put off seeing Dr Ford and Fr Tony as they were dealing with a death and a bereavement of a close friend.

Gerd was looking rather stooped, thin and pale as he waited in the station forecourt. Adam gave him a hug and took his case.

He was given the spare room before it had been redecorated for agents. It was perfectly pleasant if rather boring. Gerd seemed distracted and unaware of his surroundings.

"Dorothea is coming over this afternoon to cook us a meal."

Gerd was looking very frail. "Have you totally finished up in Germany?"

"I have moved all my stuff out. I will live in my Yorkshire home. I'll go back for holidays, perhaps but I think Bruno and the Cologne group and perhaps also Düsseldorf will be arrested. They are not active. Many are now regretting their revolutionary past. The police have left them alone in the hopes they might get some intelligence of new activities. They were suspicious to see old members go often to Aachen."

"I want to hear about Jürgen's last weeks and about his life story. Tell me when you are strong enough to tell Dorothea as well. She doesn't know your background or even your name."

They sipped a beer in the lounge.

"He was a brutal killer but when he changed, I really loved him."

"I am sorry for your suffering. Do you want a lie down?"

"Probably a good idea." He went to his room and fell asleep on his bed. He still had his coat and shoes on. When Thea arrived, Adam went to wake him but saw his condition. He pulled off his shoes and put a duvet over him.

"We'll have to wait. He's fast asleep."

They sat on the settee and kissed and cuddled. There were no creaking stairs to warn them when Gerd woke up and came downstairs. He opened the lounge door and saw them embracing passionately.

"Sorry. Hello, Diane." They looked up, straightened up and laughed. "Just like teenagers," Thea said.

Adam stood up. "Dorothea meet David Reger from Leeds." She gave him a hug too. "I have made a Shepherd's Pie. Are you hungry?"

"I don't know."

"I'll put it in the oven and the smell will give you an appetite." David still seemed distracted.

"How is your Leeds house?"

"In need of some work, just superficial things."

"Are you in the city?"

"No, to the north on the way to Otley. It's a quiet area. Jürgen killed Manfred in a horrible way. He made him suffer."

"David, would you rather talk first and eat later? Lotte wants to see you one day. She'll probably come here to see you."

David removed his jacket and put on slippers. He was becoming more with it.

"Thank you, David, for your years of service. It's amazing you did not get found out or caught in the police raids."

"Jürgen was awaiting trial. He was interrogated by several police teams. He would not give the names of any members. He insisted they were no longer active and that they regretted their atrocities."

He had been allowed a few visits by Gerd. Bruno discovered his arrest as he saw the photo in the paper. He went into hiding followed by his watchers.

David told them that Jürgen's real name was Heinrich Hartz. His father had been a guard at Dachau, living on the site. From the age of eight, Heinrich had seen his father beat the prisoners, shoot some in cold blood and take others to the Medical Experiment block. He had been traumatised but the taste for cruelty had become part of his emotional life. His mother had taken him to Munich before the Allies arrived at the camp. Heinrich heard that his father had been arrested and executed as a war criminal. The mother took her son and fled to the north where nobody knew her.

In 1967, Heinrich joined the student movement and demonstrated against the Vietnam War. He met up with Baader and became radicalised. In his hatred for his own father, he turned to hate the fascist elements in the state, as he interpreted them, in capitalism and commercialism. He soon met Manfred. He was very attracted to him but soon realised that Manfred was not interested in sex with men, only with women. Nevertheless, he became his great supporter and formed a commune in Aachen with links to Munich, Berlin, Frankfurt, Cologne and Düsseldorf. He revelled in the violence which developed after 1968. He showed great delight in shooting the American soldiers on the air bases where they also planted car bombs.

Manfred's own violence and cruelty thrived with Jürgen.

David, as Gerd, had driven with Bruno and Manfred after the attack on Diane. He and Bruno knew that execution was the only way.

They drove into thick woodland armed with pistols. Some prepared a tomb, digging deep but leaving lots of shrubs to plant on the top. Manfred knew he was going to be killed. They gagged him to stop his shouting while two men were digging. Jürgen took a pistol and shot him in the legs, in the thigh area and then at the top of the shins. His hands were tied so Jürgen ordered them to be untied and for the gag to be removed. He was too weak to shout but he groaned in pain. Jürgen then shot him in one shoulder and one elbow. He had to reload. He then put the gun to his head and cursed him. The next shot went through his right cheek and out of the left, shattering his teeth and jaw. He was still alive when he fired into his crotch three times. Jürgen was yelling obscenities. The diggers begged him to stop. Too many shots could attract attention. They pulled him to the tomb and tipped him in. Jürgen then stood at the end and fired into his head.

David/Gerd dug around the blood stains and buried them. The diggers filled in the tomb and beat the earth down before planting the shrubs. Gerd then stood back to ensure that the tomb was not obvious to passers-by.

David was weeping as he finished the story. He escaped being caught when the Cologne group was arrested. He fled for a while but returned to see Lotte and Diane in Aachen. No one knew what he had done. The Aachen group dispersed when the Wall fell and Germany reunited. Jürgen moved to a new flat and began the process of repentance and conversion. He changed his appearance and started going to church services. Bruno kept in touch and visited him in Aachen and when Gerd went, he found a very different, broken man.

They formed a caring and loving relationship. This just about brought them up to the day when Gerd met Rainer in the cathedral.

In the holding cell, Jürgen's health declined. The prison doctor wanted him to be put into hospital but he was considered too dangerous. He was soon bed-ridden and incoherent. Gerd was called in and sat with him as his life ebbed out of him. Jürgen held a crucifix as he died.

"It was a sad, lonely funeral. Bruno came but we kept our distance. When I close my eyes, I can see that terrible burial in the woods and then the simple cremation and burial of ashes of Heinrich."

David drank another beer, ate some of the pie and clearly needed to sleep.

"It was a time of madness, my love. I'm sorry you had to hear that. I hope it won't disturb you too much." She wept in his arms.

"It's a horror story."

"Do you want to stay? You should not be alone, should you?"

"I'll go. I want to be alone for a while."

"See how he is tomorrow. It might help if I brought him to your house if you can bear it."

"He won't cover that ground again. Get him to tell me his own story." Adam did not know what was best. Dorothea drove home as darkness was falling. She touched her sapphire and read the verses from John's Gospel.

"Will it ever end? Will we ever get away from those mad years, those mad people?"

She awoke after a fitful sleep and walked to the hills behind her house. Some horse riders and dog walkers were already out in the fields. She breathed her deep exercises and felt a great deal better.

Adam rang.

"I am so glad you are out in the fields my love. I'm contacting Dr Ford. The doctor she recommended has already made contact as you know so I'm going to ask him to deal with David for some weeks. He could start before we are officially open. If he is willing, he could start in Leeds!"

"What a good idea, my dearest. Are you going to bring him to mine?"

"I will ring you back."

Adam gave David breakfast and told him about the doctor who works for the Department. "He might be willing to talk with you and help you settle in to your new life in Leeds. If you agree he will come and meet you here."

David seemed much better. He was no longer sitting and staring ahead as if traumatised. "Come for a walk near Dorothea's house and we'll go and see her."

"I think I have upset her. She should not have had to hear all that."

"No, she should not. I had no idea what had happened. It is a relief that Jürgen has died in peace."

Adam checked that she could cope with David's visit. "I have made an appointment for you with Dr Ford in two days' time and after that we'll go to see Fr Tony. Thea was pleased with the suggestions and went home to prepare for the visit. When they drove up, she smiled and suggested they went to a different hill across the main road.

They walked on the lower slopes looking down at horses munching in the fields, wearing their winter coats. David was relaxing more. At home she put on some Einaudi in the background, undemanding, repetitive, gentle melodies.

"How did you become an agent, Gerd?" she asked.

"Did you see that Gerd came from the letters in my name? I had a great-grandfather who was German. His son, my grandfather often talked about our German heritage and persuaded me to learn German. I did A level and a German and Russian degree. I ended up working for a company which made and sold heavy duty working clothes to both Germany and Russia." David went to both countries and made a lot of money so that by his late twenties he was able to afford to buy his own house. The family pressure was on him to find a wife. By then, he knew that he was gay but he did not dare tell his family. On one of his trips to Germany he was contacted by an MI6 recruiter in his hotel. He was amazed to hear how he had been observed by MI6 as a very good candidate to act as an undercover agent. Of course, he had been familiar with the student demonstrations but he was not so aware of how they had turned into Marxist Revolutionaries. He learned of the friction between the various gangs and their collaboration with Jordan and the Palestinians. David had several meetings with the agents until he understood what he was being asked to do. He would keep his job as cover but try to deal mainly with Germany. In London he met Rainer who had taken over as controller of the German Department and was running five to six agents. That's when he signed the

Official Secrets Act, went to a training camp in Norfolk. He did thorough weapons and explosives training. He began by linking with student rebels in Munich. He worked at being trusted by the members and made some extreme suggestions for targets. The Munich leader asked if he would go to Cologne and work with a group who dealt with literature and had links to Baader and Meinhof. Rainer thought that would be a good idea so he put him touch with Lotte in Aachen.

David sat back with his eyes closed and breathed deeply. "Lotte's coming to see you tomorrow," Adam told him.

"Can I take you both out for a pub lunch? You have been so kind to me? What do I call you?"

"Adam and Thea, or Dorothea. Are you sure you want to do that?"

"I most certainly do. Dorothea I am very sorry about yesterday. I've told no one, talked to no one. I let it all go. I am sorry."

"We'll go to the Percy up the road. We have booked our wedding reception there. They have a deck for summer, a bar and a restaurant."

They all unwound somewhat in the pub and chose a meal each. David ate well and thanked Adam for setting up the counselling. When Lotte arrived, she and David talked in Adam's house while Adam and Thea went to see Dr Ford Lloyd. She was pleased to set up counselling with one of the new doctors but when she heard of the long horror story, she was angry and agitated.

"Doro you need protection from that kind of talk. It will do you no good. How did you let that happen?" she turned to Adam.

"I'm very sorry indeed. Doro had often worked with Gerd over the years and neither of us had any idea about what had happened. He never reported it. He's with Lotte today."

"Your instincts, what happened to them? The encounter in the cathedral was bad enough."

"How could we imagine that we would see a Marxist revolutionary in a Mass? I had no idea that Gerd had witnessed the brutal killing of Manfred. He and Lotte were in great danger of being 'blown' at that time."

Dr Ford took Thea's hand. "What's this done to you?"

"It was a shock. We are exhausted. I've wept it out and I've found great comfort in spiritual things."

"I'm glad to hear that. I'm sorry this happened."

"It's made me trust Adam more. I've lost my fear of his control, especially since I have met his family."

"You have done well. In fact, you have both done well. What a lot you've had to overcome. Now get Gerd here to meet Dr Noel Armand at 11.00 am in two days. Then Noel will go to Leeds and see him in his home. You should not have to deal with him while you are preparing your wedding."

"Dr Ford, thank you so much. You will receive an invitation to the Abbey in Chilworth and reception at the Percy. Please do come. Last Saturday in April." Doro smiled as they still gripped hands.

"How lovely, I hope I am free. I'd be delighted to come."

"Rainer, Adam, when you pick up Gerd, David, take the chance to speak to Dr Armand. He is quite enthusiastic about the clinic. David is being fully funded by the Department."

"Thank God!" Adam smiled. "Have you two found God?"

"In a way, we have. We are still searching and finding a way forward."

"You are both great. A clinic indeed. Sandbags Care Centre indeed!" She got up and gave them each a hug.

Both Adam and Thea wondered what they would find when they reached his home. They rang the doorbell to let Lotte know they were back.

"Hello, welcome home!" Lotte hugged Dorothea. "Thanks for coming, Lotte, how is David?"

"Broken, upset, not fully with it." They all joined him in the lounge.

"Good morning, Dorothea," said David. Adam opened the glass doors and invited them to see the garden by the river and the signs of spring. The snowdrops were almost gone from the grassy slope. A few daffodils were raising their heads, tight and green, in the woodlands on the opposite side of the river.

"What's that?" David pointed to the artistic, metal tree. Adam explained and showed him the painting they had called hope.

"Do you need more time with Lotte?"

"We were just sharing our info on the gang members. Lotte knows about Jürgen. I knew that Ilse got into the drug scene and Lotte thinks that Raoul and Felicity were arrested. No news of any of the others apart from a few rumours."

"David has an appointment with a new doctor from the clinic tomorrow. Dr Ford Lloyd has been very helpful. We will all miss her."

"David needs rest and recovery, like we all do at times. We'll all support him. When you feel up to it, come and see us in London. I am with a partner called Helga."

"I am pleased, Lotte. It's good to see you in retirement. Thanks for coming to see me. I'd love to come to London sometime."

"Do you want to eat, Lotte?"

"No, thanks, Helga is cooking."

"Shall I take you to the station?" Adam realised that this would mean leaving Thea with David, not a good idea, but he wanted to ask Lotte a question.

On the doorstep he asked her, "Did David tell you how Jürgen killed Manfred?"

"Yes, he did."

"Let Doro drive you back. She was very disturbed by his account. It is too much for her and too much for me." Dorothea appeared to say goodbye.

"You drive Lotte back, my love. I'll stay with David."

She saw that his instincts were now working and was very relieved.

Adam used the time to tell David what a real help the counselling had been to him and to Dorothea. He persuaded him to follow that plan for recovery, all paid for by the Department.

"Thea and I have an appointment with the priest this afternoon. Can I leave you here? We are going to our local Abbey for spiritual guidance and wedding preparation. You can choose, stay here or come with us and walk in the lovely grounds."

"I'll stay here, thanks. Sorry to be a nuisance at this delicate time."

"David, you served us for years, taking terrible risks. You are not a nuisance. We have needed to heal and recover as well. Make yourself at home."

'God give you peace' was on a sign at the main entrance behind the Abbey. They both felt that peace as they drove in. It was such a relief to be there.

"We are sorry, Fr Tony. We've been dealing with a very difficult situation, a sad death and the breakdown of a faithful old friend. We are so pleased to be with you today. Fr Tony lit a candle and they all sat in silence for a few minutes. Then he picked up a Bible and read slowly, the first few verses of St John's Gospel.

"It is wonderful language, isn't it? Did it mean anything to you?"

"The contrast of Word and World," replied Adam. "There was conflict between these two expressions. The world rejects the word. So, the word is a term for Jesus Christ. The world is a term for people who are out to destroy Him."

"I was struck by the first five verses and they did speak to me. I understood that the Word, or Jesus was present at every part of creation of the universe. He is in absolutely everything and He is life and light. Those words at the end of the book of Job just showed me that we are so small, we understand so little and that God is far, far greater than we ever imagined. He has an agenda we cannot understand," Thea added.

"It was a tortuous route through Job but the ending used illustrations in nature to show us our powerlessness. It left me with the impression that it is acceptable NOT to know, not to understand because the God who made the universe is too mysterious for us to grasp," Adam tried to explain.

"I could have you both back to give sermons!" Fr Tony smiled at them. "You have reached a place of deep understanding which gives some peace, but it does not answer the original question."

"Is there an answer?" Thea asked.

"Perhaps not but in worship and prayer you can reach a deep trust in God. Prayer is not asking God for things and being upset if you don't get them. Prayer is being in God's presence, opening yourself to Him, listening to His Spirit guiding you."

"We feel privileged to work on these things together. I loved those words, 'we have all received one blessing after another'. We have been feeling like that and this recent unexpected encounter with death and sorrow was a shock."

"Is there anything, any aspect of your marriage you want to talk about?"

"I have no one on the world and Adam has a huge family. I feel so blessed to join and feel part of such a family. I won't always know how to act with them. Having lost my own children, I'm overwhelmed by love for some of these little children." Dorothea admitted her lack of confidence and nervousness.

"I realise how much my work cut me off from so much of normal family life. I am amazed at how pleased they all are for me to have found such a lovely wife. I need to learn to share, to love in a normal human way."

Silence reigned as Fr Tony heard words he was not expecting and needed to process them. "What is your German connection?" asked Thea.

My father met Dietrich Bonhoeffer just before the war. He was teaching in a protestant college. When he saw the direction of the 3rd Reich, he left Germany and came to England, but he kept contact with Bonhoeffer. He did not know what happened to him until, after the war. He taught me German, told me all about this teacher and his sad death. I've read everything I could about him."

"Thanks, Father Tony."

"Can I give you a couple of Psalms to read through? Do read the rest of the Gospel of John if you can. So much deep teaching. Do you want to come here before your wedding?"

"I think so. Who knows what else will happen to us before then?"

"We may bring a friend sometime." Adam wanted to prepare the way for inviting David.

"I think you are telling me that this death was not the usual kind of death and that there was an element of shock, of abnormal distress."

Adam choked and tears ran down his cheeks. He could not speak. Thea went to him and held him.

"It's been a terrible ordeal, Father. You are right. For a long time, we did not know if we would mend."

"You have experienced trauma." Fr Tony seemed calm and caring.

"We have. We have had help from our superiors, some wonderful psychiatrists."

"You have put your trust in God to help you. He will help you."

Fr Tony was moved and rather shaken to see the groom so broken.

"We are broken, Father, but we have begun to heal. You and the Abbey have helped us. Now we have another broken soul to help. His name is David. Could we say a prayer for him?"

Fr Tony fetched a small candle. He read out a wonderful prayer they had never heard before. The words gave them confidence. Adam wiped his eyes.

"Sorry, it has been very difficult. We are rather overwhelmed and exhausted. Thank you so much for your prayer. Can we have a copy?"

"I'll give you one next time. It is called St Patrick's Breastplate."

They both needed to walk in the woods before they drove home. They wandered across the road and went up a sandy hill. They suddenly saw a grey stone cross at the top. When they reached it, they saw it was a war memorial. The views all around were so lovely. They could see St Martha's Church in the distance across the valley. Somehow, they found that they could face going back to David and taking him to meet Dr Noel Armand.

David had read and dozed and was sitting quietly in an armchair in the lounge. "Would you like some soup and toast?" Adam asked.

"That's just right," Thea said. She was worried about Adam and stayed the night. She cuddled him in bed and let him weep. He kept the sound down but he needed a sobbing session. She took a damp flannel and wiped his forehead. When he fell asleep at last, she fetched some whiskey. She fell asleep next to him but had set an alarm, knowing he had to get David to the clinic. Adam woke up about 4.00 am and sat up. This woke Thea who asked him how he was.

"Headache," was his reply.

"You won't want whiskey, then."

"Water and pills. In the bathroom cabinet." She brought them in and watched him swallow a couple of pills. He dozed for a couple of hours.

"What happened?" he asked about seven am.

"The trauma caught up with you, my love. How is your head?"

"All clear. I'll check on David."

They all washed or showered and had breakfast. David seemed calm but still distant.

"He was so cruel, so hard, so violent." David was in his own world, reviewing the character of Jürgen. "He loved me. He wanted to say sorry." Adam put his arm around his shoulders.

"Tell all that to Dr Armand."

They drove to the clinic to meet the new doctor.

Dr Noel Armand was a gentle giant, over six foot tall with tousled ginger-brown hair and a ginger moustache and beard. He beamed widely as Adam introduced David.

"I've read the files. Thank you, David, for all you have done for Germany over so many years."

"David is not totally coherent at the moment. I'll wait outside so you can talk to him and at the end I'd like a few minutes of your time about my future clinic."

"Good to meet you, Dr Chamberlain. Give me about 90 minutes today."

Adam left him to begin peeling back the layers of trauma in David. He walked around the water meadows, through the park and stood by the empty bandstand.

"This must be lovely in the summer, bowls, music, dog, river." Adam was longing for normal days, normal families. He sat on a bench and reread his notes. He returned when the time was up and waited in the reception room. David came through the door.

"Hello, Adam, Dr Noel is coming to Leeds with me tomorrow. He's taking me on. I'm so grateful." Adam smiled.

"Can you wait for me here?"

"Yes, I'll look at the magazines." The receptionist asked Adam to wait a little longer and he would be called in. He chatted to David about his magazine. When the time came, Adam pulled out his notes and sat opposite Dr Noel.

"Your initiative encourages me a great deal," said the doctor. "I am pleased to offer my services. My priority is the London clinic but I can already see that some agents would benefit from seeing me outside London."

"I am only thinking of sessional work, not daily clinics. Each doctor can choose his or her way of working. I'd like to invite you to my house to take in the atmosphere and advise me of any facilities needed. When you come, I'll show you the leaflets and cards we plan to print and discuss with you the other sessions for local men who will have reduced fees. The funding from the Intelligence Department will contribute to the counselling for the men."

"Who is 'we'?"

"My fiancée. We get married in April and go to Greece for our honeymoon."

"Congratulations!"

"I am just the manager or director. I am not doing the counselling. I want no payment or profit, just enough to keep the work going and pay for other qualified doctors like yourself. Dr Ford Lloyd recommended you. I am hoping you can recommend one or two others to work in a team. Please call me Adam. May I call you Noel?"

"You may, Adam. I am so pleased to be involved with your project. How will you contact the locals?"

"Through the Barber's Organisation for training barbers to have listening and basic counselling skills, hopefully to pass on the cases which need more than just a chat." Noel and Adam agreed on a date for a visit to his home.

"Where do you come from?"

"Scotland, Edinburgh but I went to school in England so I have lost most of my accent."

"I am so pleased to meet you. Are you collecting David tomorrow?"

"No, he needs to meet me here at 10.00 am."

"Thank you, he seems willing to comply and really happy that you are going with him."

"It's the least we can do."

Adam took David back and found that Dorothea had taken a call from Russell in Greece. She waited to hear about the visit to the doctor before she told him the contents of the call.

"Dr Noel is just right. He is so open and helpful and encouraging. David is travelling to Leeds with him tomorrow and they will sort out a schedule of care. He's coming here in two weeks to see the clinic area and discuss your advertising ideas. It was very good."

She put her arms around his neck and kissed him.

"Your brother wants to speak to you. He reminds me of you a few years ago, he's got it all planned out."

"That's Russell. Big hearted; treats his family celebrations like his business conferences. Did he tell you what he wanted to do?"

"Part of it was that he wants you to bring all the relatives and friends to Greece for two nights so he can hold the reception in his hotel!"

"Does he expect them all to pay the fares?"

"He says he can get reduced fares and coaches to and from the airports."

"He owns a big hotel so he'd put them all up," Adam explained.

"I'm not sure we want such a big affair, do we?"

"Well, we'd hate to leave out our dear friends like Lotte and Helga if all my family are coming."

"Have you got the energy to ring him?"

"I think so. It's a pleasant task. Do you want to go home for a rest? Are you happy for me to make the decisions?"

"Yes, dearest Adam, I trust you." They kissed lovingly.

"I'll see you tomorrow after David goes." She went into David and gave him a hug. "I haven't slept well, I'm off to rest. God bless, see you again soon."

Adam phoned his brother who then reverted to Skype. Russell had a pile of documents in front of him.

"Adam, this is a great day for us all. Our young brother, beloved uncle and great uncle is getting married for the first time at 63 to a lovely lady. I want to mark the occasion in the only way I know how. I have a big hotel, I have flats for you, I have brilliant caterers. I organise these events for hundreds of people at a time so surely, I can do it for my family plus some friends. Let me know how many. My three will all want to have you to a meal but I have left you plenty of free time to yourselves. It is your honeymoon after all!"

"Russ, you are amazing! What do I put on the invitations?"

"The hotel address and two-night stay, all meals included, then coach back to the airport. How many others?"

"Dorothea has no relatives but some good friends, probably five to six extra."

"Send me the wedding program with times. Coach for 40 should cover it."

"We are getting married in the Benedictine Abbey in Chilworth. We shall have a drinks and canapé reception in the local gastro pub. The flights to Greece need to be at about 8.00 pm.

"We won't have cakes and speeches, hopefully, not with you either."

"May be not too many speeches, but I'll get some sort of cake. I have high quality caterers. What do you want to eat?"

"A choice, one vegetarian and two or three fish and meat options."

"I'll send you photos and plans soon!"

"Russ you are so kind and generous. Thanks so much."

"I'll die happy knowing that my little brother is happy!"

"Russell I am very touched. We are ready to contribute to our own wedding. What can we cover?"

"Adamo! Your clothes and jewels, touristic entry fees, internal travels. You know how lovely it is here. Will Dorothea like a boat trip?"

"I expect so. Good idea. Thea has met everyone at Steven's and has asked Courtney and Dora to be flower girls."

"Ah, lovely! Little dears!"

Chapter 22

Guildford has hundreds of daffodils in the spring, on road sides, roundabouts, parks and gardens. The golden flowers, tall and short cheer all the residents as they go about their daily tasks.

Noel appreciated them greatly and sat filming them on his bench by the river. Dorothea told him the story of the Aachen myth which gave rise to the title, 'Sandbags Care Centre'. He had never heard of the myth nor was he familiar with Aachen.

"I usually recommend a room which is only used for consultations. Using the lounge means that you are bringing the problems into your personal living space. You cannot allow yourself to be so involved that you have no private life and private space."

"I will probably live at Dorothea's home with occasional days spent here. Her home will be our domestic base and mine will be another quiet space also used by the clinic. We have yet to make final decisions. It's hard to tell how often the clinic will be open."

"It's so important to guard your privacy."

"What do you think of the guest room?"

"For patients or doctors?"

"Both. If they both need to sleep over, I can normally be with my wife or on the couch in the lounge."

"Not ideal. You have to be aware of your own protection. Your lounge is big, could you put in a partition so the counselling area is separate from your living area?"

"You have left me a lot to consider. I'll talk it over with Dorothea."

"I have a prospective lady team member for you. She is on our team in London and loves your plans. She is Dr Glenda Grey with experience in abuse, rape, stalking and stress. She's worked with agent breakdowns from Russia and Eastern Europe. Shall I put her in touch?"

"Please, you have been very kind and helpful. Thank you for helping David, I have worked with him for 40 years."

The amicable conversation came to an end and Adam felt restored from his own stress. He was pleased to be alone with Thea once again. He had to explain to her about Russell's invitation, or rather his organised plans as well as Dr Noel's comments on the usage of his lounge.

They immediately thought about how to get a partition put in the lounge but decided to wait until after their honeymoon. As Dr Noel had approved of the cards and flyers, Thea organised the printing of these plus their wedding invitations with the address of the Abbey, The Percy Arms and the hotel in Greece.

The next task was to choose the music for the wedding and to get some different clothes for the reception in Greece.

"Just what we need, something practical to do. I'll get a long summer dress for the reception. I can ask Renate, or do you want to come."

"Do ask Renate but I will come too so you can help me choose some suits."

Dorothea discovered some musical versions of St Patrick's Breastplate and chose a modern version, simplified and shortened which began, 'I arise today in the strength of heaven'. It was named, *The Deer's Cry*. Adam loved it. He also wanted some Bach in memory of his mother and of Richard.

It gave them great pleasure to plan the ceremony which would be taken by Fr Tony. It restored their equilibrium.

David spent two days with Dr Noel who ascertained that he could make the journey from Leeds to London, to attend the clinic on a regular basis. Independent travel and regular meetings would be good for his recovery. He had seen how stressed Adam and Thea were and felt that David should wait a while before spending time with them.

The white April blossoms were thick and beautiful and in full view of his glass doors. They both loved sitting there.

"Uncle Adam, please can I bring a boyfriend to your wedding?" Shirley rang from Woking.

"Hello, Shirley, you've met someone you really like, I'm very glad. I'll add him to your Uncle Russell's list. You know about the invitation to Greece?"

"Yes, Mum's delighted. Dad won't come but he's happiest at home. My boyfriend is another social worker. He works in the department for the elderly."

"And his name is…?"

"Mustafa."

"Pakistani?"

"Yes."

"Well, welcome him on our behalf. Will he mind being in a church?"

"No, he is open and liberal and rejected by his own father because of that. We all call him Muzi. His name is Hossein of course!"

Adam was surprised but pleased to add to his international wedding guests. Russell was buying the flight tickets at a reduced price and asking the guests to reimburse him on arrival.

Wedding shopping was proving more complicated. Dorothea arranged to take Michaela and Ashleigh with the little flowers girls to buy them matching dresses. Thea drove to Brighton and met up with them both at Ashleigh's house. She showed them the photo of her blue dress from Aachen. It was a real treat for them to look through the gorgeous little dresses without worrying about the cost.

In the large Brighton store, it was clear what Michaela had to cope with when handling Courtney. The child had some learning difficulties and could not speak much but she had the habit of darting away in the wrong direction. Michaela had some reins for her when she did not settle down. Dora was her angelic self, holding on to Thea's hand and holding on to Courtney. They sat for a drink in the cafe.

"Are you sure you want to cope with Courtney?"

"Of course, Michaela. She can run around and be herself even in the wedding. It's not the Royal Wedding."

"She can be hard work."

"You cope so well. What do you like out of all we have seen so far?"

Ashleigh said that Dora had chosen hers. They laughed then went to see it. It was cream lace with a wide blue silk sash. Dora held it up.

"My dress."

They found the size for both girls, a headband and cream silk shoes and tried them on. "They look like angels. Let's hope they behave like angels." Michaela undressed her daughter and put on her normal clothes, much to Courtney's disgust.

"Well done, you have made an excellent choice." Thea held the smart bags as they went for lunch in one of the Italian restaurants.

The outing to Kingston was similar. Adam looked at suits while Renate and Thea looked through long dresses. Adam chose a light blue suit for the wedding and a light grey one for the Greek reception.

Thea showed Adam a filmy silver dress with a straight skirt and chiffon drapes from the shoulders. Her other choice was a simpler cream dress with pastel shades of flowers.

"They are both lovely. Do put them on." The little fashion show began.

"You look like a film star in silver. Gorgeous!" Renate said.

"Those pale flowers are so pretty," Adam said. "They both suit you. Film star is right. Celebrity quality!"

"Help me decide."

"What a difficult choice," said Renata.

"OK, one for the reception and the other for when we take Russell and Lesley for a thank you meal in a top restaurant."

"Dear Adam, I'm not used to spending like that. It's too much."

"Nor am I. Fun, isn't it?" Thea went to get changed and Adam took the dresses to the desk. "He spoils me," she said to Renate. "My silver shoes will already match and I have white ones for the pastel flower dress. It's like an artist's canvas. I think it needs a gold necklace, not the choker, and I already have two of those."

"It's so good to be with you, Thea and share these happy moments."

They had a quick sandwich before they braved Kingston traffic and the one-way system. "Renate, how is your new grandson?"

"He's lovely. His brother and sister treat him like a delicate doll. They argue about whose turn it is to play with him. He's not a good sleeper at night so my daughter is very tired."

"We have another doctor visiting us tomorrow. She's quite keen to join the team in Godalming."

"Now, Thea, rest up after that. It can all wait until after your honeymoon."

"Yes, Mum! Thank you so much for coming!"

Thea hung her dresses up in the bedroom and sat and admired them. Adam went home to sleep and to prepare for his next interview. He rang David and found him more articulate and alert.

"Did you get our invitation?"

"Yes, thanks, I will ask Dr Noel if he thinks I could cope with it all."

"Very good. I am sure he will agree."

Dr Glenda Grey drove herself to Adam's house. She stepped out of the car and stood looking over the river. Adam opened the door when he saw her car.

"What a lovely place! How beautiful. Just right for counselling. Hello, Dr Chamberlain, pleased to meet you, I'm Glenda."

"Dr Grey, thank you for coming. How was your journey?"

"I live in South London. I crawl through Putney and zip down the A3."

"I was very impressed by Dr Noel. He has already started with one of my agents. Call me Adam, please, may I call you Glenda?"

"Of course. I was not born GG, that's my husband's name, I was GM for Marshall."

"It's memorable, the GG. Please take a seat. This is the lounge I hope will be used for consultations. Dr Noel wants me to partition the room so the consultation area is not the same as my living area."

"It's big enough. I agree that the room should be separate from the living area."

"I want the patients to be able to see the glass doors, the river and the garden bench."

"Idyllic!"

"I shall live with my wife in her home but we were both agents and have baggage, so my home will be our quiet space."

"Well, thought out. Will she be involved in the clinic?"

"I shall only be manager, not counsellor. She will support me. She had designed these cards and leaflets and has framed the myth from Aachen which inspired the name."

"I shall have to read it." Adam served Glenda a herbal tea and explained his thinking to her.

"The Listening Barber!" She laughed at his story.

"We have agents from Hungary infiltrating the extreme right-wing groups. One woman and one man are very stressed by the rumblings of violence in some groups. They might well need counselling in the near future. Have you thought of drug security? We'll need a secure, lockable cabinet."

"I would not like that in the lounge. Can it go in the kitchen? Come and see." Glenda noted the abstract paintings as she got up.

"They are lovely!"

"Local artist, this one."

Glenda walked into the large kitchen and into the dining room with a study space at one end. "Most cupboards are in this central block?"

"Yes, we could put a secure safe in one of those and take the contents out and get an attractive cupboard put up on the wall."

"Just right. It would not be visible. I will send you a catalogue of the firm we use for safes. We would have to dispense from here on occasions."

He showed her the spare room and talked her through their ideas for decorating it.

"It's a fair size. One or two pictures of landscape or sea scape and pale colours, no big bold designs. Simple but warm."

"Thea will help me." He heard her car draw in. "She's here to meet you."

He opened the door and called, "Spaces over there. Dr Glenda came by car." He stood as she got out, embraced her and kissed her.

"Good morning, my beloved. Come and meet our new doctor."

Glenda was observing, standing by the door. Thea put her arm around Adam as they stepped towards the house.

"I am delighted to meet you," Thea said as she shook hands with the lively, dark-haired young woman. "I'm Dorothea. I was always called Doro but now I'm mostly Thea."

"Glad to meet you, Thea. I envy you your name, it's so attractive. When's your wedding?"

Last Saturday in April. Not long now. We have the flowers to confirm and we are all set. It is in the Abbey in Chilworth where I live."

"Congratulations and very best wishes."

"Thank you."

"Anything you want or need to know?"

"Adam will deal with the admin and timetable. I expect we'll meet problems and challenges we have not thought of, once we are up and running. I will not be very involved but I will probably end up supervising the food for those who stay over."

"I wonder what will come from the barber's links. If it doesn't bear fruit, try advertising in the GP surgeries and local hospitals."

"Can you stay for lunch?" asked Adam.

"That's kind of you. Thank you."

"I have some soup and things on toast."

"Shall I do it, love? Don't you need to talk?"

"You talk. I'll cook." He kissed her forehead and went into the kitchen.

"Tell me about yourself, Glenda."

"I am from London, studied at Cambridge and began clinical psychology there. I was contacted by MI6 who invited me to the London clinic and explained the Official Secrets Act. Eventually, I joined the London clinic and signed my life away. I could not even tell my husband. He does scientific research at King's."

"What subjects?"

"Psychotic drugs, cannabis and some native medicines from the Americas."

"How fascinating. My son was beginning a similar research program at Bristol. I'm sorry to say he died young before he could make any headway."

"Oh, I'm sorry. Are you widowed?"

"Yes, I was married to a musician and he died of cancer a few years ago."
"Well, I am happy for you that you have met Adam, you seem to have a loving relationship."

"Thank you. We have a deep love and a fair amount of past to overcome. The work seems to cause many breakdowns."

"I think I have seen everything! The toll is terrible." A call from Adam invited them to the dining room.

"We owe a great deal to Dr Ford Lloyd." Thea said.

"She was a wonderful counsellor. We shall miss her. I hope she has a lovely retirement with her partner."

"She has never mentioned him."

"Her." Adam and Thea looked at each other in surprise. "Will she mind us knowing?"

"No, not now she has retired."

"She still counsels me," said Thea.

"Well, I am sure you are discreet."

"She's invited to our wedding. She could bring her partner."

"I see. Shall I tell her that I let it out to you?"

"Only if you are happy to do so, otherwise, let her come alone and we say nothing."

"What a slip. I'm so sorry. That's not my usual manner but I knew she had retired and had no idea she was still working."

"Please don't worry. We will say nothing. Just let her decide to come alone. I do have a session with her next week and in all innocence, I could tell her who is coming and ask her if she wants to bring anyone. Two of our closest friends are lesbians."

"What will you think of me, Dr ex-controller? I should not have presumed. I still have a lot to learn."

"You are young to be doing such a demanding job. You will be good at it and pick up little hints as you go along."

They finished lunch as Adam ate the baked beans on toast portion left over. "Remind you of your single days?"

"Too right." He smiled. "I am looking forward to opening the clinic and working with you."

"So am I. Enjoy your wedding. Are you having a honeymoon?"

"My brother owns property on a Greek island, Aegina. We are going there."

"Have a fantastic time." Adam and Thea were so delighted.

"What a team already. Such amazing people."

"When we get back, we must see about the partition. A pity really."

"And the secure safe. Both doctors agree that a separate room is very important." She put her arms around his neck. "I expect we shall understand why one day."

Chapter 23

On the last Saturday in April, a weak sun was trying to shine, but there was no sign of rain. The florist had decorated the church with beautiful arrangements on two stands at the front of the pews. The flowers were designated for Care Homes after the ceremony. Purple and yellow flowers were scattered among the white roses and lilies and a small, trailing white bloom.

Adam and Thea entered to the strains of Bach. Adam wore his pale blue suit, Thea wearing her blue silk dress, carried a trailing white bouquet. They beamed with happiness as they walked past Adam's family and close friends. Dr Ford was there with her partner. During her last session, Thea had lightly asked her if she wanted to bring anyone. She was not planning to join the group in Greece.

"I have a partner called Candida Ford, another psychologist, but not in the same kind of counselling. She is more a social psychologist."

"I am very pleased."

Lotte and Helga sat with Renate. They wore their gorgeous, sparkly suits, while Renate was unrecognisable in a large hat and a flowery dress. Courtney held Dora's hand as they followed behind. When they reached the front, Michaela was there to seat them with her. Fr Tony had had a haircut and looked very smart as he welcomed everyone. Steven was the best man and held the rings. Dorothea passed her bouquet to Dora.

Fr Tony began the liturgy leading up to the marriage vows. Just before then they played the 'Deer's Cry' on a CD.

'I arise today in the strength of heaven'.

The vows were read and the rings exchanged, the bride and groom kissed and everyone sat down. Fr Tony said he would give a short homily. He stood at the microphone and read the words of the 'Deer's Cry'.

"That is a version of St Patrick's Breastplate. This is our prayer over Dr and Mrs Chamberlain. They are not a young couple with their life before them, heading in love to an unknown future and a family. Adam and Dorothea are in their second half of life. Behind them lies more suffering than most of us have experienced in a life time. They have fought through and they have sought God to heal their souls. They have accepted the mystery of suffering with love, support and understanding for each other and trust in God. Not only that, they have overcome their suffering to such a degree that they are using their second half of life, to show love and care for others in the form of a clinic for counselling in Godalming, 'The Sandbags Care Centre'.

"This will be opened in the near future. On their rings is engraved the word 'Gesegnet', 'Truly Blessed'. God had truly blessed Adam and Dorothea and may He continue to bless them with peace and joy and strength in their future."

Renate, Lotte and Helga had tears running down their cheeks. David was sniffing and so were some others.

There was spontaneous applause. That was the cue for Courtney to jump up and run up the aisle. Ashleigh stepped out and caught her. She sat on her lap for the rest of the liturgy. The *Deer's Cry* was replayed during the signing of the Register; more tears, more sniffs.

They collected the bouquet from Dora who played her role well and held Courtney's hand as they walked back down the aisle for the photographs. The organist played a toccata and fugue by Bach as the congregation marched out. David joined Lotte and they had a long hug. Lotte then met Dr Ford Lloyd and Candida. The weak sun shone more brightly for the photographs under the arch, under the trees and on the grass. The flower stands were placed at the top of the steps, under the archway and the couple with their flower girls posed for several shots.

Thea picked up Courtney. "You have been such a good girl," and kissed her.

"Good girl," repeated the sweet child.

She then picked up Dora. "My angel, you were so wonderful. There are some presents for you both at the Percy."

Adam found David. "You look so much better and you will enjoy Greece. Not on Gerd's passport, I hope?"

"Well done, Adam, you both look fantastic." Cars drove down to the Percy and Fr Tony went in the minibus for those without cars.

Thea found Dr Ford and met Candida. "Please tell me your name. I cannot call your wife Candida and you, doctor."

"I am Anthea Lloyd. We had our names blended before the Civil Unions and same-sex marriage." They saw that while Anthea had neat, short hair, Candida had long grey hair caught back in an artistic clip. Adam remembered Lotte's words, "I was changed to another counsellor, I don't know why." He imagined that all those years ago, Anthea had met an agent to whom she was attracted and had a conflict of interest.

The Percy was soon filling up as the wedding guests went down to the restaurant area where tables were set out with canapés and superior finger food and bottles of champagne. Wine and beer were available at the bar. Steven was filming everything for Russell.

Adam called attention by banging a spoon on a glass.

"Dear friends and family, first, thank you for sharing the happiest day of my life with us. We are having our reception on a Greek Island, so this is a little reception for those unable to travel to Greece with us."

Steven took over. "Our love and congratulations to my dear brother and his lovely new wife! We are filming all this for Russell in Greece. The coaches will be here in about two hours. I hope you have been able to organise your cars and your luggage. Now raise your glasses to toast the bride and groom."

Thea took her presents to Dora and Courtney. They were well wrapped so the girls had fun tearing off the paper. Inside she had put six rolls of silky hair ribbons and decorative butterfly slides. As they squealed with delight, she moved nearer to Fr Tony who was speaking with Melanie. Melanie spotted her and threw her arms around her neck. "You look so lovely."

"Thank you, Melanie and for making such an effort with your outfit."

"Dad!" Melanie said. Thea smiled.

"I don't know how to thank you, Fr Tony. You gave us such a wonderful wedding. Sorry you cannot join us in Greece."

"I've never heard of a reception like that, in another country."

"That's Adam's brother. He's lived there for decades with all his children and grandchildren. He owns property, a hotel and flats. He has given it to us all for two days. Adam and I have a two-week break."

"Well, you must rest and enjoy every minute. Greece is beautiful and it will be warmer than here."

"See you when we get back."

"And thank you both for the generous gift, my dears."

The coach arrived and the family climbed on with Helga, Lotte, Renate and David.

The plane landed in Athens as the sun was setting. Warmth surrounded them as they changed planes for a smaller craft to the island. Russell was waiting for them at the small airport. He hugged Adam and Thea and told them they would be in his car. He then hugged his brother and sister and greeted the rests of his relatives.

He stood on the coach with a microphone.

"Welcome, everyone. You will be taken to your hotel and given your keys. You will be hungry, so supper is served in the dining room. The main reception will be at 6.00 pm tomorrow. All your meals will be provided in the morning and at lunch time. I will be taking my brother and his wife with me. Enjoy the beautiful island and see you tomorrow at 6.00.

"Just follow the signs to find the venue in the hotel."

He left the bus to a chorus of thanks, went to his car, a chauffeur driven car, and took the bride and groom to his house.

Adam and Thea held hands and sat quietly, pleased to relax. The sky was so starry as all was darkness around them. The sound of the waves hitting rocks, the lights, twinkling now and then on the black waters gave them a strange feeling of unreality.

"You are eating with Lesley and me and getting an early night. Welcome, Dr and Mrs Chamberlain! You've met Rosamund and Steven's families and tomorrow you meet mine, 11 of them!"

The house was like a set for a television serial; white walls, arches, low walls, a blue pool. Lesley came out to meet the car.

"Don't you both look just wonderful!" She kissed them both. "Let's see you properly. Adam, you are a very lucky man!"

As they chatted and tried to get to know each other, Adam was preoccupied. "Can you tell me where various guests are?"

"I can."

"David Reger?"

Russell consulted a list. "Room 231."

"Is there a phone? Is it far?"

"On your wedding night?" Thea helped out. "He's had a breakdown. He knows our other friends but we need to keep an eye on him."

"I need to speak to him," Adam insisted.

"Use the phone in my study, you will get privacy there." Adam and Thea went to the study.

"What's troubling you, my love?"

"David could say too much to a kind relative. He could ignore his training and let his pain and grief come out. I did talk him through it all, but he is alone now and out of his usual environment."

"What's the worst he could do?"

"Talk about being a spy and reveal our past." The phone rang but there was no answer. "Can you get Lotte's number?" Thea went back to Russell.

He rang Lotte.

"Sorry, Lotte, I'm worrying about David. He could open up to a kind young man without thinking. Do you know where he is?"

"He's right here with us, drinking."

"Thanks, Lotte, can you remind him please?"

"Have done. Am doing. Will do. Go and love your wife!"

"Will we ever be free?" Thea asked.

"Sorry, my love. I worry."

"Thanks, Russ, sorry, just over anxious. I think we need to go to our flat."

"Of course. Breakfast with us whenever you like."

The flat had a large balcony with a table and chairs. They stood holding each other as they watched some boats on the dark sea, looked up at the stars, never so thick and twinkling. They breathed in the different air, the perfume of some plants or trees and the faint smell of fish.

They unpacked their clothes for the reception and hoped they would lose all sign of creases by the next evening. They sank into their large bed, kissed gently, made love slowly and fell into a deep sleep.

The different light, the unfamiliar sounds woke them early. Thea went straight to the balcony. The scene before her was just like a television holiday advertisement. Green mountains, rocky cliffs curving down to the blue sea which stretched to the horizon. The slopes were covered in white houses, some closely packed. Small fishing ports and a long beach wound around the edges of the island. Little coloured boats bobbed on the water lapping at the shore. Adam came and joined her and stood in silence for a few minutes.

"I could live here," he whispered and then turned to her and took her hands.

"My dearest Thea, thank-you so much for taking me on, for marrying me. I hope I never hurt you, never let you down. I want to love you, care for you and cherish you forever."

"Adam, I love you and I trust you. I want to love you, care for you and support you too." They eventually put on casual clothes and went to Russell's house for breakfast.

"Good morning, dear Adam, dear Thea." Russell boomed. They sat overlooking the bay from a different angle.

"I hope you don't mind; my three children are coming to meet you this morning at different times. It's too much to leave it all till tonight. You'll never work out who they are."

Thea looked at him; stockier than Adam, just as tall with the same thick, grey hair. She smiled at him.

"You are alike."

"You are not like any woman I have ever met. Adam is so fortunate to have met you before he is completely past it." They all laughed.

"Tomorrow, you have a day to yourselves. Here are some brochures and you can take my car and chauffeur."

"This is a wonderful present, Russell. We want to take you and Lesley to the best restaurant around to thank you. Possibly in our second week."

"That's the White Lady, the best restaurant on Aegina, a static ship in the marina."

"We'll book that then."

"Lesley will love it."

"What will I love?" Lesley came in with the coffee. "The White Lady. We are invited."

"True? Thank you, I do love it! It's a real treat."

"How was your man in trouble?"

"Just fine, thanks. I'll check after breakfast."

Paula, their third child and only daughter was due to arrive with her husband William. They lived in one of the large flats in the block with their two children, Vicky, six, and Vernon, four.

They had called in on cousin Rosamund on the way. Paula did resemble her and they were clearly close friends. Thea again found her heart melting as she saw little Vicky and Vernon.

"Can I see your doll?" Thea asked Vicky who was holding one hand of a doll dangling down. Vicky gave Thea the doll.

"What's her name?"

"Dolly."

"Hello, Dolly." She straightened her dress and hair.

"She doesn't speak." Vicky informed her. Thea smiled at the little girl who was not overawed by meeting great uncle and wife. She tried Vernon. "Have you got a favourite toy?"

Vernon stared at her as if asking, 'Who does she think she is?'

Paula bent down. "Vernon, tell aunty Thea about your favourite toy."

"It is a koala," he replied.

"How lovely, from Australia."

"We went there, to the Great Barrier Reef last year. He tucks his koala in bed but he doesn't carry him around."

"Glad you caught this one!" William came over. "Welcome to the family."

"Thanks, William. It is a privilege for me to join such a fantastic family."

"Uncle Adam can't be the black sheep anymore. We are looking forward to seeing Steven's video of your wedding."

Adam asked when that was happening and discovered that it was due to be shown at the reception that evening.

Chapter 24

"When we came to the island, we lived in a small flat but as Russell's business grew, we bought ever bigger properties. The children all grew up here. Adam we've made some changes since you were last here, come and see."

They started upstairs and saw the rooms which had been the children's bedrooms or dens. Two had been knocked into one to form a large bed-sit for friends or families.

"Shirley can come with Muzi sometime."

"I haven't met them yet." Thea had briefly seen them at the Percy. Muzi was tall and thin with shoulder length black hair. She wondered what his elderly clients made of him. Paula left as they had their tour. An hour later Raymond and Gloria arrived. It was timed like a military operation.

"Thursday is our day to have you," Ray said. "We're looking forward to it. Hi, Uncle Adam, congratulations." He shook their hands.

"Thanks for having us. Where are your young people?"

"Not far, coming. They're longing to go into the pool." Gloria brought over Craig who looked very mature for a ten-year-old and Sara who was 12 going on 20.

"You have grown, Sara, no longer a little girl," Adam commented.

"I'm nearly a teenager!" Sara added, kissing her uncle. "I can't wait for a swim but Mum said no as we are not staying long this morning."

"Pity. I expect you can come another time."

"Where do you live in England?" Thea described their houses and the area and explained that they were not far from London.

"I'd love to see London one day."

"We'll talk about it when we come to your home," Said Adam.

"What are your hobbies?" Thea asked.

"Swimming, reading, craft, I like making things."

"And you, Craig?"

"Football, football and football. I play with my cousin Chris as well as my team."

Like clockwork, the final battalion arrived before midday. Simon and Kate brought Chris to the terrace. Everyone made an effort to welcome Thea, who in her turn tried to engage the children.

"Three more homes to visit and a meal on a boat." She tried to take it in. Chris was chatty and talked about football and trains. He had a new train set which went along a corridor and into his room.

Adam knew that Russell had planned a timetable for them to go to each family but to have days to themselves in between. He decided to ring David and Lotte and found that all was well.

"We are on the beach. It's wonderful. Renate is with us. We make quite a foursome!" Lotte said brightly.

"By the way, I didn't know Dr Ford was gay. I forgot that when she saw me, she was Doctor Lloyd. Ford appeared later. Now I understand."

"She told me that they had made the name change long before civil partnerships and marriages came in. Quite surprising." Adam was relieved and returned to Thea.

"Shall we have a walk and then a siesta before the reception?" They sat under a parasol on the beach after walking down the slopes.

"Dear Russell," said Adam, "he's so generous and runs the family in such a military way. I often used to think of him when I sat with you in Russell square. Little did I realise that one day you would be with him in his house!" He took her head in his hands and kissed her lips.

"You two are like teenagers!" Shirley's voice came from behind a tree. "Hello, meet Muzi." They all laughed.

"I'm making up for lost time." Adam giggled and stood up to meet Mustafa Hossein. "How are you enjoying Greece?"

"Your wedding was fantastic. I loved that song. I love Greece; I've hitched around Greece before, when I was young."

"Thanks. We enjoyed it too. It's lovely to meet you and know that you are with Shirley."

"I hope I am better for her than the drunken bugger she married."

"I hope so too." Shirley laughed. "No one around here swears, language, darling."

"Whoops! I saw her when she was trying to save her marriage. She needs some proper love." He held her hand and kissed it.

"How do you like your work?" asked Adam. "It's such a vital job."

"I prefer the elderly to teenagers. They have such interesting stories to tell. I do think Pakistanis look after their elders better on the whole." A talk on comparative culture ensued. Muzi was a thoughtful, humorous man. He had rejected much of his culture including an arranged marriage. He joined in with English peers and Afro-Caribbean friends, went to discos and was thrown out of home. He shared a flat with an African when he joined the social work team in Woking.

"You will come and see us in Godalming and Chilworth, I hope."

Shirley was so happy. "We'd better find Mum, I left her with your German friend."

Russell had choreographed the start of the reception. All friends and family were drinking sparkling wine, circulating among each other while music was playing in the background. Adam wore his light grey suit and Thea had chosen her silver dress to match the sparkling venue. Russell held them in a side room and then, when the music became the wedding march, he led in the bride and groom. They had to stand a while next to an ornamental fountain while the photographers were at work. There was a gasp as the couple walked in. Thea looked surreal, floaty and romantic in her amazing dress.

She had never worn such an expensive dress, even when she dressed up for Richard's concerts. This was the grandest affair she had ever been in.

"Adam and Dorothea!" was the toast.

Russell ushered his family to process in front of them as they stood by the fountain, followed by the various friends.

"Wedding gifts are back in England. Impossible to bring them here. Well done, both of you." Lotte hugged them.

"Thanks for looking after David," whispered Thea. David came to them beaming.

"This has done me the world of good. Seeing you so happy. It's like life after death. You have given me hope. I can get better. I can have a new life!"

"You can, David!" said Adam.

Suddenly Thea felt her dress being tugged. Dora was trying to climb up. Thea picked her up and kissed her.

"You're wearing your pretty dress." She stood holding her for a while. "Dora, I love you." She visualised herself holding Dora's baby in 25 years' time. She would try not to make her the favourite but she felt there was a special bond.

"And I love you, Aunty Thea."

The film show was announced. One wall had a dark curtain hanging from the ceiling. It opened at the press of a button and a screen appeared. Steven had set up the computer and the film opened as Adam and Thea walked into the church. He allowed the music to play, fast forwarded to the song and then to the vows. He waited until Courtney's run up the aisle was seen and then fast forwarded to the photographs outside. There was loud applause.

Some music played and a few people pranced and jived around. "Did you learn at Oxford?" Adam asked Thea.

"I did but I have done none since!" He led her to the dance floor and they had a go, much to everyone's amusement. They enjoyed the fun of it. Then came the sit-down meal at round tables along two walls. Russell and Steven had prepared a speech each. They both had some childhood tales of their baby brother. He had broken up their Lego constructions and made a series of bridges. When they had set out their rows of soldiers in battle array, Adam would systematically change all the rows and positions.

"That's how he came to organise the Foreign Office!"

The brief speeches were followed by the announcement of the cake. Everyone clapped as a pièce montée was wheeled in, a high cone of chocolate éclairs.

Adam stood by the cake and took Thea's hand.

"We are feeling very spoilt. Thank you so much Russell and all my family and friends." After the cake was mainly demolished, Melanie came over with her parents.

"Melanie so loves your dress; she is thinking of becoming a princess instead of a Goth," Chantal said.

Thea took Mel's hands and twirled her around.

"You would make an absolutely beautiful princess," Thea said.

"You are so beautiful; you should be a model," Mel said to Thea.

"Well said, darling," Added Conor.

"Can I talk to you when you next come to Brighton," asked Mel.

"Of course, you can, dear." Thea smiled and saw something else in the girl's eyes; teenage angst and longing.

"I have an idea. Come with me, Mel." Thea took her hand and led her to the cloakroom. "Unhook me and try it on." Mel pulled off her clothes and pulled on the silver dress. Thea put on Mel's clothes.

"Come on." They walked out and mingled in the crowd. It took a while for anyone to notice until Conor spotted his daughter. Cameras and phones clicked as if a film star had entered the room. Thea held Mel's hand and walked her around the room. The admiration for Mel touched her despite herself. Everyone enjoyed the swop. After half an hour, they changed back. Thea felt that this had changed Mel deeply.

She visualised a feminine Mel in ten years' time.

There were several other meaningful but unexpected snippets of conversation with Rosamund, Ellie and Simon.

The waiters served tea and coffee. Adam sat down. "I'm exhausted. I need my bed, my love."

"OK. Old man. Let's say our goodbyes."

In the morning the coaches would take the guests to the airport and they would not see them again until they returned to the UK.

"You've worn them out!" boomed Russell. "Let them go to their bed." There was clapping and calls of 'goodnight' as they left.

Russell saw them out. "Ring me tomorrow and say when you would like the car. Your day alone tomorrow."

Adam unhooked the silver dress and they fell into bed and slept after a kiss.

"Our fridge is full of food!" Thea exclaimed. "There's breakfast food here. Your brother is amazing."

"Lesley had to fight for some independence in the early years. She's done well and stood by him. It can be like living in an army under his control."

"So you moved his soldiers!" Adam laughed.

"I'd like to visit the monastery and the Cathedral of St Nektarios and have our lunch somewhere up there. The chauffeur will advise."

"Fine, I'll ask for the car at about 10.00?"

"I could get used to this!"

The chauffeur took them to the top of the hill.

"I will take you to a little village not far from here for your lunch." Thea was charmed by the Greek accent.

197

On the hill top they took in the magnificent view. The pale pink of the walls and roof of the monastery contrasted with the blue of the sea and the green of the trees just budding into leaf. Such beauty, such a special place filled them with peace. They went into the cathedral and found that a service was taking place. A few people in black stood around the wide space as a small group of singers intoned a deep, reverberating song. They stood in awe as their eyes adjusted to the darkness. The candles flickering gave them enough light to see the gold painted icons. The overall effect was a spiritual, shimmering atmosphere, the sense of a powerful presence. Adam took Thea's hand. There were very few seats but they watched the people cross themselves, bow and bend their heads. Entranced, they stood in this unfamiliar atmosphere. The little choir bowed, put lighted candles in troughs of sand and left the cathedral. One by one, people did the same and the church was empty.

The priest had disappeared near the screens. They walked around a little, observing the icons of Mary and the saints. As they reached the door, the priest emerged from behind the screen and walked towards them. When he was close enough, Adam thanked him for the lovely service.

"You have been to Greek Orthodox service before?"

"No, never. It was beautiful, absolutely beautiful," Thea added. They all stepped into the bright sunlight. The three of them stood in a close triangle, smiling.

"My brother and his family live here." Adam told him.

"You are special people. I bless you."

The priest raised his arms and put one hand on each of their heads. He spoke in Greek for a while and then in his own kind of English.

"Two good souls are here. God give peace. God take distress. God take pain. God give strong. The Father, the Son, the Holy Spirit bless you, give rich days." He crossed himself and gave them a bow.

"Thank you so much," Adam said.

"Father, thank you and God bless you too," Thea added. Amazed they watched him go back into the church.

"He seemed to know our lives, our feelings," Thea said. "He gave us such a special blessing."

They visited the public areas of the monastery then met the chauffeur to drive to a restaurant. The little village nestled on the side of a valley. There were a few, smart, modern cars in the streets. A large canopy hung over the square.

"Taverna," the chauffeur announced. "I come back." He drove off and they looked at the menu, chose a seat and had a glass of wine.

"We were blessed," said Thea, holding Adam's hand across the table. The warmth of that encounter stayed with them for days. They managed to eat in the three homes of Raymond, Simon and Paula. The sense of normal families, normal life, normal arguments, normal love and care filled them both, relaxed them and gave them a sense that this is where they belonged. On their free days, they went to the Aphaia Temple, the beautiful bays of Kolona and Marathonas and the Agia Marina where they saw the White Lady. It looked smart and sophisticated. Thea had saved her second dress for the evening with Russell and Lesley.

"Which suit?" asked Adam.

She stood next to both of them. "Blue," she decided.

Lesley was wowed and said so, but she looked lovely herself in a long summer gown. They walked across the little gangplank and found their seats.

"We were blessed by a priest at the cathedral," Adam told Russell.

"After your money?"

"Not at all, a spontaneous, generous and sincere gesture in fairly broken English."

"It was wonderful," said Thea.

They expressed their gratitude to Russell and Lesley. They chose a Greek menu.

"We have invited your two oldest grandchildren for a holiday with us later in the summer."

"Great kids," said Russell.

"We want to get a dog. We'll have to find a carer for when we take them to London and when we want to travel abroad."

"What kind of dog?"

"With a tail, two ears and four legs." Laughed Adam.

Thea looked like a celebrity in her lovely new dress. They both fitted in to the luxury environment and received many complements. They went on deck before coffee and liqueurs were served.

"This is not our world, is it?"

"No, my love. It's fun but it is not our life."

"What will we do with these dresses?"

"Hold on to them for a while. We have your 60th soon and family anniversaries, perhaps Shirley's wedding." He beamed at her as they returned to Russell and Lesley.

"We go home to find our dog and to manipulate my house into a clinic."

Chapter 25

Cards and parcels greeted them in both homes. It took a few days to sort them all out. In Greece, in holiday mode it seemed easier to make plans for organising their life. Like deploying soldiers, they had decided on making Fridays their day apart. Adam's idea was to open the clinic four days a week. The building would then be closed for three days so it could again be a home. Now, in the reality of their homes they felt very differently.

"You need to move the rows of soldiers again," Thea said as they separated the piles of cards and gifts into Chilworth, Godalming and some in reserve.

Adam sat on the settee. "Let's make this our home and mine a sort of weekend home so doggy gets used to the changes. Can we begin as a normal couple and understand there will be times when we take time out? You can stay here while I spend time in Godalming. If there are other crises we will decide then how to cope."

"That sounds good. Right now, I never want to be apart from you."

Before the pleasant, emotional task of choosing a dog, Adam wanted to call in help from a company to install a partition, put in a safe and a filing cabinet. As Thea spent the first few days sorting out their clothing, the bedding, the wedding gifts, Adam had a visit from a firm to take on all three jobs.

First, he moved the TV and hi-fi to the near end, then he measured the walls and height of the room and then they showed him images of the different kinds of partitions available.

Pictures and furniture would have to be moved to allow for the folded panels.

The safe would be in the central kitchen block, drilled into the floor but out of sight. Near his desk area in the dining room, he planned to put in a wooden clad filing cabinet for the doctors' files. He had always visualised the patients being able to talk with the view over the garden and river.

Thea came to join him to organise the bedding, the towels and their clothes. He took her to meet the contractors and show her the various folding or sliding doors.

"Which ones fold back into the flattest area?" They drew out their plan for the paintings, the settee, and the coffee table and stood and walked around and eventually chose the least disliked partition.

Adam had felt that he should not label the outside of the house. He had a plaque made for the hallway wall just before the door into the lounge. 'Sandbags Care Centre' was the sign in an attractive gold colour with the Aachen statue and the print out of the myth.

When the contractors left, they both sat in the lounge trying to imagine how it would look. Adam ran over in his mind what Dr Noel and Dr Glenda had advised; the importance of the consultation room being separate from the living area.

"That would be the case if this were our only living area and if I were a counsellor."

"I think you are going to demolish their Lego and build bridges," Thea said.

He phoned the contractors who were still on the road.

"Change of plan. Sorry for the inconvenience." He explained his thinking to them and asked if they were still willing to install the other items. They went home to Chilworth to look up dogs.

"You must have one of the larger rooms as an office or a den," Thea said to Adam. "Next project after the clinic is finished. See if you want to change anything else."

"Doggy area?"

"His bed could be on the landing outside our room but in the day, he can have the run of the house and garden. We'll have to buy a bed for Sandbags to save us carrying it, bowls and toys too."

"Lots to think about. We'll ask about carers and holiday homes for dogs too."

They had a whole list of people they wanted to contact. Adam rang David to see how he was doing. He was still managing the regular journeys to London. He had a few ups and downs, but the worst seemed to be over. With their minds at rest, they could concentrate on finding a puppy. They had read all the warning about puppy farms so they looked for a local, independent breeder with a certificate.

The house was pink. The garden in the front had ornamental arches, flagstones, steps resembling a photograph in a high-class gardening magazine. Behind the house was a large lawn area where six or seven puppies were playing. The mother dog was sitting quietly while her offspring were tumbling, rolling, pulling rope toys and tossing soft balls. They were golden Labradors. Mrs Dalton let them walk out of the back door and stand among the puppies.

"They need a couple more weeks before they can leave their mother. If you choose one today, I have a collar to identify him or her when you come to collect him or her. They are popular and are going quite quickly."

"Who is left?" Some clearly had collars with a reserved tag. Two males and a female were unclaimed.

"A male, please," Adam said.

Mrs Dalton picked up one and gave him to Adam and then gave the other one to Thea. Hearts were smitten. Adam put his down and had a pulling game with the rope toy. Thea placed hers next to him.

"Sit! Stay!" Adam tried and walked away. One puppy wrestled with the toy and padded away. The other one sat looking at them.

"Are you ours?" Adam asked him. The puppy padded towards him and Adam picked him up. "He seems to think so."

They left Mrs Dalton with the payment and contact details and agreed to return for the puppy with the blue collar in 14 days.

Adam saw an email had come in from Ralph. He checked his phone and saw that he was asked to contact Ralph urgently.

"Oh, dear, I hope it is not David."

It was far worse. Ralph answered Adam's call with bad news.

The watchers had seen Gerd pack up and leave the flat a few weeks after Jürgen had died. They then noticed that Bruno made a return visit. They watched him pass the windows carrying bags and a suitcase. They decided to arrest him when he came out. As darkness fell, no lights came on in the flat. Bruno did not come out. The elderly, doddery Bruno had been too well trained. The police broke in but there was no sign of Bruno. They sealed the doors and windows of the flat to await the anti-terrorism police. They checked all possible exits from inside. One door on the stairs led to a fire escape down one side of the building. Did they not watch that? Another door on the stairs led to a flight of steps to the cellar. On the ground floor there was a door which opened out onto the back garden with direct access to the street. Bruno had taken some unknown documents or items and escaped through one of those doors. They watched the Cologne flat but he never returned there. The most worrying part was the number of documents found inside when an MI6 officer joined in the clean-up operation.

Jürgen may have converted and repented but he still kept documents dating back decades. Their fear was that there may have been evidence that Gerd had been a double agent, that other commune members were also double agents. Ralph was on the phone for two hours explaining the various possible scenarios.

If Bruno had found nothing of interest, he would have come out as normal. He must have found something that let him know the flat was being watched. There may have been evidence that Gerd had been living with Jürgen in his declining months. Gerd had confessed to Jürgen that he was a spy, but he would have carefully safeguarded the identities of Lotte and Diane. What had Bruno and Jürgen talked about? Did Bruno know about his intimate relationship with Gerd?

Ralph tried to reassure Adam that he had men looking for Bruno. Protection would be provided for Gerd, Lotte and Dorothea. Bruno was in his '80s and not in the best of health. If he tried to take revenge, he could possibly use a younger Marxist, or someone released from prison.

The search revealed hundreds of documents from Jürgen's terrorism work. There was some clothing and books belonging to Gerd. The documents were all bagged up and removed. An officer would have the task of going through them all to look for clues or information.

Ralph wanted to plan protection for the three people under threat. He wanted to send an armed officer to pose as a house guest. Adam pointed out that Bruno might not have found any such incriminating evidence, that he might not be planning revenge. He asked if there was any evidence that Bruno still had Marxist contacts. Ralph said he would have more information in two days after the sleeper agents had been alerted.

Adam wished he did not have to tell Thea. He spoke to Lotte first.

"Bruno was a kind and fair man. He authorised Manfred's killing and he ran Aachen commune for some years before he set up the new Cologne group. How would he react to double agents after all these years? Not sure. He could have changed a lot. He may be angry. Gerd would never leave incriminating pages around."

Adam finished the call and went to Thea. She knew there was a problem. Adam gave her the outline of what had happened, trying to sound reassuring. She would normally have expected to be full of fear.

"The Greek priest said, 'Give peace, give strong'. That's what we have. If Bruno found our cover names and documents saying that we were double agents, would our real names also be there? If he did find them, would he be able to discover our present whereabouts?"

"Ralph is taking normal precautions in case it is the worst case, but he has got agents working on it, looking for Bruno and checking on his contacts in Cologne."

Within 24 hours, Ralph had the report that Bruno seemed to have no Marxist contacts. Jürgen had been his only contact from those years. He could not have known about Gerd's relationship with him. He had led a very secluded life after he was released from prison. It was a mystery that he had left the flat unseen and had not returned to his Cologne flat. The German agents had found witnesses who had seen an elderly man with a suitcase at the back of the flats. CCTV had picked him up at a bus stop. The buses were going to Düsseldorf.

Ralph thought that David would be safer in Leeds and advised him to stay there while they tried to track Bruno. Dr Noel agreed to visit him and take an armed guest just in case. David told Ralph that he doubted that Bruno would be out for revenge after all these years.

Ralph tried to find Bruno's real identity.

David was questioned about what was in the flat. He talked about lots of old files but he had never known what was in them. The converted man had begun to write his memoirs. That had been found in the flat. David said they had never discussed the commune personnel or the presence of spies. He had never taken any documents to the flat himself as he usually travelled there directly from England.

Next day, Ralph said that Bruno had been traced to Düsseldorf where he had boarded a train. They checked all ferries to England but the task was more difficult because they had no idea what name he was using. The MI6 photographs were out of date but they were digitally aged on computer. After 24 hours the agents sent a surprising message. Bruno had boarded a ferry to England, but from Ostend. Bruno still had his training to fall back on. The only way they knew all that was because an elderly man with a fake passport was found dead on the ferry. MI6 agents swooped down to Dover to take over the investigation, to retrieve the suitcase, establish the cause of death and keep it out of the Press. While there was relief all round, they wanted to understand why he had suddenly fled to England.

The suitcase contained old documents showing the planned attacks on US airbases, some of which had happened and others had not been put into operation. There was a chapter from the memoir describing the murder of Manfred. There were no weapons in the case or on the body. Where was he going and why? The autopsy revealed that he had suffered a massive stroke as he was going up the steep stairs between decks. It was a mystery. Would it ever be solved?

David and Lotte were given the details. No one could offer a theory. "Give strong! I'll never forget that," Thea said to a rather shaken Adam.

"Had a good fortnight?" Mrs Dalton asked Adam when they went to pick up their puppy.

"Quite an eventful one," Adam said, cuddling the puppy with the blue collar. "I hope you won't miss your family." He addressed the puppy. Thea stroked his soft head as they received all the paper work. They thanked Mrs Dalton and clipped a lead to his collar. He walked with them to the car. He was shown around his new home, had some supper, a game and then curled up in his bed in the lounge. At bed time Adam carried his bed to the landing. Puppy could just about manage the stairs then ran up and down the landing. He sat in his bed, a soft, modern circle of comfort.

"He's so independent," Thea said as she gave him a toy.

"Indy." Adam bent down to him. "Hello, Indy, here is your own toy puppy." He moved the toy over to him.

Thea printed out a picture of him and sent it to the whole family. The great nephews and nieces were all longing to come and meet him.

The next few days were nearly filled by Indy, walks, training and playing. Adam had to meet Dr Noel at the clinic to show him the new furniture items and to explain why he had not acted on his advice about partitioning the lounge. Adam took Indy with him to show him his second bed and set of bowls and toys.

"This will not be my living area. I shall live with my wife in her home. This will be like a holiday home. The clinic sessions will not take place on Fridays, so we can come for the weekend, or use it like a retreat place for one of us. We can then keep up with the cleaning and management. We have yet to decorate the spare bedroom, but I don't expect you will need to sleep here immediately."

"Very good safe and filing cabinet, so smart and sophisticated. I quite understand about your lovely lounge."

"I had it all planned out and booked even. But I realised it made me sad and was not really needed. My desk, next to the filing cabinet, please make use of it if you want to see your patient the other side of a desk. Please take one of the dining room chairs for them."

Indy came into the dining room and sniffed at Noel, wagging his tail.

"Meet, Indy, our baby." Noel called him, patted him and Indy went wild with enthusiasm. "He could be a real help with some patients."

"If you want him, just let me know. He is not fully trained yet, still making puddles indoors."

"I think I have a patient to bring down or meet here."

"That's a good start. I presume you will try to get patients to arrive independently most of the time?"

"I hope so. You gave me the bus schedule from Guildford and Godalming station. This first one, I might need to stay with him to start with."

"Can I take you to lunch?" Adam asked.

"That's very kind. Thank you." Thea arrived to pick up Indy while the two men walked to the Côte Brasserie.

"Noel, you have complete independence. You are not answerable to me. Your sessions are in confidence. I do not need to know names or backgrounds. If, on the other hand…" The onion soup arrived with melted gruyère on a floating roundel of bread dripping down the side.

"If you do wish to discuss with me, I have years of experience with agents."

"I will keep records and just let you now times and dates."

"And sleepovers."

The main courses arrived, beautifully presented.

"I shall be occupied with Indy and we will no doubt become a hotel for my family. The first two young ones arrive at the end of August."

"A whole new life for you."

When they returned, Noel stopped at the plaque in the hallway.

"This is really lovely. Could we have our names on small plaques at the side? Very professional."

"Of course. Write out all your initials and qualifications."

"I sometimes make a recording. Can you show me where the plugs are?"

Adam found one near the settee in the lounge and put a small table from the nest for the recorder. Noel smiled. He had a very small apparatus clipped to his lapel.

"I only need somewhere to recharge."

"It will sound like a spy film. I will start by speaking to him in Russian."

Thea loved training Indy, included Renate on some walks and had visits from Lotte and Helga and David over the first few months.

Dr Glenda's first visit coincided with the arrival of the plaques.

"I am real now; I am valid now!" Glenda laughed. She was shown the desk, the filing cabinet and the lounge area.

"I might use the desk when I start. I like to have patients the other side of a desk until I get to know them."

Before she had her first patient, Adam and Thea, with Indy's help started to redecorate the spare room. They called in a workman to put up the wallpaper after hanging a pretty blind. They chose an artwork from one of the Guildford studios. Glenda loved it and longed to have a reason to stay there. A routine developed; Noel came one morning a week and Glenda came one afternoon. They each had their own set of keys for everything.

The counselling for local men had its debut. The barbers and the GP surgeries had cards and leaflets offering counselling at a reduced rate. Adam made the first consultation free so the men could decide if they were willing to commit to a few weeks of paid sessions. A conversation with a barber led to a young man going to talk to his GP about medication or counselling. The doctor asked the young man if he could phone the Sandbags Care Centre to make initial contact, and then he could ring up to make an appointment himself. Glenda was his counsellor. Wayne's father had walked out on the family when he was about nine. He became angry and hurt and tended to lash out at school if a boy talked about outings with his own father or activities with his own dad. Ten years later, he still had the feelings but did not lash out. He became depressed and could not see a point to life. He had had girlfriends but his morose character put them off. He made a suicide attempt, letting his poor mother find him in bed having vomited up spirits and pills. Wayne had been followed up by the hospital but the waiting list was long. Fortunately, he mentioned it to his barber. Adam was thrilled that his vision had become a reality.

Adam and Thea spoke regularly with Fr Tony.

"You both look radiant." He gave them a hug. They told him a slim version of the ordeal they had been through for a few days.

"I did not go to pieces because of the words of a Greek priest at the St Nektarios cathedral on the little island."

"It was remarkable," Adam joined in, "we stood enjoying the haunting music and at the end a priest came out and spoke to us at the door. 'You are special people, I bless you,' he said.

"I wrote it down; 'Two good souls are here. God give peace. God take distress, God take pain, God give strong, the Father, the Son, the Holy Spirit bless you, give you rich days.'"

"That was a real spiritual encounter, a gift of God." Fr Tony smiled at them.

Indy soon learned to be home alone for a couple of hours, knowing they would return to him. He had a window sill space cleared so he could watch the cars leave and return. No vase was safe when he wagged his lengthening tail.

Sara and Craig were their first house guests. Shirley and Muzi came next. Over the next months, all cousins, great nieces and nephews had a stay in Chilworth. Thea became a good tour guide to Winchester, Windsor, Wisley Garden, Epsom Downs. They shared Christmases with all the different families. They even returned to Greece for a holiday once they had found a couple who loved to care for dogs for a short period. They had owned dogs all their life but could no longer have a permanent dog because of the husband's health. He enjoyed having one around. They lived in Shalford so Indy had a different walking area. He treated them like a holiday home and did not whine or fear when he stayed with them.

Adam and Thea never totally forgot that because of their past a member of the commune they had betrayed could discover their identities and whereabouts. They never solved the mystery of the strange effort Bruno had made to get to England. David stabilised and settled into his Leeds home but was often a guest in Chilworth. Thea did not need to see Dr Ford Lloyd as a patient but she remained a friend and she and Candida came for meals in Chilworth.

Thea developed close relationships with several of Adam's great nieces and nephews. She knew she would be close to Dora all her life and that she would also have a special relationship with Melanie. Melanie confided in Thea and gradually dropped the Goth or Punk style and made friends with girls who wanted to study. Thea and Adam shared that they were feeling like normal people.

One Saturday, Adam was at his desk and Thea was sorting out the laundry at the clinic, when Indy let out a challenging bark. Someone knocked at the door. Thea held Indy back and opened the door to see a man in a yellow jacket.

"Sandbags, madam."

"Yes, do come in. I was not expecting you. Who do you want to see?"

"I don't need to come in. I've got a supply of sandbags for you as your stream is threatening to overflow after the heavy rain. These are to protect your backdoors. Some have already been flooded."

Adam had heard the bark and came to see what was happening. He saw the workman and heard the tail end of the conversation. They both stood laughing and apologising to the poor, confused workman.

"Look at this." Adam invited the man to come in and read the plaque.

"Well, I never. I'll just get them off the lorry. There's more at the depot if you are unlucky." He carried the bags to the backdoors and put them across the thresholds.

"If you know any men who need to discuss their problems, direct them to the clinic, the Sandbags Care Centre." Thea smiled and gave him a card.

"OK. I won't forget that. Sandbags, eh?" Thea passed him a leaflet.

"The Devil's Sandbags, actually. Here's the story."

Bibliography

Aust, Stefan, Die Baader-Meinhof Komplex, Knaur 1989 Becker, Jillian, Hitler's Children, Pickwick Books, London 1989

Böll, Heinrich, Die Verlorene Ehre der Katharina Blum, Nelson 1974

Mitscherlich, Alexander, Auf dem Weg zur Vaterlosen Gesellschaft, Piper Verlag 1963 1973

Mitscherlich, Alexander und Margarete, Die Unfähigkeit zu trauern, Piper Verlag 1967,1977

Films

Deutschland im Herbst, Kluge, Fassbinder et al. 1978

Die Verlorene Ehre der Katharina Blum, Schlöndorff 1975

Die bleierne Zeit, Margarthe von Trotte, 1981

Stammheim, Reinhard Hauff 1986